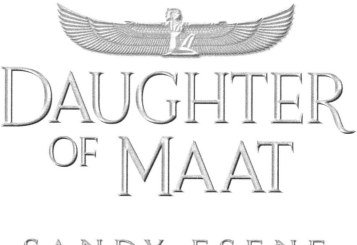

DAUGHTER OF MAAT

SANDY ESENE

BLUE BENU
—PRESS—

Published by Blue Benu Press, Seattle, Wa 2018

Cover design by Mariah Sinclair

E-book ISBN: 978-1-7328105-0-1

Print ISBN: 978-1-7328105-1-8

Hardcover ISBN: 978-1-7328105-2-5

For
my mother and fellow adventurer
and
my father and fellow storyteller

CHAPTER ONE

Beyond Raymond's shadowy blind, the shimmer of city lights scattered like a loose universe in the Los Angeles basin far below. It didn't surprise him that Marceline chose to live atop a high perch. A primordial hunting instinct had quickened within him when he spotted the dark recess of her foyer, perfect for a swift kill. He at least owed her that.

Raymond regretted the need to kill her tonight. He rolled his head from side to side. His muscles were stiff from the many hours poised like a desert snake under a cool rock, ready to strike.

His grasp on the glass syringe tightened. How easy it would be to crush it, to allow the poison to infiltrate his system and be released from this endless misery. He didn't relish the thought of killing her, or the Others for that matter, but there was no other way.

In the distance, across the large sunken living room, the mechanical thunk of a security bolt and the soft swoosh of the floor-to-ceiling glass door jolted him back to the present. He spied Marceline's silhouette outlined by the silver moonlight. Opened to the night air, the space filled with the gentle sound of palm fronds stirred by the autumn breeze. His heart pounded against his chest as he breathed in her heady scent of sweet lotus blossoms.

Marceline stepped into her house and switched on a table lamp as muffled digital tones emanated from her handbag. The sounds were notes strung together to resemble Cher's song "Gypsies, Tramps, and Thieves." It was a song they used to laugh about in better days. "Oh damn," she said as she dropped her oversized purse on an end table and rooted through it.

Doubt filled Raymond as he watched her. Maybe he was wrong about it all.

For the time being, his presence was undetected. He would have to act soon. Why on this particular night did she choose to enter through the back door? Was she aware of his plan? Could she be toying with him? Raymond's mind reeled at the possibility. Then it occurred to him: If Marceline the warrior knew his plan, he would not be pondering. He would be fighting.

Marceline swiped the phone to life and held it to her ear. "Hello, Seth," she said, her tone flat. "Like I told you earlier, no. It's completely impossible." She stared into what she must have thought to be an empty house.

Raymond's gaze wandered around the room. The golden glimmer of the Louis XIV clock he gave to her years ago caught his eye. The clock was commissioned by the Sun King as a token of love to his second and officially unofficial wife, Françoise d'Aubigné. The sight of it sickened and embarrassed Raymond. It was a garish and awkward attempt to woo her. His skin burned with self-revulsion. The clock stood as a painful and gaudy tribute among the sleek ultramodern furnishings. He always knew no matter how much he tried, she would never be his. The Others never understood. They had thought him sick for wanting her, but then again, they had all lost sight of the old ways.

Marceline leaned into the wall, bracing herself as she grabbed her right shoe and tossed it toward the entryway. "How many times do you need to hear it from me? I said no." She grabbed her left shoe and threw it into the darkness. "I know," she said listlessly.

Her all-too-familiar tone of despondency awoke within Raymond a fresh wave of disgust.

Marceline and Seth's relationship was like an eternal screening of a cheap reality show, but much less entertaining. Once, Raymond thought himself unworthy of her and longed for her to notice him. But over time he lost his taste for her as he realized she and Seth deserved every single misery they inflicted on one another.

Surety rose within Raymond. She must die tonight. She was the trial run of his toxic alchemy. Marceline was the weakest link of them all, but tonight, if all went well, she would help him cure the Others and end all of their endless wanderings through this mortal realm.

"Listen, we can talk about this later," she said, unzipping the short pencil skirt that hugged her thighs. It dropped to the white shag carpet and encircled her bare feet. "I've been hard at work. No, not that." She giggled as she unbuttoned her sheer blouse. "And I need a good swim. Work some tension out, you know." Her voice had turned soft and teasing.

Raymond gazed at her naked body. A strange cocktail of lust and anger pulsed through him. He could only guess at what they were talking about. Bile crawled up his throat like a slow-moving Gila monster. The light but discernible presence of the poison in his hand buoyed his resolve.

Marceline laughed. The sound bounced off the hardwood floors of her contemporary boxlike home. He smiled to himself. If all went as planned, this house would soon be like a massive museum vitrine, encasing something ancient and dead under its glass shell.

"Come if you want," she said teasingly, and set down her phone. Marceline stepped out onto the patio. She strode toward the lap pool with a casual grace, her nakedness illuminated by the low full moon that gave her skin the appearance of polished alabaster.

He would have to act quickly with Seth on the way. If the poison didn't take, he didn't want to fight them both. It had to be quick in, quick out. It could be a blessing in disguise that the estranged husband was on his way. Police investigations always like to start close to home. The thought of Seth being dragged in for questioning made him smile.

Raymond heard the water swallow her form, slowly drinking her in as she slipped into the pool. He waited to hear the repetitious sound of her strokes before leaving his hidden lair.

It was time.

Raymond skirted the pool's edge, traveling its length with great intention. Surprise would be his greatest ally. He stood on the grey concrete lip and watched her head turn from side to side. Excitement coupled with sorrow filled Raymond as he imagined her heart pumping, lungs breathing in the cool night air for what would be the last time, knowing he held her death—and ultimately her freedom—in the palm of his hand.

He squatted as her body moved toward him. Her arm lifted out of the water in an arc as she reached for the cement edge of the pool. He caught her wrist hard.

Marceline's legs thrashed below the surface. Her startled eyes bulged open with panicked fear, and her mouth shot open as if to speak as Raymond jammed the needle into her neck. He sent the plunger home while he struggled against her erratic flailing. Red froth unexpectedly bubbled out from her mouth as she gasped. Her body became still. Marceline sunk to the bottom like a beautiful marble Venus returning to the sea.

As the water's surface mellowed, gentle ripples refracted the moonlight, creating a disjointed illusion of motion on Marceline's body. Raymond stood at the pool's edge contemplating the crushing reality of what he had done.

Not much time before Seth arrived. He dove into the water to retrieve his precious pearl.

The worst defilement of this Venus was yet to come.

CHAPTER TWO

Alex Philothea stepped through the threshold of the ancient oak doorway. Lecture halls and libraries were always safe harbors to her—places of reassurance and comfort. Alex relished being surrounded by the warm glow of knowledge, ensconced in the lecture hall's thick and protective layers of belonging and discovery.

She sat in the back row of the wooden bench-style seats, the pews in the sacred space of her house of worship. The room was filled with a fresh batch of novices swept into this cathedral of learning by the autumn winds. An almost imperceptible twinge of envy passed through her.

The undergrads seated around her were a vast sea of untapped potential and new discovery. How she missed the simplicity of college life, where she could dedicate every waking hour to study.

Now she was in the continual day-to-day grind of her career.

The small light on the lectern pulled her gaze across the room like the lighthouse of ancient Alexandria guiding weary sailors to land. It softly illuminated the distant speaker in a halo of golden light reminiscent of a Rembrandt or Vermeer. Alex's eyes adjusted slowly to the darkness. She pushed her glasses up the bridge of her nose to make the speaker more visible. It was Dr. Thorne who summoned her. Alex shivered in the overwarm lecture hall.

As Thorne gestured, her fingers cast shadows resembling clawlike tendrils that stretched across the ceiling toward Alex. The upturned podium light carved Dr. Roberta Thorne's sharp features into high relief. The tiny but bright beam of light morphed her smile into a cruel sneer.

The room was dark, but Thorne's eyes were laser-trained on Alex. "Evisceration." Thorne spoke the word slow and clear as if relishing it, sending a message as clear as day. She would like nothing better than a sharp obsidian stone in her hand and Alex's exposed belly. "After purifying and cleansing the dead, evisceration is the first step in the mummification process." Her gaze pulled away from Alex and shifted from directed contempt to general professional detachment. "For next week, you are to complete a comprehensive fifty-page essay on the mummification and funerary processes of the New Kingdom."

The students in the auditorium sat in a stunned silence while Thorne turned the houselights up. Although the students did not protest audibly, Alex could read the posture of defeat in their slumped shoulders and downcast eyes. At the Oriental Institute one rule remained constant: never question Thorne. Unless, of course, you wanted to end up like Alex, forever damned.

"Dismissed," Thorne commanded. Her words broke the spell of disbelief that hung over the seated freshmen. As if on cue, they shot out of their seats and scattered in harried chaos. Alex's doom grew closer as they spilled into their freedom. She pushed against the oncoming current of departing students and made her way to the podium. A strange man in a prison-grey wool suit had joined Thorne.

"I am glad to see you finally made it, Alex," said Thorne. She motioned toward the newcomer. "This is C. C. Maspero. He is a national rep from KHNM."

Alex fought the urge to roll her eyes. In her experience, people who had initials in place of a first name either had impossible-to-pronounce names, or were incredibly pretentious know-it-alls. She guessed the latter was the case for Mr. Maspero. "KHNM?" She hadn't thought of that organization since her undergrad days. What could Thorne be playing at?

"Oh come on, Alex." Thorne crossed her arms. Her nose wrinkled in a familiar show of disapproval. Alex wasn't sure what she'd ever done to Thorne, but from the first time they'd laid eyes on one another it was plain that this hard-edged woman held a deep and irreversible loathing for her.

Thorne's unexplained dislike of Alex combined with her

near despotic status at the Oriental Institute allowed her great sway in Alex's career. Each interaction made her feel she was walking a sharp edge. Did Thorne expect her to pretend she knew what was going on?

Could this be a twisted loyalty test? If she went along with this, would it be possible to get into Thorne's good graces? Or was the situation a trap to make Alex look foolish?

Desperate for clues, Alex examined the newcomer, hoping something would stand out to guide her safely through this real-life Scylla and Charybdis. Would she find safe passage between the six-headed monster and the madly swirling whirlpool of Greek myth?

Alex took in Mr. Maspero's dull grey suit, pale translucent skin, and dead eyes that softly screamed bureaucrat. Adding it all together, it was a relatively safe bet he was from the organization. "Oh, yeah, KHNM," Alex said, trying to play along, but her words came out flat and unconvincing.

Maspero set his black briefcase on the lectern and opened it with a metallic pop. "You have been activated by the Keepers of the Holy and Noble Maat. You will be on the next flight to headquarters in New York for a full briefing."

"I don't understand." There were many possible reasons Alex had considered regarding her summons, but this?

"You're Alex Philothea, aren't you?" Maspero had the quick and efficient tone of a seasoned paper pusher. He pulled a manila file out of his briefcase and flipped through it, tracing the printed documents with his pale finger in a purposeful search to find the exact verbiage. He tapped the paper hard as if to permanently hammer in the lucky passage. "Here it is. Member in good standing since . . ." He whistled. "It appears you have not seen fit to keep up with your dues. From the look of it, for quite some time."

A burning, red flush crept from somewhere behind Alex's ears and quickly moved across her face. "But I haven't attended a meeting in ages. I can't be who you're looking for." Her voice pitched higher and made her statement sound more like a question. "There must be some sort of mistake."

"No, it is all very clear. I am here for you."

Alex detected disappointment in Maspero's voice, as if he had hoped to be talking to someone far more worthy. The Keepers of the Holy and Noble Maat was an organization Alex joined in college as a fun outlet to get her ancient-cultures geek on, go to meetings and lectures, and hopefully meet other like-minded nerds. The initiation ceremony was particularly formal, but all those "secret" societies had reputations for taking their traditions seriously.

This had to be an elaborate practical joke. Was her next class reunion coming up? Maybe her old KHNM cronies were pranking her. But no, Thorne would never be playful enough to go along with it. This couldn't be a joke.

"I can see by your vacant stare that this is a complete shock to you," Maspero said. "People sign up all the time, never thinking they will be called to duty. It doesn't happen often, but believe me, this is real."

"Called to duty?"

"If you had read your handbook before taking the initiation rites, you would've known activation was possible. But apparently you didn't deem it important." Maspero made a sweeping gesture with his arms to the empty lecture hall. "Why do you think you received the invitation to work here at the Oriental Institute? You must have realized there were many others far more talented and qualified than you in ancient Egyptian studies. And yet you were selected? Did it ever occur to you to question exactly why you were here? I assume not. But then again, you don't impress me as a natural questioner. Not at all like your father."

His sharp words stabbed at her. "You knew my father?"

Thorne chimed in, "Of course he did. Your father died in service to KHNM."

"He died on a dig. Everybody . . ." The ground seemed to shift under Alex as she leaned against the tabletop behind her for support.

Thorne's eyes shone with a sweet victory. "Everybody what? Your facts are wrong, Alex. Whatever you've been told is probably a fairy story cooked up by your mother."

Had her mother lied to her all these years? Would she? "If he didn't die on a dig, then how did he die?"

"Sorry, it's not for me to tell." Thorne's tone implied that she was anything but sorry.

"Can't or won't?" asked Alex.

"Since your mother declined to tell you, that makes the topic classified agency information. Ask Buxton. He's got the clearance to tell you anything and everything you want to know."

"Buxton?"

Maspero reached into his briefcase and handed Alex a packet. "You'll meet him in New York. Here are your travel documents," he said, snap-locking the briefcase. "Once you arrive at JFK, you will be delivered to headquarters for a full briefing."

Alex's travel folio trembled along with her hands.

Thorne addressed Maspero, as if Alex wasn't there. "It's shameful the apple fell so far from the tree. Had Phillip not died so young . . . well, who knows?" She stiffened her angular frame and gazed toward Alex. "What a waste. It's the least you can do. Finally step up and do something that would have made your father proud."

Alex knew Thorne was baiting her. She forced herself to breathe in deeply. Her hatred for Thorne solidified at that moment and became a levee that held her words at bay.

Alex pushed down the fresh rush of anger as a vision of her smiling father flashed brightly in her mind. Phillip was her father. He loved her. She was his child. What was this woman to him? A colleague? What made Thorne of all people think she was any sort of authority on Alex's own father? Although she knew Thorne was wrong, her words hurt. Alex turned and walked away with her travel docu-ments in hand, vowing to find out exactly how her father died. Escape now to fight another day. She grabbed the door handle and glanced back. Thorne's face had softened from an angry sneer to what could only be a genuine look of concern.

Alex walked through the door in a daze. She could have sworn she heard Thorne say, "Khnum keep you safe." The concern voiced in those words by the granite-hearted Thorne filled Alex with a deep sense of dread.

CHAPTER THREE

ost of the clothes she'd tossed into the suitcase were dirty. There was no time to wash them. Maspero didn't give her much time to pack before her early-evening flight. Hopefully, she'd be able to deal with it in New York. Alex imagined there had to be a dry cleaning or laundry service on every block in fashion-centric Manhattan.

She was grateful to her coworker Kathy, who quickly offered her cruise bag when Alex mentioned she didn't have any luggage. At first the bag's size seemed preposterous, but the steamer-trunk-like bag made the decision-making process easier. Alex could bring whatever she wanted. After forcing the top down, she pushed with all her might to latch its brass fasteners.

Alex tucked a lock of hair that had slipped out of her ponytail behind her ear as she surveyed her work. She cursed herself for allowing her bangs to be cut in the first place. They were taking forever to grow out. A prick of annoyance perforated her thoughts. As of late she'd come to realize she might just die by a thousand small cuts of people running roughshod over her. Was she terminally too nice? Was her propensity to treat others well her Achilles' heel?

She glanced in the distance at her bedside alarm clock wondering how much time she still had. Her pulse quickened as she grabbed for her phone. Her flight was in less than three hours, and she hadn't even called a cab yet. This was real. She was going to New York City, a place she'd always wanted to go, on a mysterious errand for KHNM. She wasn't certain if her anxiety outweighed her excitement or vice versa.

A soft dizziness overtook her as she sank into her tattered sofa. She cradled her head in her hands and closed her eyes, attempting to slow the sudden uptick in her breathing. Alex opened her eyes and pulled her phone near as she googled local cab companies. The dispatcher who answered laughed when she told him her address and proclaimed that today was her lucky day. A cabbie on a call was just stood up by a fare. A car would be there shortly.

In good traffic the ride to the airport would take thirty minutes. She should be able to get there a hair shy of the suggested two hour check-in window. She willfully avoided the temptation to contemplate a bad traffic day as she hauled herself and her trunk out of her apartment.

With all her belongings stored in the cab's trunk, and

the cab pulling away from the curb, her anxiety level dropped from overwhelmed to generally agitated. As she watched her neighborhood whiz by, it warmed her heart that the driver valued speed. If they continued at this pace, there would be nothing to worry about, and she'd be at the airport in plenty of time.

Alex lived in a small one bedroom apartment in an affordable area of the Hyde Park neighborhood of Chicago. She moved from California once she'd gotten the job at the Oriental Institute. Her mother followed her to be near. It wasn't the normal, everyday maternal ties that made her mother trade in sunshine and oranges for deep-dish and the Windy City; it was so she could be near her caretaker, Alex. The thought deflated the minimal level of excitement she'd managed to achieve upon setting off in the cab. She knew sooner or later her mother's dependency on her would have to stop. It was slowly leaching away her energy. One of Alex's friends had a term for people like Roxanne: an emotional vampire. It seemed to fit, but habits of an entire lifetime were hard to break.

The small neighborhood shops flashed by—the nail salon, coffee shop, and bookstore. The last word rang in her head like an overloud alarm clock. She'd forgotten tonight was book night.

Alex leaned into the front seat. "I have to make a stop before the airport." She rattled off her mother's address to the driver.

"The meter will be running," the driver said flatly.

"It'll be quick." She was just going to pop in to tell her

mom the basics. It bothered her that she would be so close to the one person who would know exactly what happened to her father all those years ago, but couldn't ask her. She knew that the conversation, when it did come, would be a doozy.

The driver sighed and said again. "The meter will be running."

When the cab pulled up to her mother's house something about it seemed off-kilter. Over her lifetime, Alex had developed a sixth sense for aberrations that could tell of trouble to come.

"I'll just be a couple minutes."

"The meter will be running." The driver's tone continued to have the enthusiasm of a bored toad. Alex wondered if he was an automaton, and those were his only programmed words.

She stepped out of the cab and peered up at her mother's three-story town house. It was late afternoon, so her mother wouldn't normally have the house lit up, but there was a strange darkness about it. Alex stopped at the first stair and tried to read the house like a clutch of loose tea leaves at the bottom of a teacup. The caw of a crow drew her attention to the top floor, where her mother's bedroom was. It was the drapes. Her long, velvet European-style blackout curtains were drawn. A familiar dense stone of disappointment fell hard into her gut.

Bernadette, her mother's housekeeper and sometimes confidante, emerged from the house and into the slanting autumn sunlight. Alex opened her mouth to say hello and quickly shut it. The housekeeper had raised a finger to her mouth as she strode purposefully down the stoop to where Alex stood.

Bernadette leaned in close to Alex and spoke in a whisper, as if a normal speaking voice could be heard from the house looming above them. "Your mother's been ill."

Alex must have shot her a knowing look, as her mother's helper quickly answered the unspoken question. "No. Dear me, not that. She is still securely on the wagon. Although I have noticed her usual period of pining for your father, like she does this time of year." Bernadette sighed. "When the leaves turn, so does your mother's mind."

"You make it sound so poetic. For me this season has always been the unsettling calm before a titanic storm breaks."

"Their love was something special. Her memories must be golden." Bernadette's gaze turned toward the yellow-tinged trees that lined the street, her eyes brimming with soft tears. She'd only worked for Roxanne for a year or so, but her mother and Bernadette managed to form a quick bond. Alex more or less chalked it up to Bernadette's overly accessible and tender heart rather than anything to do with her mother, who didn't make friends easily. "Roxanne caught the flu a few days ago and was up all night coughing. I finally got her to sleep. It's been the first time in a number of days she has gotten good rest. I wouldn't want to wake her. I was going to call you to cancel book night. I know you both look forward to it, but I told her sleep was more important, and book night could happen anytime."

Alex's hackles rose. At times Bernadette's angelic nature rubbed her the wrong way. She always managed to see things in a positive light. Especially when it came to issues around her mother. Like book night. Bernadette viewed it as quality time for mother and daughter, but in reality it was an excuse for Roxanne to get her daughter to format the images for her upcoming coffee-table book for free. She tapped her fingers against her thigh. Thoughts of her cab ride and impending flight were weighing on her mind as time slipped away. "Could you give her a message for me?" The words came out harsher than she wanted. She checked herself and softened her tone. "I am heading out to New York on business for a couple of days. I shouldn't be long. Could you tell her I will give her a call when I get there?"

"The Oriental Institute has an office in New York?"

"I guess the work isn't literally for the Institute. It is for an affiliate organization. KHNM."

Bernadette's normally rosy complexion turned white as the cabbie honked his horn. Alex touched Bernadette's arm. "Thank you, Bernadette." She walked down the stairs and hopped into the waiting car. As the cab pulled away, Alex glanced up to see Bernadette standing stock-still on Roxanne's stoop, her stony stare unchanged.

CHAPTER FOUR

No matter how Raymond tried to distract himself and tamp down the memory, Marceline's dying stare kept resurfacing in his mind's eye. How her beautiful face crumpled as recognition and confusion dawned on her. It must have been a cruel end to realize who her killer was. The ultimate betrayal, murdered by kin. Her unsuccessful struggle to utter a last word as her Ba-soul took to the skies. Although she wasn't able to speak the word aloud, Raymond knew deep in his heart what it had to be. *Unworthy.* The word rattled round and round in his head like a maleficent prayer wheel. No matter how he justified what happened last night, he knew she deserved better.

She was the first to be given the gift of death. Trial runs were never pretty, especially for the chosen specimen. Raymond took comfort in the fact that her freedom from this eternal curse had come. Her sacrifice would smooth the path to eternity for the Others.

He glanced up from his desk. His daughter Salima stood in the doorway dressed in lab whites. A deep sense of foreboding flooded him at her cat-who-ate-the-canary smile. Either she was far too excited about hearing of Marceline's demise, or she was delighting in some other bad news, or both. She was continually full of surprises.

She walked toward him with her usual steady grace and straightened her lab coat as if getting her armor in place before going to battle. Salima settled into the seat across from him. "So how did it go last night? Not well, I assume, if you are already back here."

Her tone struck Raymond as cheerful. Had she despised Marceline that much? A chill ran down his spine. He realized involving Salima in this project might have excited her taste for blood. In the days before these troubles, the Others had taken to calling her She-Beast. He was starting to understand why.

"I need to refine the dose." His thoughts returned to pulling Marceline from the pool's depths. Her body limp and wet in his arms, and her warrior's light forever extinguished. The memory made him feel sad and strangely powerful at the same time.

"Were you able to collect her vital fluids?"

"Just barely." He pointed to a stainless steel credenza. "The vials are over there in the bag. I nearly had to abandon the scene. Seth was on his way."

She walked to the black duffle and unzipped it,

exploring its contents. "How fitting it is that he found her drained body." She pulled out one of the vials. Marceline's essential fluids glowed, illuminating Salima's face in a soft, golden light. "It might work well for us. You know, buy us some time. Throw off those bumbling fools at KHNM. Estranged husband and all. You know they always look close to home first," she said.

"So true." Maybe he and his daughter weren't so dissimilar. The idea of it horrified and pleased him at the same time.

Silence deepened between them as she inspected the newly drawn specimens.

Salima returned to the desk and rolled one of the vials filled with Marceline's essence toward him and leaned in. "So you think the ushabtis will rise with this stuff?"

Raymond caught the tube in his hand just before it rolled off the table. "That's what keeps me up at night."

Salima's green eyes sparked with anger. "But either way it will work. Right?"

"All I know is that having helpers will make it much easier, and faster." He didn't like the dangerous way her mood was changing. He lowered his voice to be as soothing as possible. "If we are able to bring the ushabtis to life with the God-fluids of the Others, and they heed our commands, they'll be our boots on the ground. That way you and I can deal with bigger issues, while they bloody their hands. Without having minions, you and I alone can achieve our ends. It will just take more time. And personally, I've done enough waiting."

Salima sat down and smiled. "Getting itchy, are you?"

"I am ready to rule again. To put things right. But I know we can't rush it. We don't want to jeopardize our chance."

"So you would send these newly created minions out to kill the rest?" Salima's expression sank into disappointment.

"It was always my hope I wouldn't have to personally make every kill. If it comes down to it and the magic does not work, have no fear, daughter, I will kill the Others."

"What next? Should we collect the ushabtis?"

He loved her use of the euphemism. The collecting would require absconding with someone else's illegally purchased treasure. It suited Raymond well to steal from a thief. It was a further blessing of his endeavor and balanced the scales of Maat.

"Could you go it alone?" asked Raymond.

"Sure. But why?"

"I have unfinished business to take care of." He didn't want to tell her, but he had one more kill he would personally deal with. This one he'd always looked forward to. But not out of spite or a lust for blood, but out of a deep friendship and respect.

CHAPTER FIVE

From her bar stool perch, Alex scanned the tiny airport pocket bar, watching the steady stream of passengers en route to their gates. A drink seemed like the perfect remedy to help her unwind and contemplate her current situation. The small watering hole had one bartender. His attention was singularly focused on the only other customers, a large group of boisterous German tourists who had taken residence at the opposite end of the bar. Judging by their flushed, ruddy faces and frequent outbursts of laughter, they were accumulating quite a tab.

Even without a drink, it was good to get off her feet for a few minutes. A wave of exhaustion rolled through her body. Between the summons from Thorne and the disturbing news from Bernadette, the past few hours had been taxing to say the least.

She tried to get the barkeep's attention. Maybe she should head to her gate and forget the drink altogether.

It wasn't that Alex had anything grand to celebrate, far from it. But a champagne bar was the last thing she expected to see at O'Hare airport. The neon sign glowed with the promise of the bar's name, Bubbles. The clusters of champagne bottles displayed in neat little cubes behind the bar served as a sign of divine providence that drew her off course to the small lounge.

Champagne always had a magical quality for her. It was as if her worries floated up and away, bound to the bubbles by some sort of alchemy. If ever there were a time when she needed her concerns to disappear, it was now.

A burst of laughter erupted from little Bavaria. Alex caught the bartender's fleeting glance while he turned away from the chorus of laughter.

"Veuve Clicquot." The tall, thin glass of golden liquid therapy appeared in front of her almost immediately, as if her words reached out into the universe and called it forth from the void.

A wish of sorts before drinking champagne was a superstition she'd managed to pick up somewhere along the way. If Alex didn't make one, it was like inviting bad fortune to walk into her life. It could be grand or modest in concept, silly or serious in sentiment, or somewhere happily in between. The only requirement in choosing the toast was that it needed to suit the moment.

Alex held her glass and watched the tiny bubbles dance their way up as she tried to think of what to toast to. Safe journey? A grand adventure? She wasn't sure what would perfectly fit this singularly unique situation. The delicate edges of a wish-idea started to knit together.

A low voice close by startled Alex.

"What are we celebrating?"

He had materialized out of nowhere and sat on the bar stool next to Alex. He wore an old-school, well-tailored, shiny burgundy silk suit that was in direct conflict with his twentysomething appearance. He exuded confidence like waves of heat cascading across desert sands. Alex sensed the energy in her personal space change from contemplative to complicated as he sat next to her. She wasn't in the mood for company, no matter how quirkily attractive—if only she'd had the time to bring her drink-wish into reality, maybe it would've cast a spell of protection around her and barred his arrival.

Despite herself, Alex played along. "I'm sorry, what?"

"No need to be sorry. I just came over to thank you." He tipped his champagne glass toward her. "For the Veuve."

"What?" She choked on her champagne, the bubbles creating a mean fizz in her throat. "I didn't buy that for you. I didn't know you existed until twenty seconds ago, let alone having any insight into your current state of hydration."

She took a sip of the cool, crisp champagne. Peering up from the edge of her glass, she caught a passing glance of his deep blue eyes. Something drawing her toward him, and it was more than her usual weak spot for nonconformist oddballs. There was something fiercely unique about him. "I don't know who your secret admirer is. Maybe it is one of them." She nodded toward the boisterous group of men at the other end of the bar who were now singing what seemed like a European soccer club fight song with great gusto.

"That would be just my luck." He had the hurt look of someone who was told his birthday party was canceled due to lack of interest. "So, it really wasn't you?"

"Really."

He paused and turned his head toward the other patrons, as if pondering the notion. "I don't quite feel up to courting a group of drunken German bears tonight. How about I stay here and you and I start over." He smiled an embarrassed and somewhat neighborly smile and reached across the space between them with an outstretched hand. "I am Niles Greene, importer-exporter extraordinaire and part-time life coach."

She gingerly took his hand in hers. An odd sensation like a warm, dull shock emanated from his flesh. His name flitted around her head like a moth beating against a porch light, over and over, as she tried in vain to locate the long-forgotten memory attached to it. Niles Greene. It sounded so familiar, but how? Alex was certain she would remember him if she had ever met him before.

"So what do you do when you aren't picking up strange men in bars?" He beamed a bright smile in Alex's direction.

She rolled her eyes.

"Too soon?"

"Too soon." The muscles in her face rebelled against her as she mirrored his playful smile. "So, what exactly does a life coach do? It always struck me as the perfect occupation for con artists."

"Since I do it part time, that would make me mostly honest."

"Mostly? Is that your final answer?"

"In all honesty, I don't think you can expect any more than mostly from anyone. Especially from those who consider themselves high-minded and pious."

"So you are a con man and a realist."

He smiled and shifted his gaze to the bar napkin he'd been doodling on. "Sometimes, when we think we are being completely honest, we are lying to ourselves," he said in a soft, almost inaudible voice.

"I sense the life coach awakening within you like a ushabti being called forth by an ancient work spell." Alex instantly realized how odd that must have sounded.

"Whoa, ushabti? Interesting word choice for casual conversation in an airport bar."

"Sorry. I don't get out much. I've been spending too much of my time cloistered with other academics and forget myself when I am around civilians. I work at the Oriental Institute, as a research archaeologist. My specialty is in ancient Egypt."

"Civilian?" he gasped in a mocking air of high drama. "What do you take me for? Some sort of ancient-Egypt neophyte? If you weren't such pleasant company, I would be completely offended." He shook his head and raised his almost-empty glass. "You can make it up to me by getting me another."

Alex gave him a searing look.

He chuckled softly. "What I meant was you could erase the stain on my reputation by purchasing, for the very first time ever, a glass of champagne for yours truly."

The Germans roared with laughter as if punctuating Niles's overplayed dramatics.

She matched his charade of hurt feelings with a hint of sarcasm. "As much as I would love the honor . . . I don't think I have the time to try and get the bartender's attention." The barkeep stood like a conductor, waving his hands dramatically as if to keep his symphony of European laughter in time. "It appears the maestro might be in the middle of his greatest verbal symphony yet."

Their gaze lingered. Feeling exposed, Alex looked away. "So, if you are not an ancient-Egypt neophyte, where exactly do you land on the scale?"

"Depends on how you measure it. Knowledge is a relative and movable beast."

"Very philosophical. Okay, where do you land between, oh, let's say . . . occasional watcher of Discovery Channel documentaries and truly rabid enthusiast?"

"Neither. My import business is based in Cairo. I am just returning from a fairly intense purchasing junket." He glanced at his large and expensive watch. "Oh crap, I hadn't noticed the time." He reached into his jacket and retrieved a card holder. It was embossed with a turquoise rendering of an ibis bird with its heron-shaped head and long bill. The silver case flashed bright as he opened it.

"I find myself in Chicago often. Maybe we could have dinner sometime and discuss the Amarna Period or something." He smiled and handed a business card to Alex. "Oh wait!" He grabbed it from her and quickly jotted something down. "Give me a call if you ever have a sudden ancient-Egyptian emergency and need another geek to chat with outside of your usual academic circles." He winked at Alex as he placed the card on the napkin in front of her and then touched her forearm.

His touch was comforting as the strange energy thrummed from his fingertips.

She gazed deeply into his eyes. Alex sensed a connection of spirit between them that felt oddly at home. He let go of her hand, and without another word, he walked away and was lost in the steady stream of humanity that coursed around the island-shaped bar.

Alex picked up the small business card. Beside it, on the white-marble bar top, was his midnight-blue Montblanc pen with a mother-of-pearl inlay. Did he conveniently leave the pen in the hope that she would be compelled to return it? She laughed as she read his scrawled note on the back of the card, written in phonetic hieroglyphs above his cell number. *In case of emergency.* Alex marveled at his fluid ability to communicate in the archaic language. There was definitely more to Niles than met the eye. She picked up the pen and glanced at the napkin that he'd doodled on. The symbol he drew was both foreign and familiar, much like the mysterious Mr. Greene. The fluttering moth awoke in her mind once more.

Alex slipped the items he left into the scribe's bag her father made for her all those years ago and glanced at her watch. With a start, she leapt off her barstool and ran toward her gate, hoping against hope that she could somehow bend time and make it before they closed the jetway.

CHAPTER SIX

The past twelve or so hours were a tornado of events landing Alex at baggage claim in JFK. The path she followed to claim her luggage was not a yellow brick road, but an endless corridor of industrial beige flooring. She ambled through the secured area, her welcoming party comprised of tired and travel-worn passengers who scowled at her as they wheeled their luggage carts past her. Not a single singing munchkin in sight, or anyone sent by KHNM for that matter.

As time crept on, fewer bags thumped down the gaping maw of the stainless-steel- tongued baggage carousel, until only a couple orphans remained. The all-too-familiar duo of black bags with hot-pink surveyor's tape wrapped around their handles passed by her once more. The eye-catching brightness signaled to no one in particular as the unclaimed bags took another lonely turn around the empty metal oval.

A new wave of fatigue washed over Alex as she realized the gargantuan bag her cruise hound of a coworker let her borrow was plainly still in Chicago. The bag was so large whoever used it would never want for anything, no matter how many formal nights there were. She remembered wincing when the ticket agent at O'Hare explained how much her bag fee would be. However, Alex had been sure it would be well worth the expense. It would have been a small price to pay for easy access to everything she could possibly need right there within Big Bertha. Some might have thought it excessive to bring one's own pillow, favorite tea, and reference materials, but Alex fully embraced the travel approach of having all the comforts of home readily available.

Agent Maspero was no help at all. She could be looking forward to a research project, field work, or just about anything. It was comforting that among all the uncertainty she would be ready for anything, even if that meant packing everything.

Alex spotted the baggage claim agent standing across from her in the distance. She wore a midnight blue, almost black airline uniform, clipboard clutched tightly in her hands. She had the uncomfortable, wound-too-tight appearance of someone with a short fuse. She projected an aura of contempt for humanity.

Alex marched toward the agent and steeled herself for

what she could guess would be an entirely unpleasant experience. "Excuse me," Alex said, reaching deep for any remaining positive energy she could muster, believing always that you will get more with honey than vinegar, witches included. "It appears that my bag didn't make it."

The agent grabbed her boarding jacket. "Unfortunately for you, this was the last flight from Chicago for the day. Your bags may not be here until . . ." The agent lifted the claim ticket to a handheld scanner. "Oh," she said, her voice trailing off meaningfully. She lifted up her two-way radio. "Supervisor to baggage claim."

"So, where's my bag?"

The agent paused and smiled a plastic sort of smile. "Your bag caught on fire."

A strong female voice boomed behind Alex, "What do you mean, caught on fire?"

Alex turned to look at the stranger. The woman had piercing green eyes against rich olive skin framed by a long and luxurious mane of onyx-black hair. She radiated a powerful charisma that created a golden aura, illuminating her otherworldly beauty.

The agent's attitude of authority switched gears, as if she realized a sleek lioness had entered her alley-cat domain. "The trunk was unloaded from the aircraft, but it was much too large to fit in with the other bags. So—"

"Listen," the newcomer said, "we don't need a play-by-play. We need to know what happened."

"We?" Alex appreciated this stranger's help, but it

seemed she was going a little far by claiming she needed to know what happened to her bag.

"Oh, sorry, I didn't introduce myself." The stranger's tone was cool. "I am Salima. The agency sent me to collect you." She shook Alex's hand. "I am your underutilized and overly educated greeter." Her voice became a whisper. "Leave it to the agency . . ."

Apparently Salima had brought her own baggage with her to the airport.

Salima rolled her hands at the baggage agent in the universal motion for *hurry it up* coupled with an agitated stare. "So, what happened to the bag?"

The agent spoke tentatively. "One of the large leather handles got caught in the wheel of a baggage cart. It was dragged across the tarmac, where it sparked and caught on fire. The fire crew came, but by the time they put it out, your bag was . . . " She smiled a nervous smile. "Completely destroyed."

Alex couldn't help but admire Salima as they slipped into the agency's black limo. Her powerful presence had immediately rebooted the baggage agent's desire to serve, like a quick flick of a circuit breaker.

Alex's body sank into the deep leather seat. A dull but heavy pain came to life from behind her eyes, the familiar portent of a piercing migraine to come. The reality of trying to replace all her possessions was hitting Alex hard. The umbilical cord that connected Alex with all of her familiar goods was severed in a millisecond. How could this be? Was her father's excavation tool kit gone forever? One-third of the sparse number of items he'd left to her, lost to fire? She played with the gold djed pillar pendant around her neck, rubbing the raised horizontal lines that depicted the spine of Osiris, a symbol of strength. The pendant's presence comforted and grounded her in times of trouble. Now it magnified the realization that this tiny trinket strung around her neck and her scribe's bag slung over her shoulder were her last two remaining physical connections to him.

Back at the airport, when the ramp agents appeared in their zippered beige jumpsuits and dragged the massive bag out for her to identify, it was like a sad burnt offering to a capricious and uncaring god of travel. It was charred black, nearly unrecognizable. If it weren't for its unusually immense size, she could have convinced herself it wasn't hers.

She'd picked through the remains searching for any of her father's tools that might have survived. Nothing was salvageable.

The airport's fire chief peppered Alex with a barrage of questions. Once he learned that Alex's coworker purchased the bag years ago in China, he speculated the materials the bag was made of might have caused the intense heat of the fire. He was impressed with the combustible nature of the fabric and was genuinely dismayed nothing survived. Alex's heart sank at the thought of the few but precious items that were lost to her forever.

Alex rubbed the stiff leather of her scribe's bag made from a vintage binocular case. It was comforting that she still had it. She traced the familiar grooves of tooled leather depicting Isis, Nephthys, and Hathor. Above the Goddesses, the text *Girl Gods Rock* was transliterated into hieroglyphs. It was a gift from her dad on her ninth birthday. He'd spent hours in the garage working the leather himself. It was the same year he died. She smiled to herself. Most who saw it probably assumed the text contained something far more intellectual than a slogan for girl power. Alex recalled the spark in his eyes when he told her that the scribe's bag was a special place for her found treasures. Although the scribe's palette, ink, and two sticklike pens were long gone, she used it as a makeshift carryall that was nearly always slung over her shoulder.

Her fingers returned to the pendant around her neck. A gift she'd found by accident from a false bottom in the case that her father hadn't told her about. She smiled at the memory of finding it.

It had been a cold autumn day. She missed him terribly. As she flopped onto her bed her elbow knocked into the bag. It tumbled off her nightstand and onto the floor. When it hit the ground, it made an unexpected popping sound. She peered over the bed's side for a quick damage check. The necklace lay in a shaft of afternoon light. Its glimmer uplifted her mournful heart. Lying next to the necklace was a piece of paper folded into a tiny square. She slowly unfolded it. At its heart it simply said, *Strength Always. Love, Dad.*

Since the day she'd first put it on, the necklace had never left her neck.

Alex reflected on the comfort those words had given her over the years as she stared out at the unfamiliar grey cityscape. Her head throbbed as her mood slipped into an all-too-familiar spiral of negativity. Alex endured a childhood filled with her mother's "black days." It made her supremely aware of how quickly a sad pondering could turn into an ocean of despair. She pulled down hard on her mental safety cord.

She emerged from her musings becoming more aware of her surroundings and the stone-quiet stranger sitting across from her. The naked silence thrummed with awkwardness. Alex blurted out the first thing that popped into her mind. "So, how long have you worked for KHNM?" She regretted saying it almost immediately. Powerful women like Salima always made her feel self-conscious.

Salima spoke to Alex's reflection in the tinted window. "Oh, I imagine it would be longer than you could possibly contemplate. So, you'll be seeing headquarters for the first time, I am guessing." She smiled a sad, world-weary smile that never quite reached her eyes. Then she grabbed a small bottle of water from the mini-fridge and handed it to Alex. "Compliments of the agency. Nothing but the best for KHNM operatives."

Alex cracked open the white plastic lid and slugged down the cool water. She hadn't realized how thirsty she was.

"Drink it up," Salima said. "If you are going to save the world, like Buxton and all the other dimwits at the agency seem to think, you will have to keep yourself properly hydrated."

Alex half choked on the water as it bulged painfully in her throat. She coughed. *Saving the world?* "I got the impression from Dr. Thorne that—"

"That you were being called to duty for a neat little research project or emergency conservation work on a high-value artifact." Salima turned away from Alex toward the tinted window. "I guess, in a way, it is nice they would want to ease you in gently. To put off telling you the hard truth until you're here and committed."

Alex leaned into the deep leather seat as she struggled to grasp Salima's words. "Save the world?"

"Apparently they didn't feel it appropriate to divulge your mission before your debrief. I certainly would not want to break protocol."

"Haven't you already?"

"Oh, heavens no. I only gave you a few conversation topics to think about, to keep your mind occupied while we are in transit."

Alex felt like a mouse being toyed with by an angry and bored cat that was cheesed off at being locked in the house for too long. Salima leaned forward and turned on the TV, cranking the volume to a level at which conversation would be impossible. Alex smoldered as she ignored how the loud noise exacerbated the throbbing in her head. She retrieved a prescription-strength ibuprofen from her bag and chased it down with some water.

Message received.

CHAPTER SEVEN

The limo stopped in front of an expansive staircase crowned by a large, many-pillared building that resembled a fancy wedding cake with a flourish of white buttercream embellishments. Attached to the pillars were large jewel-toned banners that billowed in the wind like grand sails on an ancient royal barge, bringing to mind Cleopatra's grand ship engineered with the sole purpose of impressing upon Mark Antony the splendors of Egypt.

The chauffeur opened the door, snapping Alex out of her Ptolemaic reverie. Salima leaned forward and exited the limo. As her body brushed by Alex, a strong and complex scent wafted by. It was familiar and exotic, comforting and yet unsettling.

Alex climbed the stairs. In the dim evening light, she could pick out the supersized images of gold-and turquoise-encrusted artifacts from Mesoamerica silk-screened onto the richly colored fabric. The text read *Diablo City of Gold* with the Metropolitan Museum of Art logo.

Alex stopped in her tracks. "I thought we were heading to KHNM headquarters."

Salima faced Alex and rolled her eyes. "Talk about flying blind."

"Flying blind?" Alex asked as Salima continued her march toward the gold-hued brass doors in the distance.

"I don't know what the agency is thinking," she shouted into the night air. "But, I really don't appreciate being tethered to someone who appears to be completely clueless."

Alex was starting to lose her patience with Salima's bad attitude. It was one thing to come off as unabashedly confident, but continually rude? That was a completely different story. She scaled the stairs two at a time to catch up with Salima. She leapt in front of her, stopping her in her tracks. "Clueless? How can you talk about me like I'm not even here?"

Salima's expression thawed for a quick moment and then returned to an icy stare. She pushed past Alex. "I think it would be better if you weren't." Salima motioned with her arm. "You'll want to move." She pulled out a cell phone and swiped it to life. "We're here." Her voice was all business.

Alex jumped away from the brass doors that whooshed open as if on command, nearly knocking her down.

"Following instructions is not one of your strong suits either," Salima mumbled as she stepped inside.

Alex walked through the threshold. Salima's last jab evaporated at the sight of the Met's Great Hall before her. She'd heard the architect modeled it after the ancient Roman Baths of Caracalla. Doric columns led the eye to the second floor. Her eyes traveled further to the massive domed ceiling. The Egyptian collection's entrance was to the right.

Surprisingly Salima led her to the left. "Shouldn't we be going that way?" asked Alex. Salima continued her march without uttering a word.

Alex turned the corner and stood in a deserted moonlit atrium. Ghost-white marble statues filled the space, standing like stiff and silent witnesses to this off-hours incursion.

As Alex's eyes adjusted to the dim light, she could see a dapper elderly man walking toward them. "Glad to see you made it. We were starting to wonder what was taking you so long." His soft, kindly face broke into an odd smile of familiarity that held an equal mix of pride and joy. It struck Alex odd that she didn't recall ever meeting him.

"The little dear's bag burned." Salima's voice was flat. "Had to fill out an insurance claim. Took ages."

"I am sorry to hear that. What a trying experience." The old man shook Alex's hand. "Buxton's the name, Charles Buxton. I used to work with your father. I am sure you don't remember me. I met you years ago, when you were just a sweet child."

"Not much has changed," Salima muttered while she turned and walked away.

Buxton hooked his arm through Alex's and escorted her away from Salima, leading her through the crush of ancient Greek and Roman statues. "Don't mind her. Her bark is worse than her bite."

The warmth of his arm was reassuring in the cold air of the museum. His tweed jacket had the familiar dusty-musty smell of old scholar. He patted her arm. "I have so looked forward to meeting you again."

They walked side by side in silence, as if on hallowed ground, past all the wonders on display from the ancient Greek and Roman worlds—war regalia, jewelry, masks, and pottery galore—until they came to a simple plain-brown door marked *Museum Staff Only*.

Buxton swiped his ID, then ushered her through. Alex glanced back. They'd somehow lost Salima along the way. "Salima won't be joining us?" She hoped her joy was not too apparent.

"Urgent matters are afoot. We may not see her for a while."

Alex followed Buxton's lead down a beige utilitarian metal staircase and wondered what urgent matters might be keeping her catty companion occupied. The empty clank of their steps reverberated through the bleak stairwell. This leg of their journey was a stark contrast from the riches of humanity they'd just viewed. The staircase led to a vast subterranean labyrinth of corridors and offices making up the grand museum's underbelly.

It occurred to her that maybe she should be feeling a little uneasy at the situation, walking through a hidden underground maze with a complete stranger. Ever since being summoned by Thorne, it was as if she were being pulled toward the unknown, caught up in a fast-moving current. At this point all she could do was hang on and trust that she was being drawn into a safe embankment and not into a nest of famished crocodiles.

Judging solely on looks, Buxton appeared to be completely harmless. The fluorescent light shone off his balding head, and the leather patches on his tweed jacket screamed scholarly gent. His warm and friendly gaze flashed in her mind, not exactly what you would conjure when thinking of a crazed killer. But then again, when serial killers are caught, it is common to hear the neighbors say, "He was so quiet, kept to himself." Her fatigued mind leapt from calm to fright like a skittish cat repetitively attacking then retreating from its own shadow.

"Here we are," Buxton said as he stopped in front of a large oak door. Dead center at eye level was an etched brass plate with *Charles Buxton — Custodian to the Ancients*. He opened the door, revealing a large office space.

Alex knew she had so much to say to him, and so many questions that needed answers, but somehow in his well-appointed office all she could come up with was, "Nice office for a custodian."

"It's kind of a play on words. The museum staff thinks it's pithy, tongue-in-cheek, you know. Apparently, they are under the impression that I am here to clean up all the ancient messes and keep them in order. And in truth, they are not far off. As chief conservator of the Egyptian collection, I do a lot of dusting." He ran his finger across a book-case, then frowned. He rounded his massive wooden rococo-style desk and sat in his giant leather chair. He gestured to the seat across from him. "Have a seat."

Buxton's office was a far cry from the dull grey hallway outside. Antique glass-fronted bookcases edged the room. It was as if she'd stepped into the library of an old-time gentleman's club in London.

"So much to say, so little time. Where shall we start? I'm sure you have a million questions. I know your father always did."

"I guess that's as good a place as any to start. My father's death, that is." Might as well grab the bull by the horns.

"Did your mother ever speak of your father's work? That is, beyond his scholarly research?"

"Dad was a forbidden topic. I learned to avoid it at all costs." Alex's mom continuously wavered between highly depressed and not-so-highly depressed. Alex tiptoed through her childhood realizing one mention of him or the slightest reminder of her father would tilt the scales to a very dark place; usually that place was rehab for Roxanne. Her mother moved from booze to pills and then back again like a wounded bird whose migration cycle was out of whack. The roles between mother and daughter were inverted. Alex learned the role of caregiver very early on.

"All my life my mother told me he died during a site excavation near Tell el-Amarna. That he was bitten by a horned viper. They couldn't get him to the clinic in time for the antivenom. Yesterday, Maspero and Thorne hinted at something very different. But they refused to tell me the whole story." The words came out in a rapid fire. She feared if she slowed down and talked normally, her emotional facade would crack and tears would be streaming down her face in front of this stranger. "I understand my mother was thriving and vibrant before Dad left for that last dig." Alex paused to conjure the courage to say what she'd always thought but never spoke aloud to another soul. "It's as if that snake killed two with one bite."

Buxton removed his glasses and rubbed his eyes. His fingers came away with a glimmering streak of moisture. "I tried my best to console your mother at the funeral, but she wanted to have nothing to do with me, or really any of us. I was your father's superior at the agency."

The doctor seemed to visibly age in front of Alex, as if the memory of Phillip's death etched deeper creases in his careworn face. "I guess his death rests squarely on my shoulders. Last I heard, your mother picked up and moved to points unknown. I've always wondered about you and how you dealt with it. Your father was like a son to me. It broke my heart when he died . . . so much promise." Buxton gazed down at the ink blotter in front of him. "Your mother told you a partial truth. He did die in the mountains surrounding Tell el-Amarna, but he certainly wasn't working on an excavation. He was on assignment for a high-level retrieval mission for the agency. His death is still, for the most part, unsolved. We believe we know who killed him—"

"He was killed?" Alex's pulse raced as the room seemed to spin around her. Her father had been murdered?

"Yes, the evidence points to it. The only one who can prove it has gone off the grid completely. We've searched high and low, but whenever we get close, he is two steps ahead of us."

"How can it be? That you can let a murderer run free for all these years?"

"No, he's not a murderer, but he was there. He witnessed the whole thing, and went underground. We can only speculate that the circumstances around your father's death point to something other than natural causes. Phillip did die by snake venom, but the evidence leaves a lot to question."

"So who is this non-killer, who happens to know how my father died?"

"He was your father's partner at the agency. He was devastated when Phillip died. After filling out his incident report the next morning, he disappeared without a word, not to be heard from again. Don't worry, Alex. Your father served honorably. Always. Don't think we have given up. I know the damning evidence is somewhere out there, it's just a matter of locating it."

Alex absentmindedly toyed with the djed pillar pendant around her neck. Buxton's gaze snapped to her hand. "Where did you get that?" he asked.

"It is one of the few things my father left me." Alex clasped it protectively in her hand. "I wear it always."

"Unbelievable. I didn't think it possible." He got up and walked to Alex. "May I?"

Alex nodded. He squatted and held the pendant in his hands. "Your father's amulet is intact. I never would have guessed it." Buxton's expression took on a faraway look. "We always thought it was destroyed along with him," he said as if speaking to himself.

Destroyed. The word hit a hard and unexpected blow. How could this man who professed to care for her dad speak of her father's death so dispassionately?

Buxton placed his hand on Alex's shoulder. "Sorry, that must have seemed callous." He returned to his desk and grabbed a pyramid-shaped paperweight and rhythmically flipped it from end to end. "I am not quite sure if I am coming or going lately . . . ," he mused as he continued to toy with the paperweight.

"So, why am I here? Salima mentioned saving the world. I figured she had to be kidding, right?"

"Salima said that?" Buxton shook his head.

"She'd mentioned it in the limo."

Buxton sighed. "I guess that shouldn't surprise me. She's always had her independent, unpredictable ways."

Was the old man avoiding her question? Alex was frustrated with the lack of answers so far. "Look, I thought you were going to brief me, get me up to speed."

"Yes. Of course. I apologize for an old man's ramblings. Now keep in mind, what I am about to tell you is going to seem completely unbelievable. But please, try to keep an open mind."

"I will do my best."

"All I ask is that you hear me out. And after you have heard everything I say, please consider what I have told you, even if you think I am an old man with crazed delusions." He opened the book in front of him. "Will you, for the memory of your father and his sacrifice for KHNM promise that to me? To listen with an open mind?"

"You have my word."

He picked up the crystal paperweight he'd been worrying earlier and set it next to the gilded leather journal he'd opened. "What if I told you the ancient Gods of Egypt walk among us?"

Alex searched his face, looking for any signs of mirth, but found only a deadly serious stare looking back at her. "I see through your strategy." She laughed nervously. "Start out with something ludicrous so the next thing you say won't sound so outrageous. Please, tell me what you brought me all the way from Chicago for."

"I did. Remember what I said about having an open mind?"

"I assumed what you were going to tell me wouldn't be sheer nonsense. Next you are going to tell me the ancient Egyptians were an alien race that used their superadvanced technologies to build the pyramids or something like that?"

"What do you take me for? Ancient aliens, really?" He snorted with disgust.

"So, let me get this right, you are totally cool with the ancient Egyptian Gods existing, but not aliens?" Alex was bemused by his illogical distinctions.

"It's no joke. I have yet to tell you the most troubling part."

"Let me guess, five thousand years of rent is due? The Gods are demanding a grand sacrifice of all the world's virgins?" Alex immediately regretted her words. Obviously, Buxton was off his rocker, but that didn't give her license to be rude. Maybe the guilt about her father's death had pushed him over the edge of sanity, like her mother. A newfound empathy flooded her for the sweet old man sitting across from her.

"Okay, what's the worst of it?"

"They are being murdered."

CHAPTER EIGHT

Raymond wove his way through the crowd of beautiful, drunken dancers. The club lights revealed a thin sheen of sweat that coated their skinny designer-clad bodies, bouncing as if on invisible pogo sticks to the thumping bass. Lasers cut through the man-made fog that rose up from the dance floor to the VIP suites above. That was where Horatio would be, surrounding himself with fragile humans, pretending as much as he could that he was one of them, and for all intents and purposes looking every bit as young and beautiful as the rest of them. Immortality did have a few perks.

Raymond's pace quickened, influenced by the strong rhythms, speeding him ever closer to the moment of truth. Would Horatio welcome death? Or would he shun it? He hoped with all his heart that his friend would see the sense of it.

Over the years Horatio had become a power broker in the entertainment management world. A recent spread in *Rolling Stone* magazine referred to him as "The New King Midas" because every act or album he backed turned to gold. Anybody who wanted to be somebody yearned to be pulled into his influential orbit. He'd built up a clientele of A-list talent that would make the most seasoned agents lose their cool at the mere thought of possessing it.

Over time he managed to collect a varied group of hangers-on. They were generally young, shiny, pretty things from every corner of the world, hoping to catch his eye.

Raymond watched from afar as his friend perfected the expected extremes of the celebrity lifestyle. Lately his tabloid appearances slowed to a dull roar. The press was openly mournful at his sudden loss of a death wish. They yearned for the good old days when Horatio could be relied upon for a sensational tabloid shocker or one of his many brushes with death. Like that time he did a free fall with the Flying Elvi and forgot to attach his chute. He somehow managed to survive the fall. Some liked to speculate it was the luck of falling into Lake Mead that saved him. Others favored more fantastical versions, asserting he was abducted by aliens and returned safely to earth.

Or there was that incident when he broke into Siegfried and Roy's tiger habitat, on a night of a full moon, with a case of bourbon, wearing a suit made entirely of steaks. Some try to end their days through death by cop, but tiger suicide is pretty rare. He was found the next morning sleeping it off in a large pile of slumbering striped beasts.

The tigers were never the same after that visit from Horatio, and neither was he. That was about the time Horatio's desire to end it all seemed to cease.

Being an Immortal, Horatio's death wish was a sincere although impotent dream. No matter how hard he tried with this hard-core party life, it would never affect him like his mortal groupies. He could drink any of his sycophants under the table dozens of times over. Alcohol, although enjoyable, burned quickly within the furnace of eternity that burned deep within all the Others.

In a twisted game of Horatio's making, he exposed his followers to the endless excesses available to rock royalty. Acting as a secret angel of death until their freedom from this life was granted. He probably thought he was doing them a favor. Horatio was continually dying vicariously through others.

Until tonight, that is. Raymond hoped Horatio would see his gift for what it was: a sweet release. Raymond gently wrapped his fingers around the glass vial that held the golden liquid promise. The terrible memory of killing Marceline, how she struggled as she fought the gift, swept over him as he climbed the stairs to Horatio's VIP party loft. The betrayal and hatred he saw in her eyes as her Ba-soul escaped made him want to retch. He consoled himself with the thought that tonight would be different, as the dose of ambrosia-infused toxin had been tripled.

"Look what the cat dragged in," Horatio shouted at Raymond as he entered the crimson-hued VIP suite perched above the dance floor. Large double-paned windows kept the noise of the riffraff down below to a minimum. Horatio's voice was easily heard over the muffled din below. "Long time no see."

Raymond bowed deeply, swinging his arm to the side with a theatrical flourish in comic deference to his friend. "I have given my coin of passage to the large-muscled cyclops guarding the iron gate of this netherworld. I survived the churning sea of debauchery over which you rule from this suspended Olympus." His hands swept out to each side to indicate the entire VIP suite and smiled. "Do my efforts grant me an audience with a God?"

Horatio laughed. "You must be in a playful mood comparing me to those relatively new Athenian Gods. Which of those self-important prods would I be in your fictitious pantheon? The great and mighty Zeus?"

"Hardly. You would resemble more the three-headed dog. But in this case I'll allow you to be Prometheus in my imaginings."

Horatio visibly winced. Did the parallel of the helper to humans hit too close to the mark? "I have missed your dramatic tendencies. Where have you been hiding yourself?" The playfulness in Horatio's voice had changed to weariness.

"Is there somewhere we can go and talk?" asked Raymond.

Horatio was different from the Others. He felt things more deeply, almost humanlike. Raymond had always thought this ability to empathize with the mortals contributed to the fertile black soil that sprouted the seeds of Horatio's dissatisfaction and obsession with death.

"How about here?" Horatio raised a glass. "The night is young and on the verge of running wild." He took a sip of his martini. "The vodka is flowing like a clear and pristine aquifer below this fair kingdom." He motioned to the personal waitress in the corner. "Called at a whim to quench your thirsty needs. The fun has only just begun. Let's paint the town red, like the good old days."

Raymond surveyed those crowded around Horatio. "I need a moment, just you and me. We need to talk."

"Of course. My penthouse awaits."

Horatio's entourage of bodyguards escorted them through the casino to his private elevator. When they stepped in, the gold doors closed, leaving them alone and cocooned in silence. They were instantaneously cut off from the cacophony of the lobby below. It had been a long time since they'd seen each other, maybe too long. While the gilded glass box pulled upward, the silence grew around them.

"Why the Luxor of all places?" Raymond was never certain if Horatio was making an attempt at irony by living there, or if the environment in some queer way made him feel at home.

"I love feeling surrounded by pharaohs. The only other time I've seen such blatant abuse of the nemes headdress was in those hokey old movies from the fifties and sixties starring Elizabeth Taylor and the like." Horatio pointed to the casino workers below who wore the headdress that in ancient times was reserved for the divine ruler. "Now it perfectly suits waitresses and bellboys. It makes me feel like I am constantly surrounded by greatness." Horatio's sarcastic and cocky smile faded into a weary one.

Raymond gazed down at the miniature army of Egyptian kings relegated to serving drinks. He was amused by the thought of it.

The elevator doors slid open to reveal Horatio's palatial nest. It had a panoramic view of the Vegas Strip. Raymond recalled the many wild times he spent in this space partying it up with his old friend. "So why all the body-guards? Certainly you don't need them." Raymond knew Horatio to be a strong warrior. Not as strong as he was, but a challenging opponent all the same.

"Oh, it's all a part of the game, I guess. Think of it as an economic stimulus. I am a job creator. Who'd have thought? Horus, once Lord of the Sky, now an immortal employer of mortals." His words lengthened as if he pondered them as he spoke. "In reality, being the master of the human entertainment realm dictates a certain standard of living. It's expected that an entourage surrounds me at all times. They would follow me into the bathroom if I let them."

"No kidding."

"As a matter of fact, the two that followed us to my private elevator are going to stand in the lobby until I leave again or they get relieved by the next shift."

"I had no idea life at the top would be so complicated. As a scientist, I find my admirers are few and far between.

It's funny, though, when I do get the occasional science-geek fan, they can be surprisingly intense. I had one guy sending me disturbing photoshopped pictures of him and me at locations around the world."

"So you were his stolen scientific garden gnome?"

Raymond laughed. Things between them were rolling along like the old days. Maybe this would be an easy one. "I guess you could say that. But in this case he'd have to have a fetish for his gnome. Some of the pictures were pretty blue."

"Well, you are a looker. I could see how he couldn't resist. Brains and beauty all in one immortal package." Horatio laughed.

"Seriously, you and I have seen a multitude of crazy things over the long course of our being, but I have to tell you, that guy was something else."

"Tell me about it. I have my own bulletproof limo."

"The letters stopped. So I didn't need to go that far. Since I had the pictures he'd sent me, a few stern letters from my lawyer seemed to curb his enthusiasm."

Horatio guided Raymond toward a sunken living room and waved him toward a faux-leopard-skin sofa. "Take a load off. I am sure you must be weary from all those scientific breakthroughs you're always working so hard on . . . It is funny, really."

"What's that?"

Horatio pressed an unseen button on the table, and from its center appeared a small but well-stocked bar. He grabbed a cut crystal decanter and poured a liberal amount of its contents into two square glasses. "Scotch?" He held one up to Raymond and handed it to him. "It is strange to think how opposite you and I are. I am constantly working to help humans self-edit their lives, and you spend your days in the lab trying to allow them to add more chapters."

"Don't make me out to be a hero."

"I wasn't." Horatio took a sip of his drink. "Just stating facts. Some people have gone so far as to call you the Golden One. The great giver of life or some kind of crap like that. It makes me laugh a little, considering—"

Raymond interjected, "Considering that I ended the old ways and trapped us in this constant state of nothingness."

"In a nutshell."

Raymond took a long pull from his scotch as he thought about what to say next. Would Horatio want an apology? Should he come out and slay the three-hundred-pound hippopotamus in the room? Tell Horatio he regretted the course they all took? That he was sorry he talked them into sacrificing their Godheads to live in this shell of immortality? At the time it seemed to be the only way to preserve the family against eventually losing their powers altogether. Maybe it would've been better if they'd faded into oblivion instead of becoming the shallow and narcissistic creatures they had become since the change. No, he knew he would have to respect the God that Horatio was. Horus, his friend, the most reasonable of them all, would not want to hear excuses. "I've come tonight to try and make it right."

Horatio shook his head. "That is impossible, Ray."

"Nothing is impossible. I came here to give you the gift

I gave Marceline." He reached into his jacket pocket and retrieved the small vial and held it out to Horatio. "Here's to a happy end to your misery."

Horatio's eyebrows knitted together in a look of confusion that quickly changed to anger.

He shot out of his seat and towered over Raymond. "You killed Marceline?"

Raymond stood, equalizing the space between them. The last thing he wanted was a brawl. He would have to try to keep the conversation calm.

Horatio's eyes shimmered with tears. "Did she agree to drink it?"

"There was a struggle." Raymond turned away from Horatio's angry glare. "But it had to be done. You, if anyone, should understand."

"You killed her?"

Raymond kept his voice steady and soft. He knew he had to quell the dangerous spark of anger that ignited in his friend's eyes. "I found an answer. An answer that is the best for her and all of us. Finally, an answer to end this misery."

"How?" Horatio's voice trailed off.

"It was an accident in my lab. I was trying to figure out why ambrosia is the one thing that can affect our state of mind. I spiked a sample of my own blood with a high dose of it, and under examination I could see it was attacking my cells furiously."

"You thought this would help Marceline?"

"That is what got me started. I wanted to figure out

how she'd become addicted."

"So you came up with a poison instead of a cure?"

"I believe the poison is our cure, Horatio. Believe me, when I figured this out years ago, I kept the fact that we could end this all to myself. But over time I have come to realize we are all miserable. Can't you see what we have become? It's sickening. I can't watch another day of us squandering our greatness."

"But why Nephthys—I mean, Marceline? Why was she your guinea pig?"

"You know as well as I do, she is the weakest of all of us. She had to be first."

Horatio spoke softly. "Last time I saw her she was elated—almost giddy with how this life was going for her."

Raymond held the vial with one hand and gently gripped Horatio's shoulder with the other. "Accept this end. We can erase this tragic mistake. It is time."

"You have got to be kidding." Horatio slapped Raymond's hand away. "Who do you think you are?"

"I am like you, miserable. Your reaction is completely counterintuitive. All these centuries you have lived your life searching for death. Now I offer a clean end, and you reject it. You look at me like I've lost my mind. But it is you who has lost touch with reality." Raymond paused, hoping to see a sign that Horatio was considering what he'd said. "Drink it, and I will assure you your name will live on."

Horatio shook his head and shifted his gaze to the table. "You have truly lost it this time, Ray."

"It is the greatest of mercies I can give to my family.

Like the desert lion who leads the pride, making the hard choices and taking down the sick and feeble. This is an offering of love."

"You're mad."

"And your trying to kill yourself for centuries is a sign of sanity? You, if anyone, have to see the sense of this."

Horatio's eyes burned with fury. "What you have is a sick sense of propriety. No matter what you say, this end doesn't justify the means. You shouldn't be making these wholesale decisions for everyone. And in case you hadn't noticed, I haven't tried to kill myself in years."

"You call what you are doing living? We all used to be Gods. The world was ours. We had the divine right and the obedience of humanity. None of us were perfect, and we had a bit of fun here and there, but mostly what we did was for the good. For the good of Gods, humans, the world, the cosmos. Now we've all become petty, soulless beings." He toyed with the vial and chose his words carefully. "I grew tired of watching us sink ever lower, living shallow, desperate lives. It is time to make it right again."

"What will happen then? Once you've killed us all and you are the last one standing? Will you take the poison? Or will you gladly stay behind and leach out all the powers we sacrificed and banked into that infernal orb you talked us into?"

"Someone will have to stay."

"I knew it." Horatio backed away from Raymond. "You like to sound benevolent. Like you are doing this for the greater good. But don't fool yourself, Raymond. All you have in mind is your own self-interest, again. Don't think I forgot what happened all those years ago, when you conspired against us with that malformed poet of a king. I should have known something was up when you appeared out of thin air after all this time. You and I are going to round up the Others and you are going to tell them what you've done. I know you, Raymond, better than all the Others. I know deep down inside you think you are doing the right thing. As a friend, I am here to tell you that you are gravely mistaken. We will initiate a council with the Others and decide as a group what your punishment is. You can wipe the slate clean." Horatio crossed to the door and grabbed the handle.

Raymond slipped the vial into his jacket pocket. He shot toward Horatio, slamming him hard against the door. As Horatio struggled against him, Raymond seized a large obelisk-shaped doorstop and hammered it onto Horatio's head. Keeping Horatio pinned to the floor was like trying to wrestle an angry bull. Raymond braced himself against Horatio's frantic surges. Being stronger than all the Others made him confident that if he was patient and determined, Horatio's pain would soon be over, no matter how gruesome the outcome. All he had to do was knock him out and inject him with the poison.

Blood gushed out of Horatio's expanding head wound. Raymond was sick at the sight of his friend's life force spilling out. This wasn't what he wanted for Horatio. He pushed past the self-revulsion, knowing this was no moment of betrayal, but of ultimate love. He brought the obelisk down with all of his might, channeling the timeless bond he had for Horatio. A sickening crack sounded, and Horatio's body slackened. Raymond stepped back to let the unconscious Immortal slide onto the foyer's cold surface.

He dropped the heavy granite ornament; it landed with a dull thud. He would have to act fast. Horatio was merely dazed by the onslaught of blows, and he would be coming around very soon.

Raymond had hoped Horatio would accept this gift. By fighting his destiny, he purchased a coward's death.

He fumbled through his pocket to retrieve the vial. Instantly, his fingers burned as if they'd been dipped into acid. He jerked his hand out and shrugged his jacket off. Raymond gingerly held the pocket open and peered into its contents. It was filled with broken glass, and the fabric was completely saturated with the poison. He hurled the jacket across the room.

He closely examined his palm as it shook with excruciating pain. The skin that had come in contact with the poison was an angry red mess. Instinctively he walked to the wet bar and shoved his hand into the ice bucket. He'd never come in contact with his concoction before. He hoped surface wounds were survivable.

He took stock of the situation. He had no backup poison. The plan was botched. Even with Horatio lying there he would not be able to kill him. The only way to kill the Others was poison. He needed more.

Raymond walked across the room and pushed Horatio out of the way. He stepped into the elevator and pushed the lobby button. As he gazed down at the casino he realized his gamble on Horatio did not play out as expected. He needed more help. More help than Salima could give him. He needed one more kill to create the minions.

The elevator doors opened. Raymond jammed his wounded hand into his pants pocket. A sharp fiery pain shot up his arm. He forced his face into a calm smile directed at Horatio's bodyguards, telegraphing that everything was as it should be as he stepped out, unfollowed, into the lobby.

Horatio's refusal made plain who the next death would be. Seth. And as luck would have it, Raymond was the only one of the Others who knew exactly where he was.

CHAPTER NINE

Buxton's eyes went soft with concern. Alex's disbelief in his pronouncement must have been crystal clear. "So . . . the Gods are being murdered? Let's assume it is true. Why does it matter? And why me? Why am I here?"

"I promise I will answer all your questions. However, I have to ask one more thing of you."

Alex glanced at her watch, guessing the next flight home wouldn't be until morning. "Your wish is my command."

"I need to show you an object. Something I'm sure you will find amazing. In fact if you don't, you are welcome to leave, no questions asked."

He crossed the office and opened the door. His expression turned hopeful. "We'll have to make our way to the museum's exhibit spaces. What I am going to show you would never fit in a space as small as this."

Alex slipped out of her seat and made her way past Buxton and into the bland corridor. "What is it?" she asked.

"Have patience. All will be revealed."

As before, they wandered through the labyrinth of hall-ways and office doors in silence. Alex figured she could suspend her disbelief a little longer. And truth be told, she found it delightfully strange to wander through the empty museum at night. As they strolled through the immense maze of exhibits, her pulse raced with excitement. It was as if they were trespassing on hallowed ground. Around each corner she expected to see a night watchman who would toss them out unceremoniously into the night. Alex couldn't remember the last time she experienced such a giddy enchantment.

If she were able to stand still for a moment and truly listen to the silence around her, she believed she would hear the echoes of the innumerable whispered conversa-tions that layered these grand halls over the years.

Alex's gaze was drawn to a dull glimmer ahead on the floor. Her treasure-hunting instincts kicked in. Like a magpie, she loved found souvenirs. Instead of buying a T-shirt or any other mass-produced trash and trinket, she was always on the lookout for nontraditional keepsakes. Some-thing that would transport her back to the moment she found them.

Alex swooped it up and peered at her new find as

Buxton charged on. In her palm rested a single purple-blue crystal bead the size of a robin's egg. It must have fallen off a visitor's bracelet or key chain. Even in the dim light of the hallway it gleamed with a bright radiance. She etched the moment in her mind and then dropped it into her scribe's bag, quickening her pace to catch up with Buxton.

He walked toward a long, gently sloping ramp. Moonlight flooded in at its base. Absent of drafts or the scent of autumn air, the space ahead seemed incongruously open to the night. Alex knew it couldn't be. Museums had stringent climate controls to ensure the proper temperature for the longevity of the art and artifacts housed within their walls. When she caught up with Buxton, the space revealed itself to her. A two-story slanting grid of glass allowed the brilliant light of the full moon to illuminate the ancient sandstone jewel that lay before her. It was a temple under glass.

It was the Temple of Dendur. A gift of thanks to the United States in the 1960s for help in relocating the ancient temples that would have been swallowed by the newly created Lake Nasser, when the Aswan High Dam was completed. The sandstone blocks of the temple glowed in the bright, yet ethereal light that streamed through the massive glass panes.

The design of the exhibition space for the temple allowed visitors to amble in and around the temple. She imagined crowds of clamoring tourists, some chewing gum as they wandered through this marvel, some wondering what they should have for lunch, most without truly experiencing its immense beauty.

She grinned from ear to ear. "Thank you, Buxton. It is truly amazing. But I don't see how this proves anything at all."

"Have patience," he said. "The temple alone is stupendous. However, it pales in comparison to what I am about to show you."

Buxton linked arms with Alex and led her up the shallow stairs leading to the massive granite platform on which the temple rested. It surprised her that they passed the main temple and headed straight to the relatively small stone pylon that rested in front of it. In ancient Egypt the pylons were the gateway that signaled to visitors they were entering into the realm of the holy.

Buxton motioned for her to stand under the pylon, its ancient stones towering overhead. "Your pendant is a key of sorts. Hold it in your hand. Then close your eyes, and in your mind say, 'Khnum, Creator of Man, Lord of the Crocodiles, keep me safe.'"

Buxton's kind and trusting expression made her feel awkward and disingenuous in continuing this charade. What harm could it do to humor this gentle old soul? Alex grasped her djed pillar pendant gently in her hand and closed her eyes. Her mind tugged against the pretense of it all. Maybe she should open her eyes and be done with it. She rubbed the notches of the pendant, pressing them against her skin, thinking about the man who left it to her —a man who would expect her to respect his old colleague —and remembering her promise to hear him out.

Alex squeezed her eyelids shut and took in a deep

breath. The words rolled smoothly across her mind like a news channel ticker tape. A sharp jolt shot through her, and she fell to the ground. Her arms instinctively flew back to break her fall. The soft flesh of her palms skidded against the rough floor surface and burned with pain. Her eyelids popped open to see where her attacker was. But only Buxton's kind face gazed down at her.

"What the hell?" Alex took in her surroundings. She was in an impossibly large stone cavern. The only source of light was the dull pulse of a large glowing orb suspended in space. She stared wide-eyed at the mystery ball hanging in front of her.

"What the hell?" Buxton mimicked Alex. His mouth broke into a broad smile that rose to his eyes. Her unabashed astonishment seemed to be the only scorecard he needed to determine himself victorious in convincing her.

Buxton grabbed her forearms to pull her up, avoiding her scraped hands. "It can be tough the first time."

"I'll say." Alex wasn't sure what she was agreeing to, but it seemed like the thing to say at the time. "Where are we?"

"We are directly below the temple. Some believe the time we live in is the apex of technological advancement. I beg to differ. Add a touch of ancient magic and the wonders never cease to amaze."

"Magic?" The question came out as if it were a dirty word.

"What do you think is suspending that great mass?

Fishing line?" Buxton's tone was playful. "No, that is powerful ancient magic out there."

The massive sphere made Alex think of a giant plasma ball with scaled-to-size white-blue lightning bolts dancing across its surface. "So what exactly is this?"

"That is what I like to call the God machine, although that is a complete misclassification. It functions more like a storage unit than a mechanized system or tool. But I like the sound of it—God machine." He spoke with a deep-throated mock theatricality. "But for now, think of it as a battery of sorts."

"So what does it power?"

"How do you contrive to explain the mysteries of the universe in a quick few sentences? If only I were more like Carl Sagan. He made the expansive knowable to anyone."

Alex tried to take in the cavernous space around them. In the distance, beyond the God machine, she noticed a bank of monitors where people were busily working. The great span between her and the operators made them appear miniature in size. Alex smiled at the visions of Oompa-Loompas that danced in her head. These workers did not have snazzy matching outfits, just ordinary street clothes. "What are they doing over there?"

"Everything in time. I think in this case the best place to start is the beginning, or at least very close to it." Buxton motioned toward two burgundy leather chairs and a low table that appeared out of the darkness. Had they already been there? Had she completely overlooked them?

It was entirely possible; however, she couldn't shake the feeling they had somehow materialized out of thin air.

The moment almost felt carefully orchestrated, like a fireside chat with her newly found fairy godfather. All they were missing were steaming mugs of hot cocoa. The heavily cushioned chair embraced her as she sank into its depths. She leaned into its high back and let herself relax. The slight letting go made her realize exactly how tired she was. She would have to fight against her fatigue and Buxton's soft voice.

"We will need to turn our minds back to approximately 23 BCE."

"About the time of Cleopatra's suicide?" Thankfully, Buxton was looking away from her and didn't see the scowl she could feel overtaking her face as she realized how epically long this explanation could be.

His gaze returned to Alex. "Exactly. Centuries after the last true Egyptian pharaohs perished, the Greek Ptolemies ruled Egypt like a successful business. The ancient Egyptian language and arts withered in the harsh desert sun. They put on airs as if they were keeping the traditions alive, but most of what they produced were artistically void fabrications, and their hieroglyphic scribblings were a bunch of nonsense. How can you pay meaningful tributes to the Gods if no one can speak the language any longer or read the script?"

Alex fidgeted in her chair. "You know I am an Egyptologist. You could save a lot of time and spare me the basic lecture."

"Please, Alex, be patient."

Alex let out a sigh as she stared at the flickering light of Buxton's God machine. "Sorry, this chair is starting to affect me like a big, soft, leather-upholstered sleeping pill."

Concern washed over his face. "You've been running at a breakneck pace. Maybe some coffee is in order." Buxton pressed a button on the table and a speaker appeared from its depths. He spoke directly into it. "Would you please bring us some coffee?"

"Right away, sir," replied the disembodied voice.

With a flash of light, a man appeared, holding a serving tray in hand with two black ceramic coffee mugs. The newcomer placed the items on the table and strode away, vanishing with another flash of light.

Alex sipped the warm liquid energy. "What do you call that?" Inspiration struck her instantaneously. "Mr. Coffee?" She laughed in a punchy, wound-too-tight way.

"Actually, his name is Luke. He's one of our top analytical minds here, an excellent archivist, and a good man to boot. I believe he was the one who chauffeured you to our doorstep tonight. We all pitch in around here. KHNM does many amazing things, but you still need someone to drive the car and bring the coffee." He winked at Alex and set his mug on the table. "So back to our task at hand. The Gods' powers were diminishing over time. As you know, the ancient Egyptians believed the secret to immortality was to ensure your name was spoken throughout eternity. The Gods were growing weak as the practice and knowledge of the rituals that powered them became obsolete. Offerings were not made and their names were not spoken. The language was quickly dying, and the sacrifices became close to nonexistent. They foresaw a time when their powers could entirely diminish, forgotten and buried under desert sand. Which would not only be detrimental to them, but catastrophic for humanity."

"How so?"

"The existence of our world as we know it hangs together by a constant equilibrium of countless ancient energies. Cutting out one of these energies could spur a chain of events that would completely alter our realm. Depending on the severity of the disruption . . . our existence could be annihilated or make life so miserable we wish it would have been."

"Some sort of celestial-warming effect?"

Buxton laughed. "I guess it does have some parallels to global warming. Both situations originate in the lapses of humans. In this case the Gods searched for a solution. They pored over the ancient magical texts hoping for an answer. They searched a vast sea of spells and incantations that were created after the primordial chaos was tamed."

"What happened to those books? Do they still exist somewhere? Are they here under KHNM's care?" Her questions shot out in rapid fire.

Buxton sighed. "Now wouldn't that be something? Imagine the wonders and knowledge they contained. Nobody knows what happened to them. Not even the Gods themselves. Some say they've been deposited into the Netherworld so no one may find them."

"Somebody has got to know. How can you not be all about finding those books?"

Buxton gazed upward and paused as if contemplating what Alex said. "There have been attempts, but the subject of those books of magic, no matter how intriguing, is not the subject that brings you and I here today." He cleared his throat and continued. "Eventually the Eternal Ones stumbled onto an ancient loophole in one of those time-worn texts. If they relinquished their Godheads and stored their powers in a magical vessel, they could go on living, not as Gods, but as Immortal Beings. They would simply take on their anthropomorphic forms. That is when KHNM was formed as a sort of system of checks and balances."

What Buxton told Alex left her with more questions than answers. She followed everything he was saying, but it was too implausible, not to mention fantastical. The giant orb hovered in front of them. It appeared to be real, although she'd not had the opportunity to come close to it. "So, let me guess." Alex pointed at the orb. "That is their storage vessel?"

"In a manner of speaking."

"Why is it here? New York doesn't seem to exactly be a natural habitat to store the essences of the ancient Egyptian Gods."

"As it is, they all happen to live in the US."

"Why in the world would they pick the States? Are they free-market capitalists now? Since they are, or were, Gods, I can't imagine they came here in search of freedom of religion."

Buxton chuckled. "No. It has nothing whatsoever to do with either economics or religion. Over time they migrated here and eventually settled. There were issues with the God machine being located so far away in Egypt, so when the temple was gifted to the Met, it seemed like a perfect time to move it over."

"But I thought it was the horror of every ancient Egyptian to live on foreign soil. That's why the Pharaoh sent his military out each year to re-subdue the subjugated lands like the Levant and Kush. To be separated from the black land of the Nile valley was viewed as a hellish prison sentence to the average ancient Egyptian."

"Necessity makes strange bedfellows. This is a land where people say their names often, giving them power, keeping them alive. So like the moth to the flame or the fly to the carcass, they all made their way here."

"You mean the Gods are powered by new agers and Egyptophiles?"

"Each tarot card set with the faces of the Gods, every decorative knickknack or pendant with the form of Isis or Thoth is like a prayer that keeps their names being spoken, therefore keeping them charged up, so to speak. The second choice was the United Kingdom, but the United States beat them by sheer volume."

"Crazy." Alex looked around her. Could what Buxton said be true? If she hadn't been magically teleported into a cavern underneath the Metropolitan Museum of Art with a massive glowing God machine, she might have had a hard time swallowing it all. "So why are you telling this to me? Why now?"

"Have you heard of Marceline D'Benneux?"

"Only what I have read about her in the tabloids. Isn't she that psychic to the stars?"

Buxton stared at his empty hands. "Was. Marceline was murdered in her Hollywood home last night. Murdered and drained of all of her God-fluids. At the hour of her death the God machine's pulse sped up." He rubbed the back of his neck. "How do you go about killing a God?"

"Marceline was a God?"

"That was her Immortal form. Her God form was Nephthys, sister of Isis, wife of Set."

Alex, at a loss for words, gazed at the hypnotic pulsing of the orb. These supreme beings were not just cartoonish idols in the ancient myths. The Gods actually existed and could somehow be killed. Her familiar view of the natural world just tilted into the unknown. "Does KHNM know who murdered her?"

"I believe we do. In my opinion, the reason for Nephthys's death yesterday reaches back to the ancient Egyptian ruler Akhenaten."

"The modern-day poster child for starting monotheism?" Alex's wry tone made no attempt to hide her bias on the subject.

"The Amarna Period certainly does have its controversies, doesn't it? From your reaction, I would hazard a guess that you fall in with the camp that believes Akhenaten's attempt to eliminate the pantheon of Egyptian Gods and leave one single God came from political ambition and not a poetic instinct."

Alex shrugged her shoulders. "To me the poetics camps are dreamers who want to romanticize the past instead of looking at history through the lens of human behavior."

"But what if I told you both were wrong? That all of the heated dinner conversations about Akhenaten at scholarly conferences were moot?"

"For one thing, attendance would plummet. Akhenaten is the Pharaoh all scholars love to hate. They roll their eyes when someone asks about him or writes a book about him, but it's been my experience that they secretly relish watching every cheesy Discovery Channel documentary on him and covertly order the books online."

Buxton lifted his cup of coffee. Alex caught a glimpse of a smirk before it disappeared behind the heavy mug.

"So what actually happened during his rule?" asked Alex.

"The situation was not initiated by Akhenaten, but by the Sun God Re. He found an ancient rite to eliminate the other Gods and amass their powers into one. His intent was to gain this power, then rule over humankind. Re figured Akhenaten, or Amenhotep IV, his name before he ruled, was a perfect patsy for his plan. Amenhotep IV was never meant to rule. Were it not for his older brother dying, he never would have. The parallels between Amenhotep the IV and King Louis XVI of the French Revolution are not far off from one another. They were both second sons who were never groomed for kingship. Amenhotep was happy writing poetry, just as Louis only wanted to chase skirts and tinker with clocks. Both met bad ends. Louis lost his head, and Akhenaten's bones were more than likely scattered in the desert for jackals to feast on. His chance at the afterlife obliterated."

"So the whole Amarna Period was instigated by the God Re?"

"In his anthropomorphic form of today we call him Raymond. Raymond Sol."

"The genetic scientist?"

"The very one. I believe it was Re, or Raymond, who killed Marceline. I have always wondered why he chose the cover of a geneticist in this lifetime. He never seemed so overly fond of humans that he would want to cure cancer. I am convinced he must have found a new way to take over. His last attempt failed because he couldn't figure out how to actually kill the Others. For lack of a better word, he could imprison them, but nothing more. This time it seems he has figured out a way to kill them and use their power. We must do everything we can to stop him. If we fail, the world as we know it will never be the same. Humanity will have a new master. And I know firsthand of his cruelty."

"Do you think he would have to kill the entire pantheon? I've never counted them, but I am guessing there are at least fifty. That could take a lot of time."

"There are two schools of thought about that. Some think he would have to kill them all. I believe he only needs to kill the "royal family" of those Egyptian Gods who took part in the pact. If he kills those five, I believe the rest of the pantheon will fall. He will become the Aten, The One True God, and will have control over the powers banked in that orb."

"Osiris, Isis, Horus, Nephthys, Set? That's it?"

"There are Others who took part in the pact that also may be in play as well: Hathor, Thoth, and Bes. However, as they signed on with KHNM to keep the Others in check, I am not one hundred percent sure that their lives are in peril."

"Bes? It seems strange he would be a part of it. I have never thought of him as being particularly powerful."

"He was the God most worshipped by the average ancient Egyptian. As protector of the home and hearth, he was a pretty important one."

Alex slouched into the soft leather and gazed out at the pulsating bulb. Was it her imagination, or was it speeding up? She turned her gaze away from the hypnotic light to Buxton's warm brown eyes.

"You look tired, Alex. Would it help to walk around a little?"

Alex nodded in the direction of the great orb. "Can we go closer? I'd like to see it up close."

"Of course."

Alex pulled herself from the warm embrace of the chair and fell into step with Buxton. Her body was slightly stiff from sitting. "One thing you have yet to answer is why me? Why am I here? You have Salima and Luke and God knows who else to figure this out. People who already know what is going on. Why pull me into this?"

"So, your mother never told you anything about your father?"

"Like I said earlier, my father was a forbidden topic. I had to major in art history when I first went to college instead of archeology. My mom was adamant I not follow in my father's footsteps and die in a foreign land."

"You could have split off and paid for your own studies. If it was your passion, it might have been well worth the extra work."

"I thought about that plenty. But it wasn't only about the money. I've always felt I needed to be no further than a short flight away from her. She was never the same after Dad died." Alex had been working toward severing the dependency her mother had on her. But it was hard to break habits formed over a lifetime.

Buxton stopped walking and touched Alex's forearm. "You are here because you are your father's daughter. I believe you may be the one of the prophecy."

"Prophecy?" Her knees buckled at the implication.

Buxton hooked his arm in hers and pulled her toward the God machine. "When the Gods altered the realm of man by walking among them, a great temple burned down in the faraway city of Ephesus. From those ashes a great and ancient seer foretold of a calamity to come. I think what is happening with the Immortals *is* that calamity. If that is true, you may be humanity's one hope."

Alex faced the God machine and was caught up in the elegant dance of the energy within. "So there are others?"

"There have been thousands of years since your family

tree took seed. We are aware of other branches that have—Don't!" Buxton grabbed her forearm as she touched the orb. He relinquished his grip as her hand made full contact.

The orb's warmth radiated softly on her cool hands. The glowing bolts were scattered in all directions, then knitted into one. The light moved toward her palm as it pressed against the clear surface. Little tickles against her skin turned to intense pinpricks. She jerked her hand away and turned toward Buxton.

His eyes were wide and his expression verged on rapture. "You touched it." Buxton pulled Alex close. "It must be you."

CHAPTER TEN

Raymond rushed down the stone stairway leading to his cavernous lair. Stray pebbles skittered to the ground below. His usual grace was lost to fatigue. Killing Seth drained him emotionally and physically. The scene was one of great violence, Seth becoming a regrettable outlet for Raymond's frustrations with Horatio. As Gods, none of them ever experienced exhaustion until they chose to walk among humankind as Immortals. He couldn't wait to never feel it again.

The ushabtis would ease his burdens. He already had too much familial blood on his hands. Once the ushabtis were brought to life, they would serve at his bidding and kill the three remaining Others. Or at least he hoped that would be the case, that the ancient magic would still take hold and breathe life into their cold stone forms.

Two minions were what he needed. In time he would

create an entire army of servants. But before then, two would be sufficient.

Marceline was always going to be the test. The Others would be on high alert once her Ba-soul had flown. Horatio had always seemed a natural second. A gift between friends. But Raymond misjudged that situation completely. With that failed attempt, Horatio would be on guard. Seth was the obvious choice to have been the next sacrifice, as his powers were weaker than those of Isis and Osiris.

Raymond had guessed that as soon as Horatio regained consciousness in his penthouse he would search for Seth himself. There was a time, before the change, when Horatio and Seth fought epic battles, but once they walked among mortals the two of them formed a strange kind of friendship.

It hadn't taken Raymond long to track Seth down. Over all these years each of them became creatures of habit. The fact that none of the Others knew where Seth was bought Raymond much-needed time. After the last breakup between Seth and Marceline, Seth had taken to the life of a transient. As much as he could, he cut ties with the Others. Until the day when he came to Raymond's lab asking if he could use science to cure Marceline's ambrosia addiction. It was ironic that fateful meeting sealed all their paths toward this current trajectory.

When Raymond reached the bottom, he took in the vast rock-hewn cave that stretched out before him. The upturned lights created hard-edged shadow patterns on the dome above.

Suspended from the dome rested his glass-clad circular laboratory. The visual contrast of the ultrasleek lab and the craggy grey mountain rock filled him with an aesthetic joy.

Up against the glass walls Raymond could pick out the distant shapes of what must be the sarcophagi his daughter promised and, most importantly, the creatures within. Hopefully they were ready to serve.

Walking toward his lab he thought about the first time he'd brought his daughter here.

The look of shock that flashed across her face. He wasn't sure if it was disgust he detected when he shared his plan with her. Maybe he was just getting paranoid. Planning to kill your entire family certainly could cause a number of psychological tremors.

This partnership with his daughter could bring misfortune like his past trials. A bitter tang filled his mouth as he remembered the failed partnership he initiated all those eons ago with that misfit of a pharaoh Akhenaten. A wave of disgust filled Raymond. Bargaining with a mortal was a big mistake. Eventually the king became so enraptured with the powers he gained through their pact that Raymond had no choice but to finish him off, close shop, and wait.

The Pharaoh got what he deserved, an unmarked grave in the endless desert outside of his newly built city. His name was disgraced, known to the ancients from that day forward as the heretic. After his day in the sun, it was a curse to say his name aloud. It wasn't until modern times, when his story was viewed through the eyes of monotheism, that he got the reputation as a poetic visionary. This always struck Raymond as odd and ironic simultaneously.

He would continue to use his daughter . . . so long as she was useful.

He entered the security code in the keypad, and the door swished open. Raymond made haste to the upright sarcophagi at the far end of the lab, excited to see what awaited him. His eye caught a glimmer of dark royal blue on the table in front of the coffins. It belonged to a deep-blue ribbon that bulged atop a long white box. He pulled out a card that was slipped under the silky fabric. *To vanquish your enemies*—Written in his daughter's hand.

He pulled at the ribbon, and it slid away with a soft swoosh. Inside, cushioned by a layer of thick blue velvet, lay the most beautiful weapon he'd ever seen. It was a long rod with a ball at the end, a mace finely crafted of electrum and encrusted with turquoise, lapis, and carnelian.

Along its shaft were magical victory texts engraved in tight vertical columns. It was perfect for bashing in the heads of your subdued enemies.

He recognized it instantly: the Mace of Prophecy. He pulled the mace out of the box, examining the intricate metalwork. She must have understood the implication. Whoever possesses it masters the future of the human race. Could it be his daughter was true of heart? Raymond set the heavy scepter into its velvet nest with a soft thud.

He wandered over to inspect the two newly made coffins that stood upright at the opposite end of the room. He leaned in and smelled them. The strong lacquer-like smell of bitumen enhanced his high spirits. He swung them open and gazed at the stone faces lifelessly staring back at him from their diorite eyes. Propped up in a row beyond these two specimens were other ushabtis to be used if needed.

Raymond rubbed the rough edges where the magical spells were carved into their legs. Pride welled up within as he examined the fine handiwork of his daughter. No matter how well written the texts were, the question still remained: Would the old magic work on these centuries-old statues? Would they hear his call as they did over two millennia ago? Or would his voice be forever silenced to their ears?

Neatly folded stacks of clothing lay at the feet of each ushabti, like practical offerings. They would need to wear something once awakened. He picked up a khaki sun hat that lay next to the Set statue's feet and smiled to himself. *A cover of tourist garb will do well enough to hide them.*

The moment of truth was upon him. Would these life-sized statues animate to do his bidding?

On the small table behind him lay a silver ceremonial adze, the ancient tool used to magically breathe life into the inanimate, and two crystal vessels that contained a small portion of the golden-hued lifeblood from Nephthys and Seth. Raymond knew the value of this rare liquid. He would use it sparingly. The delicate chalices were engraved with the donor's magical name in beautifully rendered hieroglyphs. Raymond picked up the one marked Nephthys and swirled the golden liquid around. The movement made it separate and bead like gilded mercury.

Everything was ready. He grabbed the adze with his free hand and placed it on the mouth of the ushabti nearest him and tipped the crystal cup, allowing the liquid to slowly move toward the immobile mouth as he spoke the spell. "Oh ushabti figure of the great Goddess Nephthys, Lady of the Mansion, daughter of Geb of the Earth and Nut of the Sky, you live again, you breathe again."

Nephthys's essence rolled across the statue's mouth and down its chin. The black stone surface of the statue lightened until it was the color of flesh. He rubbed the ushabti's forearm; not only did it look like skin, but it felt like skin. His spirits lifted. The face morphed into that of Nephthys. The spell was working. Elation filled Raymond. "If I be called, or if I be judged—behold, let the judgment fall upon you instead of upon me always, in the matter of smiting of enemies, of filling my vessel with power, and of bringing the sands of the east to the west."

Her eyes fluttered open. "I am here and will come wherever you bid me."

Raymond's heart skipped a beat.

The ushabti continued on, "I have come to be your protection. My protection is behind you eternally. Your summons is made by Re, your voice made true of the Gods. Your justification is raised after what was done against you. I will fell your enemies. There is decreed action against your wrongdoer. Your head is not to be taken from you for eternity."

His heart swelled with elation. The old magic was not dead. He quickly recast the spell to awaken the other. Within minutes both ushabtis stared at him with wide, expectant eyes, awaiting their first command. It was both sad and appropriate that Nephthys and Set would be the first to serve him. If they couldn't be together in this life, they would be together in death.

Raymond pointed at the one he'd awoken first with Nephthys's essence. "Your name is Victory in Thebes, born of Re, but you will be known only as Victoria, so no one will know your true name, and will therefore be unable to lay a curse upon you. You will find and follow the One of Prophecy. Do not engage. Report back to me what you find."

Victoria locked eyes with Raymond and nodded in assent.

He turned to the other, who stood stock-still. His head was topped with a long mane of red hair just like Set. "I name you Mut Is Satisfied, but you will be known as Neith so no one will know your name and be able to curse you. You will find Horus and kill him."

Neith bowed.

Raymond pointed to the clothes that lay on the floor. "Remove your starched sheaths, collars, and jewels. Replace them with the ones at your feet. I command thee, minions, make haste toward your task."

They replied in unison, "Yes, Master, Sacred Ram of the West." They grabbed the clothes and quickly dressed. Without a word, they ascended the stairs to the outside world. They had a stiff gait, but looked suitably human. Mortals were reliably unaware and more than likely would never take a second look at them. Raymond chuckled as he watched them depart.

If humans do notice, they will be in for quite a surprise.

CHAPTER ELEVEN

Buxton looked at the God machine and then back at Alex. His expression was filled with awe. "No one else has dared touch the vessel. There has always been an edict against it. Its power must have called to you." He hooked his arm through Alex's and pulled her away from the pulsing orb. "If you are not the One of Prophecy, there is something very special about you."

"So what's wrong with touching it?" Her mind felt scrambled, as if all the neurons in her brain had been flung around willy-nilly.

"I am not certain exactly. No one has tried to for centuries. The last record of someone attempting it included the words *bodily inferno*."

"It was a strange sensation. It did feel as if it was calling to me. The desire to connect with it was undeniable." Alex tried to shake her discombobulated feeling as Buxton guided her to the spot they'd originally arrived at.

"Transporting will be easier this time. No matter how you try to prepare the person for the first run, it always ends up with a bodily spill across the floor. Now you will know what to expect and brace for it properly." Buxton looked at his watch. His eyes widened with surprise. "Oh my, it is late, already two in the morning. I think we've covered about as much as possible for one night. Tomorrow we need to come up with a plan to stop Raymond. But right now, it is time for you to get some rest. The agency has a residence close by. Luke and I will escort you there."

Buxton was right. The teleportation back to the temple space was considerably easier the second time. She didn't fall backwards but still managed to feel a little woozy afterward. She guessed that it might be a constant effect no matter how many times your body gets magically zapped through tons of stone, dirt, and concrete.

In the distance, beyond the temple, Luke was waiting for them at a nearby exit. He swiped an ID card, and they were out into the night air. The full moon was so bright it shone like a spotlight on the path they followed to a main road and then onto Fifth Avenue. It surprised Alex that the immediate area would be so quiet at this time of night. It had an eerie ghost town feeling to it. Granted, it was after two in the morning, but she'd always imagined life in New York was always hopping. As they crossed Fifth Avenue, the large-scale, mansion-like townhomes made her realize any neighborhood flanking Central Park and located on

Museum Mile would be epically expensive. Unlike the Sinatra song, this probably would be the neighborhood in New York that did sleep, and more than likely on hand-stuffed eiderdown mattresses with sheets nearing a ten-thousand-thread count.

Although Alex felt safe in the company of Buxton and Luke, she couldn't shake the feeling that they were being followed. Her neck prickled at the sensation that someone was watching them as they strolled down the boulevard. Maybe her fatigue and the new information she'd been exposed to in the past few hours were making her mind run toward the fantastical.

She looked at her companions on either side of her. They seemed relaxed. Maybe all she needed was a hot shower and a deep, uneventful sleep.

They approached a five-story townhome that was sandwiched between two much taller buildings in an urban canyon. The small building's limestone exterior glowed against the silvery moonlight. Near the arched wrought iron doorway was a lantern that burned like a bright beacon of welcome. Alex tilted her head to take in the understated and elegant structure. The architecture style seemed Georgian with its clean lines and strict sense of symmetry. Each floor had two large windows with delicate, scrolling ironwork creating false balconies. The top of the building was crowned with a large rectangular balcony fronted with a demure string of pillars, creating a decorative ledge. Tucked behind it were two arched windows from which a diffuse light emanated.

Buxton reached into his pocket and pulled out a massive brass ring lined with keys. "No need to wake Jeeves. Alex, not a sound till I get you to your room. You wake up Jeeves and you wake up the entire house."

"You've got to be kidding me—you have a butler named Jeeves?"

"Hopefully, you won't know the answer to that question until tomorrow morning," said Luke with a chuckle.

Buxton smiled knowingly at Luke and pushed the key into the lock. He slowly opened the door and crept in. Luke and Alex followed close behind. As Alex closed the door behind her, Buxton flicked a light on, revealing a richly appointed foyer. The entrance to this grand urban townhome was glorious. A large marble staircase with dark mahogany handrails swept up to the second level and split as it rose in a graceful fashion to the next floor, repeating itself all the way to the top. Alex stepped in closer to the stairs and glanced up the elegant atrium.

Suspended from the topmost floor was a delicately rendered but significantly sized stained glass chandelier. Its rich colors and naturalistic lines were typical of the art nouveau movement popular at the beginning of the twentieth century. Could this colorful masterpiece have been created by the master hand of Louis Comfort Tiffany? She itched to ask but respected the silence imposed by Buxton. She would save that question for later.

Luke silently saluted Alex and Buxton and strode up the stairs, presumably to his bedroom. Alex followed Buxton's lead away from the staircase, toward large wooden doors with decorative bronze lion-headed knobs. Alex figured the room hidden behind the doors would be the salon in this stately old house. Buxton veered to the right just before the doors and slid a panel away revealing a small lift.

As he motioned for her to step in, a loud crash-bang broke through the silence. Alex almost jumped out of her skin. A high-pitched and insistent dog bark emanated from above. Buxton shook his head. "Sounds like Luke woke up Jeeves." Alex followed Buxton to the atrium. He yelled through the continued barrage of barking, his voice barely making it through. "Are you okay, Luke?"

Luke's head popped through the support rods of the staircase handrail. "Just tripped over one of Jeeves's treat balls." He winced a little as he pulled himself up. Luke was favoring one leg as he stood. His voice barely carried over the incessant noise. "Might have a sprained ankle. Jeeves, bad dog. No barking."

By the continued onslaught of barking, Alex assumed that *no barking* was not within the dog's lexicon of human words, or maybe it was more a case of willful ignorance. The little dog looked to be a schnauzer, a breed Alex knew liked to play by the rules that suited them and ignore all others. Luke hobbled off with the small salt-and-pepper beast trailing behind him like a very loud live-action pull-along puppy toy.

Buxton and Alex returned to the lift. "Jeeves takes a bit of getting used to. He came with Luke and has over time become sort of our house dog. He gets especially testy when Luke is not around enough from his point of view.

Luke usually bears the brunt of the anger." As the elevator closed, Alex could still hear Jeeves barking in the distance. Buxton pushed the topmost button. "Hopefully, Luke can get him to quiet down shortly. The record was over an hour, but that was when Luke was sent away on a mission. Given that he was only gone for half the day today, Jeeves's anger should be sated in short order. Relatively speaking, of course." Buxton let out a soft chuckle.

The elevator door slid open, revealing a spacious bedroom fit for a king, or a Vanderbilt. "You get the penthouse suite tonight. This building is the residence of the chief custodian. This room is pretty much the best in the house. It always seemed a little ostentatious for me, personally. It's the only room with elevator service. When I took over years ago this became our guest suite. It's been a while since we've had anyone stay here."

"I would have to guess that, being a secret organization, you wouldn't encourage visitors."

"Quite right. Only staff reside here. Salima and I have fairly large quarters below this one; Luke and some of the technicians you saw earlier reside on the second and third floors. The first floor is the library, salon, dining room, and kitchen. It's good to know, in case you need to pop down for a midnight snack. Which at this time you would be terribly late for. I know you are tired and probably want to fall into bed. So I will leave you to it." Buxton moved toward the elevator and then paused before hitting the button. "I almost forgot. I had Salima order in some new clothes for you. She had to guess at the sizes. I hope they fit. The walk-in closet is adjacent to the bed." He pointed toward a door to the right of a large canopy-style bed. "Good night, Alex. Glad you are here." He stepped into the elevator and smiled wearily as the door slid shut.

Alex flipped through the hanging garments that Salima had purchased for her. She was surprised to see Salima's guesses were not so far off. Everything chosen for her was perfectly suited to Alex's conservative, if not boring, dressing aesthetic. Salima's apparent consideration of what Alex would actually wear impressed her. She halfway expected the closet to be filled to overflowing with skintight vampy things that were more akin to Salima's sexy style. She selected a pair of khaki pants and a plain sky-blue blouse for tomorrow. She was pleased that, although she'd lost all of her personal effects to that ramp fire, at least Salima supplied her with things that would not make her feel like anyone other than herself.

Alex had to admit, in hindsight, all the supplies she'd brought with her were completely out of scope for what KHNM actually had in mind for her. How would tea bags and reference books help with saving the world? She chuckled to herself as she contemplated the clothing, wondering how Salima was able to purchase all these things during off-hours. It wouldn't surprise her one bit if someone as stylish as Salima had an all-hours personal shopper.

After laying out her clothes, she took a quick shower. The near-blistering hot water felt good against her skin. It was refreshing and relaxing to have the thin layer of travel funk stream off her body and swirl into the drain at her feet.

Alex emerged from a cloud of steam as she opened the bathroom door in search of pajamas. She returned to the walk-in closet and didn't see any. Either Salima must have spaced it out, or maybe the KHNM agent slept in the buff. On the top shelf was a white box, with a lavender ribbon. Alex pulled the box down and carried it to the immense bed. The silken ribbon slid away with a soft swoosh. Alex lightly grazed her hand over the thick-gauge cardboard top embellished with the look and feel of snakeskin. Whatever was inside came from an expensive boutique. Not merely because of the cost, but because Alex never allowed herself much in the way of indulgences. As she lifted the box, her eyes rested on an exquisite lavender peignoir set. She pulled the nightgown and its robe from the box, their material ran like a cool silken river down the length of her arms, making her shiver.

She felt indulgent, almost naughty, when she dropped her towel and slipped on the beautiful garment. Her go-to nightwear was usually a random oversized T-shirt and maybe fleece bottoms in the colder months. As the nighty slid over her body and came to rest, Alex checked herself out in the mirror. It fit her perfectly, and there were no seams that she could see. It was as if magic silkworms that could spin it whole-cloth to her exact proportions created the gown. The soft lavender color warmed her brown eyes. Or was it the thought of that peculiarly strange and admittedly cute guy she met just a few short hours ago at that champagne bar, Niles. Her face flushed a deep red.

Alex laid the beautiful robe on the tapestry-cushioned chair next to the bed, in case she needed it in the middle of the night. She placed the ribbon in the fancy box and returned them to the top shelf in the closet. As she placed it on the shelf for safe keeping she had to laugh at herself. Her habit of saving quality ribbons and boxes would do her no good here.

She made her way to one of the room's arched windows that reached from the floor to the ceiling and gazed out beyond her balcony. She stared out in awe at the majestic Metropolitan Museum of Art across the street and the vast park that surrounded it. She grabbed the large brass handle and cracked the window open. She was exhausted and certain that sleep would come easily; however, she always seemed to sleep more deeply in a cool room with fresh air.

She followed a shaft of moonlight from the open window to the immense bed and pulled back its weighty down comforter. She slipped under the covers. The mattress embraced her as she sunk into its cushiony depths.

Now that she lay in bed, she couldn't sleep. Her mind seemed to be spinning at top speed, going all directions but getting nowhere. The conversation with Buxton wound through her head like a visitor through an untended Victorian maze. Did they really think Alex could save the world? And did the world need saving? Although Alex thought she had a better handle on what was going on, she was still at a loss about most of the finer points. It was like what Buxton said in the God machine room. *We all have our part to play in the agency.* And whether or not Alex believed it, Buxton certainly thought she was the key to the survival of humanity. An idea flew out of her chaotic thoughts. It was so obvious it surprised her that it had taken so long to hit her. If Raymond's intention was to kill the other Immortals, why was he draining them?

CHAPTER TWELVE

Alex woke to the sound of determined scratching coming from the balcony. A flash of movement passed by the opened window. Was it a street-wise pigeon or a mischief-seeking crow? Given the late hour, it seemed odd to be either. With her curiosity piqued, she flipped the heavy comforter back and kicked her legs over the mattress to investigate.

The bed had a small wooden staircase to enable a gentle descent from its great height. It struck her as a grandiose approach to exiting a bed, and she chose instead to slide down the mattress until the balls of her feet rested on the floor. No longer protected by the thick cocoon of blankets, the room was decidedly cold. It hadn't taken long for it to fill with crisp autumn air, or maybe she'd been asleep longer than she had thought. Alex grabbed the silk robe from the bedside chair and slipped it on. The delicate fabric provided a surprising amount of warmth.

She grasped the window's brass knob and pulled it open further to inspect the bird. Instead of a dove or crow, Alex was startled to see a large bird of prey on the balcony's ledge. It stood a regal two feet tall. A buff-and-black dappled pattern ran down its belly and continued on to the downy feathers that covered its legs like an odd pair of gaucho trousers. The bird's beak was a pale yellow except for the very tip, which was ink black. Its head tilted as if appraising her.

Alex squinted. There was something in his beak. Was it a piece of paper? Maybe a card?

She'd never thought of hawks as treasure hunters like crows or magpies. Had this bird found someone's discarded love note or random business card? Paper seemed an odd choice for aviary treasure. It was neither shiny nor sparkly, the qualities Alex thought attracted most feathered collectors of ephemera.

Intrigued, Alex moved onto the balcony with as much grace as she could muster. She didn't want to scare the odd creature away. She inched closer and closer still. The bird, stoic and immobile, continued to gaze back at her. If it weren't for the spark of intelligence in its eyes, she could have convinced herself it was one of those plastic birds you affix to your house to keep pigeons away.

Alex stood directly in front of the bird, so close she could reach out and touch it, if she'd wanted to. It jogged from leg to leg and dipped his head the way she'd seen parrots do before. It was as if he wanted her to grab the paper. She reached out and gently took hold of the card that protruded from its beak. It was embellished with a small puncture in the paper fiber where he'd been holding it tight. She dropped her hand to her side and backed away. The falcon turned around and plunged into flight, disappearing into the dark depths of Central Park.

She drew the card close. Her heart raced at the realization it was addressed to her.

Alex,

Meet me at the park entrance near the Dendur enclosure. I have information that will help you with Raymond. And I KNOW you need my help. I fear there is a mole working within KHNM. Please come alone. I also know information about your father's death. – H.

Befuddled, she scanned the salutation once more. How could it possibly be addressed to her? The top corner glowed bright orange and burst into flames. She let go as the heat singed her flesh. The small flame consumed the card. Grey remnants of ash drifted away as they were caught in the autumn breeze.

How did this mysterious *H* know about Raymond? Or know who and where she was? That he claimed to have information about Raymond could be helpful. She'd like to be able to contribute new information in the strategic planning tomorrow, but what if this mysterious *H* abducted her, or worse?

She peered out at the park. The road that passed by the entrance was well lit and easy to scope out from a distance. She could cautiously make her way. If she saw something or someone that did not look right, she would march back to the residence and return to that amazing bed.

The assertion that this *H* could tell her about her father's death compelled her toward meeting with the stranger. Could this person actually be able to prove who killed her father? If all went well, maybe she would have many things to tell Buxton in the morning. She would have to be on high alert and turn back at the slightest suspicion.

She threw on some clothes and made her way to the elevator. Her private lift would allow her to leave the residence without waking up Jeeves, or anyone else for that matter. The small wood-paneled box quietly lowered her to the first floor. The doors parted, and she stepped into the large and silent foyer. She slunk quietly toward the large frosted-glass door. An eerie light penetrated through, illuminating the entryway with a strange glow. A chill rushed up her spine. She steeled herself as she opened the door and stepped onto the stoop.

She guided the door closed, not wanting to wake any of the other inhabitants of the KHNM residence. The bright moon that was out earlier was nowhere in sight. It must have sunk past the visible horizon. It was that strange time that was neither night nor morning. The streetlamps were garish in the ethereal blue light of pre-dawn, like party guests who didn't realize the party had ended hours ago.

Alex made her way down the cement steps, her eyes

and ears on high alert. From the crosswalk she could clearly see the drive that cut through the park and passed by the Dendur Temple enclosure. Standing under one of the many streetlamps was the presumed Mr. H. Even from across the street it was evident that he was attractive in a Hollywood sort of way, five o'clock shadow, tousled hair, and a pair of stereotypical celebrity perma-shades.

His chiseled good looks gave him the appearance of someone who stepped off an action hero movie set, including a large-sized bandage near his forehead. Had he gotten into a bar fight, or did his stunt double not show up to work one day? The thought made Alex smile. As she approached him, he waved to her.

Alex stood at what seemed like a safe distance from him. The man crossed his arms and gave Alex an appraising look. "I am so glad you decided to come. I thought it would be best to meet in an open space, since you don't know me."

"But you know me?"

"I have known about you for a long time. However, I have only been following you since yesterday."

She bristled at the thought that someone really had been following her. "You've been following me? Since when?"

"Since you arrived in New York. I had my scout keep an eye out for you. I knew eventually KHNM would bring you here."

"And who am I?"

"Isn't that the eternal and elusive question we all ask from time to time?"

"No really, who do you think I am?"

"You are Alex Philothea, daughter of Phillip, most likely the One of Prophecy. That is who you are."

"So you've had someone trailing me?"

"The feathered greeter on your balcony."

"The bird?"

"He and I have a long-term arrangement."

"You are a falconer?"

"I guess you could say that."

"So, who are you? And why are you following me?" It surprised Alex that she felt more intrigued than creeped out at the thought of his following her. Was it because he was easy on the eyes? Or was it the strong sense of confidence that radiated from him? She sensed he meant her no harm. Or was it wishful thinking? She rankled at the thought of how easily she came when he summoned her, like an obedient ushabti.

"I am sure you have many questions." His voice turned wistful as he gazed across the street to KHNM headquarters. "Never would I have thought that I could ever truly run out of time."

The mixed messages Mr. H was sending confounded her. The note held a sense of urgency, but his tone was reflective, if not bordering on philosophical. She cleared her throat to break the reverie that had overtaken him.

His gaze returned to Alex, his smile gone. "Once I

found Seth dead I knew I had to find you. No matter what it took."

"Seth?"

"Seth Redland, Marceline D'Benneux's estranged husband and . . . Immortal," he said as his breath caught in his throat. "Sorry. I can't believe it has come to this. Immortal, that is, until yesterday." He tented his hands in front of his face and pulled in a long, deep breath. "We don't have much time; I am sure Raymond is hot on my tail, and capturing you would be the icing on his twisted mental cupcake. If he had you, all would be lost. In fact, I think it might be best if we didn't stay in one place too long." He pointed to the bandage on his head. "You are in danger. This is a souvenir of when Raymond and I last met. I am a door prize compared to you. He wants to kill me. Lord knows what he has in mind for you."

Alex wasn't going anywhere with this man until she got some answers. "For the last time, what is your name?"

"I am the key to your survival. I am one like Seth and Marceline."

"So you are an Immortal?"

"I am for now. That is, until Raymond catches up with me. I tried to find Seth to warn him, but I didn't make it in time. When I found him he'd already been dead for many hours." His voice cracked with emotion.

"I am sorry for your loss." Two Immortals were now dead. Raymond was making fast progress. If he needed to kill all the Egyptian Gods, he had a lot to go through, but if it were only the five top royals, as Buxton surmised, he was already nearly halfway there.

The man gently clasped Alex's forearm. "Listen, Alex, I realize this may be hard for you to believe, but I have no reason to harm you. But Raymond does, and I fear if we stay in this highly lit space, we could be found too quickly. I didn't know your father well, but he was a good man who had the respect of most of us. There is so much you need to know." He linked his arm with hers and walked toward the park.

Alex allowed herself to be led onto the pathway. There was something in his presence that was meditative and calming. They walked through a canyon of fall colors that flanked them on both sides. The bright-colored leaves danced in the autumn breeze and reflected the illumination from the light posts, creating an illusion of brightness in the pre-dawn half-light. "How do you know Raymond is behind the killings?"

"He showed up at my place in Vegas, acting like a deranged wish-granter." He shook his head. "He actually thought I would willingly drink the poison. It was as if he saw himself as a damn angel of mercy, giving me what he thought would be a great gift . . . my own death."

"So you are suicidal?"

"I guess you could call it that. For a time, I most definitely was. My escapades made it into the entertainment news." He shoved his hands in his pockets and looked away.

In a flash, she knew exactly who he was, his chiseled

good looks, the many suicide fails, his face on a recent cover of *Rolling Stone*. "Damn, I knew you looked familiar. You're Horatio Diogenes, death-wish Diogenes."

He slipped off his sunglasses and turned to look at her. Alex was shocked to see his left eye was a dark lapis blue with a silver-white ring around the iris, and his right was a rich deep brown with a corresponding ring of fire encircling it. The closer she looked, Alex realized his right eye was not brown at all. It was a deep, dark red.

"Where are your bodyguards? I hear you never go anywhere without them," said Alex.

"The fight I have ahead of me is beyond the abilities of mortals. To survive, I must battle the strongest Immortal among us, or whatever powerful magical servants he may have created. I am here to save what is left of my family and humanity, not squander innocent human lives. You know me by that nickname the press has given me. I know they thought they were being clever. Little do they realize, I've had hundreds of names over the centuries. Before Raymond had us make our pact, I was Lord of the Sky. But my friends called me Horus."

Alex's thoughts became a muddled chaos as she attempted to weave this new information into making sense. "So, you are a God?"

"Used to be. Not so much now, thanks to Raymond."

Other than being unavoidably handsome, he essentially looked like any other person.

Could she actually be walking through Central Park with Horus, son of Isis and Osiris, Lord of the Sky? Alex hadn't given much thought as to what she might see when she eventually ran across one of these Immortals, but she never imagined they would seem so normal. "So why the death wish?"

"It is hard to explain to someone who always knew they would die. At first, giving up my powers and walking the earth for eternity didn't seem so bad. As the harsh grind of time wore on, I noticed a small but growing void within my Ba-soul. This chasm was fed by long years of loneliness and boredom. Over the years it became an unbearable burden. There was nothing to live for."

"So you are saying it is like winning the lottery that ends up ruining your life?"

Horatio smiled. "I guess you could say that."

Alex's thoughts twined together, and a strange inconsistency in Horatio's story pushed itself to the forefront of her mind. "But that makes no sense; as Gods you would have already been immortal. I don't get what the problem is. Wouldn't it be more of the same?"

"We were growing weak. But even in our weakened state we still had our powers, or more importantly we still embodied the essence of what made us who we are. Once we banked our powers, it was like we became vague shells of our former selves. It is as if you magically made it possible for a shark to live on land and out of his natural realm. How successful would it be?"

"So you tried to end it all?"

"I was continually staggered by the short but beautiful human life span and frustrated by your kind's empty use of it. So we have to sit by and watch as you live your short lives like the delicate butterfly that dances on the wind for a short flicker of time. To live amongst humans in a powerless foreverness became a hurtful prison."

The deep sorrow that lay in Horatio's voice tugged at Alex's emotions. By his description his life seemed as cold and empty as the park they were walking in. His views on humans seemed bittersweet. A tinge of embarrassed recognition filled her as she thought about her own inability to live in the moment and see the exquisite beauty around her. Horatio, or Horus, or whoever it was she walked with, seemed to have a gentle and beautiful soul. "But couldn't you have found solace in the Others? You are family."

"In this form we are more solitary creatures. We stake out our own territories and don't tend to mix much. I did have the misfortune to fall in love with mortals three times. Each time I lost dearly. I am not sure what was worse, to see them fade and die, or to witness them implode emotionally as they realized they would die and you wouldn't. There was nothing I could do to make it right. The dream of forever never was. Each romance started with the belief that time was not the enemy. Eventually, I gave up and retreated into entertainments of my own making. I watched as the Others found comfort in mocking human weaknesses. How they settled into a hedonistic existence. I am the only one who became disenchanted with our life."

"So why didn't you take Raymond's remedy? It sounds to be just what the doctor ordered, a merciful release."

"It's one thing to desire an end, but to have someone decide for you is an entirely different sort of scenario." A glimmer of mischief lit in his mismatched eyes. "Also, I had given up some time ago and resigned myself to the entertainments of the human realm. Whatever the Others are today, they are still my family, albeit a clan of loners. I have to do what I can to save them."

The trees rustled as the falcon burst through the foliage. It screeched and circled above them and then dive-bombed their heads. Alex swiveled her head to follow its flight path. It landed on a branch behind them and let out a second earsplitting call. Beneath the falcon the bushes parted, revealing a massive goon with a shock of red hair who was striding toward them. Its movement lacked any natural grace or fluidity. It was as if a mannequin had been brought to life.

"What the—?" Alex shouted.

Horatio twisted around to see the oncoming creature. "It can't be . . . Seth is dead." His voice held a sad combination of disbelief and horror. He yelled at Alex. "Run!"

The Seth-creature snapped off a very large, low-hanging branch. It was roughly the circumference of the light posts that lined the path. The creature charged toward Horatio, wielding the giant pole as if it were a stage prop made of Styrofoam and paint.

Alex turned on her heels and sprinted down the path, away from the confrontation, her scribe's bag bumping against her as she ran. She didn't hear the sound of pursuit and paused to assess the situation.

The creature lunged at Horatio with a single-minded focus. It was as if it had no idea Alex was there. Horatio jumped to face his attacker with a beautiful agility.

Alex leapt behind a large hedge underneath an oak tree. She was paralyzed by her conscience as she watched them fight. She didn't want to leave Horatio to battle the monster alone. However, he'd told her to run. Should she run back to the residency for help? Call the police? Or bolt to save her own hide?

The creature swung the mighty branch and brought it down with great force. Horatio blocked the blow with his forearm, throwing him off balance. His knees buckled, and he fell. The creature took advantage and pinned him to the ground, straddling his chest. Horatio's body jerked violently as he struggled to buck his attacker.

"I said run!" Horatio screamed as the creature's hands clawed at his face. Gruesome rivulets of Immortal blood streamed down his cheeks.

He was losing. She had to help him somehow. How could she defend an Immortal? She scanned the area for something useful. The creature had laid down the massive tree limb to concentrate on mutilating Horatio's face. It was far too heavy for her to lift. Next to her foot lay a massive rock. She lifted it with both hands and lumbered toward the creature that was now crouched over Horatio. Alex clumsily flung herself onto the creature's back and then heaved the rock upward using all of her strength. She brought the rock down again and again, raining blows onto the creature's head, her muscles screaming at the force of each contact. Each time the stone connected there was a flash of light and the sharp cracking sound of cleaved rock.

The creature reached back as if to swipe her off like a pesky fly. Alex clung to it as she ducked away from its sweeping blows. Unable to knock its parasite off, the creature shifted its weight and heaved itself from Horatio. Alex held on tight, bracing herself for the creature's attack.

As the creature rose, Alex could see Horatio's hands covering his face as he writhed in agony on the pathway.

The creature grabbed Alex's leg. She screamed at the searing pain as it yanked hard on her calf. Her flesh threatened to tear away from bone. A frightening vision of her leg popping out of its socket like a perfectly baked chicken made her release her grip. The creature swung Alex from its back and slammed her face down into the turf.

Alex was able to brace herself with her hands. Her face was inches away from the musky, dew-filled carpet of grass below. Before she could try to stand, the creature flipped her, so she was belly-up. Exposed. The unforgiving force of the impact had knocked the wind out of her. She struggled to catch her breath. The creature stared at her with cold, dead eyes as it wrapped its viselike hands around her throat and squeezed. The pressure on her windpipe burned as she gasped for air. Alex flailed, punching at its arms as her vision was turning black, erupting with silver starbursts.

Suddenly, the pressure was gone. She inhaled deeply. The intake of oxygen cleared her mind. She was no longer in the creature's grip. She sat up and rubbed her raw throat.

In the distance, Horatio was once again locked in battle with the creature he called Seth. A river of blood flowed openly from where his right eye used to be. Horatio had retrieved the creature's weapon. It was now or never. She had to take advantage while Horatio had the upper hand. Alex sprinted toward the creature and leapt on its back. The unexpected contact made its body sway.

Alex slammed her fist onto the creature's head. Her hand reverberated with waves of pain with each blow. It shrugged her off in one sharp move. She flew off its back and onto the ground, her bones jarred on impact. She willed herself up. It looked like the creature held something small in its hand, but Alex couldn't make out what it was. Could it be a syringe?

Horatio swung the weapon. The creature swerved unexpectedly to take the blow and stabbed the object into Horatio's neck. As the branch made contact with the creature's head, a sharp, crisp smell of electricity flashed with a crackle of light. Horatio's powerful swing had knocked the creature's head clean off its shoulders; its body shattered into a million pieces like molten glass thrown into a frigid night.

Alex crawled to Horatio's side. He was bent over, hands on his thighs, breathing hard. He craned his neck to look at her. His once handsome face was now completely disfigured. Not only was his eye gone, but it looked as if the creature had raked Horatio's face with a fist full of steel spikes. He grimaced as he yanked the syringe out of his neck. "It burns." As he stood, he rubbed the area where the needle punctured his skin.

"What?"

"Raymond's death tonic." Horatio handed the syringe to Alex. "We've got to get out of here. I'm certain Raymond had a locator on that thing." He kicked the pile of rocks that was once a creature. "And he will be sending backup soon." He grabbed his sunglasses and winced as he placed them on the bridge of his nose.

Alex held the syringe. "It looks like only a third was delivered. Maybe—"

"It's a done deal, only a matter of time." He grabbed her hand and pulled her further down the pathway. "It won't be long before another minion shows. Follow me. We have work to do."

"Minion?"

"Salima was right about you."

"You know Salima?"

He somehow managed to look concerned and irritated at the same time. Horatio sighed.

"Let's get some cover, and we'll work everything out from there."

"How about the residency? I am sure Buxton could—"

"No. Not there. I have things you need to know. No one else. Especially KHNM." He dropped Alex's hand and walked up the path.

CHAPTER THIRTEEN

Horatio led Alex under a grey stone bridge. He motioned for her to sit on the path. He hadn't spoken a word since they'd left the minion's remains. Horatio sat next to her and immediately slumped onto her shoulder. The small amount of poison injected into his system was starting to take its toll. "Listen, Raymond is probably scrambling to locate us. We don't have long. I am growing weak."

"Shouldn't we be at a hospital? Maybe a doctor could fix you up somehow."

"Nothing can save me now. I hunted Seth down thinking I could save him, but I was too late." Horatio gazed at the asphalt pathway. "He died all alone. Now Raymond has somehow managed to use Seth's essence to power one of those things." He shook his head with disgust. "You know, there was a time when Seth and I fought tooth and nail . . . but neither of us was ever meant to die. I was born from the chaos of creation long before man walked this earth. Now my immortal light will be extinguished."

Horatio's falcon swooped in under the bridge at a fast clip like a large feathered bullet directed at his torso. Before Alex could react the bird plunged into Horatio. He rested his hands on his belly and leaned into the wall of the bridge and closed his eyes. "Now my friend and I are one again, ready to take our final flight together."

In the shadowed space a dull glow radiated from him. She put her hand over his. Her fingers experienced that strange and yet familiar warm throb of energy. A dim, pleasant memory fluttered in her mind, then quickly disappeared.

Horatio grimaced with pain. "I know it is hard to believe, but this is real. When Raymond tried to kill me, all I could think of was to escape and to warn the Others."

"So why go to Seth?"

"I was certain Seth would be his next victim."

"Set, Lord of the Red Land, your uncle?" Uttering those words felt surreal. How was it that today she was talking to a God? Or at least the anthropomorphic Immortal form of one.

"I was certain Raymond started with Marceline because she would probably be the easiest to overpower. I was an easy second, as he thought I would take it willfully. Seth was the next logical step, hitting him while mourning his lady love. They had a rocky relationship, but eternity is a hard thing to get over. There definitely was a method to Raymond's madness. Once I knew Seth's Ba-soul had flown, I knew I had to find you, the one of the prophecy, at all costs."

He'd said it so regular-like. It rolled off his tongue, like one of the prophecy was an everyday thing. It hit her how little she actually knew about her role in this foreseen situation. "One of Prophecy. What exactly does that mean?"

"All I know is you are the chosen one. You are a descendant from a long line that is known to be called upon when that which is foretold comes to be. The Immortals never put much weight on the prophecy. I think, more so than humans, we have the ability to delude ourselves about things we think are impossible. As Immortals, we tend to see ourselves as infallible and indestructible. There were a few of us who joined KHNM to help humanity, should what was foretold come to be. I was not one of them. I need you to promise to act as my angel of mercy." He handed her the partially spent syringe. "You must drive the plunger home and give me the lethal dose."

"But—"

"By escaping that minion we bought some time." He grabbed her hand and squeezed it softly. It was something her father used to do when he wanted her buy-in on a matter of grave disagreement between them. "Once I have gone West you will need to use the empty syringe to draw out my vital fluids."

"You've got to be kidding." Alex couldn't believe what

he was asking her to do. Not only kill him, but extract his blood?

"I wish I were. I don't know exactly what Raymond is up to, but I do know he extracted fluids from Marceline and Seth. The minion we fought was the embodiment of Seth. Raymond must have used his essence to bring old ushabtis to life in the form of a minion or servant. We don't have much time. There was powerful ancient magic within that minion. We are more than likely being tracked as we speak."

His breathing became ragged and his body spasmed with a fit of coughs. "I have yet to tell you the worst task yet. I have one more request before I die. And I know you are not going to like it." He pulled off his sunglasses, exposing the red crater that once held his eye. Now it gleamed like a golden pool. "There are few things more powerful in your realm than immortal body bits. As you can see, my blood no longer runs red. And as a learned Egyptologist you are well aware that my eyes—"

"No." Alex turned away from Horatio.

"You didn't even let me finish."

"No."

Horatio grabbed her arm, forcing her to look at him once more. His steely gaze shot through her. "As much as you probably don't want to hear this, your father sacrificed his life so you could be here in this moment. This is not about you, this is about humanity. This is not about something horrible you need to do. This is about having as many weapons as possible at your disposal to battle Raymond. Much is riding on this, and even more is riding on you."

"So, just buck up? Like it's just so easy?"

Horatio chuckled, then cringed in pain. "How do you think I feel about this? Do you think I woke up this morning thinking nothing would be better than to experience both my eyes being gouged out?"

"Of course not, but . . . what do you mean, 'experience'? You want me to do this now, while you're alive? No way." The thought of digging the eye out of his living socket seemed like more than she could bear.

"The magic is more powerful if I am alive. It has to be done. That is the reason the Seth creature went for my eyes before trying to kill me."

Alex scooted closer to Horatio.

"After you remove my eye and fluids, keep them safe. Trust them with no one. Promise me, Alex." His voice was starting to fade. "You must do this. Think of it as retrieving a stubborn olive from a small jar. Reach in and pull with all your might."

Alex winced as she lifted her hand to his face, stopping mid-air. She clamped her hand against her mouth. "Oh god, I think I am going to puke."

"Do it, Alex. As quick as you can. Do not stop if I scream. This eye was a gift from Re himself, it contains the power of the moon. I have to imagine it could be useful to you. You must do this." He ripped at his shirt, producing a rag. He tied it tightly around his head. It held both eyebrows as far up his forehead as they could go in a constant involuntary stare.

"Like a Band-Aid," Alex said, her voice wavering.

The corners of Horatio's mouth curled up in a tight smile. "Like a Band-Aid." Alex lifted her hand and hesitated.

"Please." Horatio's voice gently pleaded.

Oh god, what am I about to do?

Her hand shot out like a cobra, penetrating the socket's flesh. Her fingers slid around the ball of Horatio's eye. His body jolted stiff. As her fingertips brushed against her thumb, she imagined them as a basket made of steel to encase and protect the fragile cargo. Alex yanked her arm back.

Horatio screamed as the eye came loose with a sickening snap. Blood flowed freely down his second empty eye socket.

Alex leaned over and threw up. She wiped her mouth with her shirtsleeve, then opened her hand. The object she held was less like flesh and more like a large corkscrew marble, except the swirl in this case was what appeared to be a charge of lightning.

"Please finish me." Horatio's voice was rough with pain.

Alex reached for the syringe, held it with a gentle strength, and plunged the needle into his neck. She pulled him toward her, his head resting on her chest. He would not die alone. Alex gazed at Horatio as a radiant peace spread over his face. It was as if the thousands of years of pain were scattered in the desert winds. "Remember your promise," he mumbled. "Do not trust easily. Find Thoth."

The Immortal Falcon flew to heaven.

CHAPTER FOURTEEN

Ｉt felt so wrong to leave his body, as if Horatio were nothing but a discarded mass of flesh.

She couldn't lift him, and dawn was coming. Soon workers and tourists would descend onto the city streets. She needed to get back to the residence before another minion came calling. After retrieving his fluids with the syringe, Alex searched Horatio's body and found his cell phone. She figured she would call the police about the body as soon as she had cleared the park. She looked at what should have been her bloodstained shirt. Instead of a dark red bloodstain all over her chest, Horatio's fluids had transformed in the open air. The stain was lightened into a rose-gold color, like his eye socket had. It made sense these Immortals would be made of different stuff.

Alex's brisk walk turned to a run. Visions of minions close at her heels ran through her mind. As she ran toward the residence, Horatio's dying words drifted like a dark shadow over her thoughts. Was he telling her to trust no one at KHNM? Should she tell Buxton about the eye now hidden in her scribe's bag? What would she tell the others about what happened with Horatio? Could Buxton be the mole? Alex found that hard to believe. Until she could glean more information it might be best to keep it all to herself.

Once she was out of the park she dialed 9-1-1 and told the officer who answered about a violent fight she'd witnessed. She dumped the phone in the trash and made her way to the residence. At the door, Alex realized she didn't have a key. She pounded on the door, fully aware she would wake the entire house. As soon as her fist struck the wood, the high-pitched bark from Jeeves accompanied the flicking on of lights.

Alex turned to look down Fifth Avenue. Her arms became populated with a tiny mountain range of goose bumps. Could a minion be following her from a hair's breadth away? Alex's pulse raced at the thought.

The door swung open. Luke's hair was standing up in sleep-sculpted tufts. He leaned into the door and rubbed his eyes.

Alex pushed past Luke. He barely seemed to register what was happening. She slammed the door shut and twisted the bolt lock with a satisfying thunk. She leaned against it and sighed with relief.

Salima descended from the main staircase. "Look what the cat's dragged in. Have you been out all night?"

Buxton wasn't far behind her, looking flustered. "Alex? Where have you been?" He rushed past Salima.

"Horatio is dead." Saying the words aloud made the impact of an Immortal dying in her arms feel more real than when it had happened. Alex walked toward Buxton, who stood like a beacon of offered comfort. The movement made her head spin. Her body crumpled. Instead of landing against the hard floor, she was gently supported. Luke had caught her. She leaned against him as he knelt down. His earlier injury inflicted by Jeeves's treat ball did not seem to be paining him any longer.

Buxton stood over them. "Luke, bring her into the salon. I'll grab some brandy. I think we need a plan."

Luke helped Alex up. She leaned on him as he guided her to the salon. After ushering her to a nearby chaise lounge he retrieved a crystal glass of cool water from somewhere and held it in front of her nose. "Drink."

Alex sipped as instructed. By the time Buxton scrounged up the brandy, Alex shooed it away. It was the last thing she needed.

Salima had taken a seat in the far corner of the room. Luke and Buxton took the chairs opposite the chaise lounge. Both leaned in toward Alex, their faces intense with concern. "How do you know Horatio is dead?" asked Buxton.

Alex gazed out at the tableau in front of her as if in a fog. "I killed him."

Salima shot out of her seat and instantaneously loomed

over Alex. "What do you mean? How could you have killed the Lord of the Sky?"

"Raymond sent a minion. They fought. Before Horatio could put a stop to the creature, it injected him partially. He made me push the plunger home. Horus is dead."

Salima shot Alex an odd look, then returned to her faraway perch. Alex wasn't sure if the expression was one of disgust or fear.

Buxton sat in stunned silence. His body hunched forward. "So Raymond already has three. Only two more to go."

"Well, maybe you are wrong, maybe he needs more than the main five." Luke was trying too hard to sound convincing.

"So did Horus tell you anything of interest before he died?" asked Salima.

Alex resolved to only tell the three of them the one thing she thought would be safe to tell them. "He said we should try and find Thoth. Do any of you know where he might be?"

"He went underground after your father died. They were partners, you know." There was something in Salima's tone that made Alex cringe whenever Salima brought up her father. It was as if she was taking an odd pleasure in believing she knew things about Alex's dad that Alex never had the chance to know.

"Are you saying nobody knows where to find him?"

"I didn't say that. I just don't know where he is. I'll bet you Captain Medjay knows." Buxton's expression brightened. "Luke and I will try and locate Isis and Osiris. Hopefully, we can talk them into going to a safe house. Salima and Alex, I want you two to find Captain Medjay and see if he knows where Thoth is."

Salima smiled. "I know where to find Medjay."

"I figured you would." Luke stalked out of the salon.

Was there something between the archivist and Salima?

Soon after Luke left the salon the meeting ended. Alex made her way to her private elevator. As the lift closed she reached into her bag for a ginger chew. She hoped the intense spicy-sweetness would energize her. Something cold and metallic brushed against her hand. She peered into her scribe's bag and caught a flash of blue. She smiled at the thought of Niles the half-time life coach. Would she meet up with him again? If only to return his pen?

She pulled out a ginger chew and worked at its wrapper.

An old memory of better times fluttered through her mind. It was nighttime. She and her parents were sitting on a beach around a bonfire with a cadre of friends. One of the friends was playing guitar by the flickering firelight, and all were singing heartily. There was something about the singer that made Alex think of Niles. She shook the thought away, realizing how ludicrous that thought was.

Alex couldn't remember the last time she'd allowed herself to mentally peruse the happier days, when her father was alive and her mother was joyfully engaged with the world. When he died, her mother entombed those memories six feet below the surface of the earth. After the last shovel of dirt was cast onto the coffin, it was as if they'd been willed away forever.

She could see the beach scene as clear as day. Roxanne's body relaxed and reclined against a driftwood log. Her parents' heads inclined toward each other. Their enthusiastic voices joining in with the boisterous shout-singing of those who are not accustomed to singing out loud. Alex couldn't remember the exact song they were all caught up in. But something about it had struck her as comedic, judging by the verve put into the performance.

She popped the candy into her mouth as she stepped into the bedroom. The early morning light pulled her toward the balcony. Down below was the park entrance where she'd met Horatio. A wave of exhaustion rolled through her. She looked over at the phone half-heartedly.

She would call her mother after some sleep. Since the moment she stepped off the jetway at JFK, her life and world had become somebody else's. Was it only yesterday Thorne had summoned her? Alex had never run a marathon, but she imagined if she had, her body would feel less tired than it did now.

She pulled the heavy drapes closed and headed to the bathroom for a long, hot shower.

Her mind was certainly jumping at shadows. Her subconscious mind making any sort of connection between Niles and her father was proof of that. The two men were very dissimilar. Judging Niles solely by his looks, he was probably Alex's age or slightly older. There was no way he was a part of the sing-along. She needed rest, and she had time to take it. The next stop on her itinerary wouldn't happen for quite a few hours. The only place Salima knew where to find Captain Medjay was in a midtown bar for an after-shift cocktail.

After washing away her battle funk, Alex picked through the clothes Salima ordered for her. She reached past the fancy silk nightgown and grabbed a roomy T-shirt. Something about slipping into the elegant silk sleepwear seemed inappropriate for a quick nap. Satisfied, she scaled the massive bed and sunk into its warm embrace.

CHAPTER FIFTEEN

Alex woke, startled.

Salima was perched on the bed stairs and was looming over her. "Man, are you a heavy sleeper. I've been trying to wake you. For, like, five minutes."

Salima leaned out of her way as Alex sat up and rubbed her bleary eyes. "What time is it?"

"It's time you put some clothes on and meet me downstairs. If we don't hurry, we might miss Medjay."

"Why didn't you wake me up earlier?"

"Before Buxton left, he told me to let you sleep until it became absolutely necessary to wake you. The old softy thought you could use some rest." Salima rolled her eyes.

Alex ran a hand through her sleep-tossed hair. This small action revealed the sore aftereffects of the earlier minion combat.

The scent of cinnamon filled the space between them. It

struck Alex as odd. She vaguely remembered using rose-mary-scented shampoo last night. Or to be more precise, this morning.

Salima climbed down from the bed, then made her way to the elevator. After pushing the button she turned to face Alex. "Ten minutes?"

"Fifteen."

"Luke and I will be waiting in the car." The elevator doors opened. She stepped in, then turned to hold the door open. "To be clear, Medjay can know we are looking for Thoth, but nothing else. KHNM doesn't want what's going on to get out in the civilian world." She removed her hand and the door slid home.

Alex carefully navigated her way off the bed, realizing just how stiff her entire body was. It wasn't just her arms; every muscle complained loudly at their abuse. She reached into her bag and shelled out a few of her prescription-strength ibuprofen. She was getting low. If this adventure was going to continue at this pace, she might need to call in a refill.

It took her less time than she thought to get ready. However, as she arrived at the limo idling outside the residence, Salima had a perturbed air about her. Alex was starting to think that was her go-to state of mind.

Traffic was surprisingly light. Alex imagined rush hour in the largest city in America to be constantly chaotic. It was anything but. Luke dropped them off at a bar called Lucy's. The exterior was neither fancy nor run-down. It looked like a quiet place where you could sip your beer and be left alone.

Inside, there were a sparse number of patrons. Alex figured it would be packed once people clocked out from their workday.

The bar ran the length of the space. Small faux-wood-topped tables filled the center area. Opposite the bar were large leather booths. The far end of the dimly lit bar was illuminated by the florescent glow of an old jukebox. Alex wondered if it was one of those new ones built to look retro, but instead of vinyl, all the songs were stored digital files. At the bar, an elderly barkeep was pouring amber liquid into a short, round glass.

Salima nodded at the barkeep as they wove through the tables toward the furthest booth in the back. A man sat alone in the center of the large curved pocket, his only company a beer. If this was Captain Medjay, he looked too young to have already made captain. Alex assumed it took time to rise through the ranks of the New York Police Department. He appeared to be in his early thirties.

Salima leaned into the tabletop and motioned to the booth. "May I?"

"It's good to see you, Salima." His voice was warm, almost seductive. He motioned to either side of him. "Have a seat."

The corners of Salima's lips pulled into a sly smile. She slid in one side. Alex slid in on the other.

A smile? That was something Alex had yet to see from

Salima. It wasn't your everyday, run-of-the-mill smile either. It melted her cold, focused demeanor. The atmosphere slipped into something a little more comfortable as Salima's personal energy shifted from a tall, cool cedar to Venus mantrap in the blink of an eye. "It's been a long time," Salima purred.

Alex took in the man's slim, athletic build, dusky-brown skin, pearly-white teeth, and bright, intelligent eyes. *Not bad, Salima. Not bad at all.* The space filled with a sweet, spicy smell. She figured he must be a clove smoker.

"Michael Medjay, this is Alex Philothea."

Medjay shook Alex's hand. "I didn't know your father personally. He was before my time. But I have the utmost respect for him and all he'd done. I am not sure how much Salima told you about me. I am no longer a KHNM agent, but my family has a long history of service to KHNM."

"You traded the glamour and gold the agency had to offer to go into the service of humans, not the Gods," said Salima. Disapproval salted her words.

A shadow of discomfort passed over Medjay's face. He turned away to flag down a waitress. After she took their orders and was out of earshot, Salima expelled a soft, breathy sigh. "The agency lost a good one when you became a civilian."

Well, I'll be . . . Salima has a crush. A hint of pink flushed the captain's cheeks. *What was the story between these two?* Alex tucked the thought away for later. She cleared her throat. "We are wondering if you know where Thoth is." The scent of clove was now almost stifling.

She glanced across the room. Was the barkeep burning

incense? It seemed a strange choice for a seemingly crusty old bartender. Maybe he was an aged hippy of sorts, although he certainly didn't look it.

The waitress had returned to their table with their drinks. Medjay pulled out his wallet and paid for the round. "I haven't seen him in ages."

Salima pouted. "We need to find him. You don't have any idea where he is? I know you two used to be thick as thieves."

"A lot of things used to be." Medjay took a long pull from his beer. Alex did the same, to occupy the awkward silence that ensued.

Medjay cleared his throat. "Any New Age conventions going on?"

Alex choked on her beer. "New Age convention? What would Thoth be doing there?"

Salima laughed and pulled out her phone. "Is that where he has been hiding all these years? Makes sense. He'd never find one of us at one of those things. Let's see . . ." Her fingers flew over her phone's interface.

Medjay pulled his attention away from Salima and her search and looked at Alex. "You know how in ancient Egypt you were kept alive in the afterlife by people saying your name? How they would hire professional mourners, to ensure their names would be spoken. Knowing they couldn't rely on their relatives over many generations to continually remember them."

"No surprise there," Salima said as she worked at her search.

Alex wondered what Salima's story was. What life events had turned her into this strong but angry woman? Medjay glanced at Salima with a tenderness verging on pity.

"So what does that have to do with Thoth?" asked Alex.

"Well, Thoth is pretty smart. He found a loophole the other Immortals never saw."

"Most of them thought it beneath them," Salima interjected.

"Be that as it may. Thoth has come up with a line of meditation products and other trinkets basically ensuring those who buy them will speak his name. He manages to gain a little extra power by it. I don't think it's much, but I assume it helps him feel more like himself. Or at least that was what he said when he started the company. Now I think he gets a kick out of being around a bunch of nutty mortals."

"But don't the Others benefit if their names are said? Why wouldn't they do the same?"

"It's like Salima said. Some of the other Immortals have ideas about what is below their station. They want mortals to say their name, keep them alive, but don't want to seem like they are groveling for attention from lesser beings."

"So he sells these products at conventions? Couldn't he sell them online?"

"It keeps him busy. Eternity is a long time," quipped Medjay.

Salima gazed up from her phone. "Here's one. New Mexico. The Full Life Awareness Conference started yesterday. Albuquerque, here we come."

"Will you be catching the first flight out? Or will you be in town a little longer?" Medjay's eyes shone with hope. "Maybe we could—"

Salima cut him off. "Alex, could you go flag Luke down? I'll be out in two shakes."

It was more of an order than a suggestion. Alex slipped out of the booth. "Nice to meet you, Medjay." As she turned away Salima leaned in close to Medjay.

Alex wondered about the history between them as she stepped onto the curbside and waved at Luke. He'd parked across the street and was leaning against the car. He mimed doffing an imaginary hat and popped into the car. It didn't take much maneuvering from him to get the large black automobile to where Alex waited. She hopped in the back of the limo. The glass window between them rolled down. "Where to?" asked Luke.

"New Mexico."

"I guess I'll have to fill up a few times along the way. This thing is a hog."

Alex's eyebrows pulled together. Were they really going to drive all the way to New Mexico?

Luke chuckled. "Just pulling your leg. I'll call headquarters and get them working on the arrangements." The quiet buzzing sounded as he rolled the small window up. The street-side door swung open and Salima slid in. The rear compartment was engulfed with the scent of cinnamon.

Salima wore a scowl on her face, her brow was furrowed, and her arms were resolutely crossed over her chest. If the moment were rendered in cartoon style, Salima would have exaggerated steam clouds shooting out her ears.

"Do you smell cinnamon?" said Alex as the car pulled out onto the street.

"What?"

A fresh wave of Red Hots candy scent rolled through the compartment. "I was just saying it smells like cinnamon in here."

"Oh that." It struck Alex as if Salima hadn't even heard her. As if she was distracted by her own thoughts. Medjay must have stirred up Salima's emotional pot.

Alex considered the woman sitting across from her. There was something about Salima that Alex couldn't help but envy a little. Her current state of agitation only seemed to heighten the effect. Salima had a rare combination of exotic and easy beauty. Alex was certain that whether waking from a restful sleep at the crack of dawn or being dragged through the center of the earth, Salima would only ever display sheer perfection. Her masses of silky hair, wide beautiful green eyes, and luminous olive skin gave her an otherworldly appearance. A random thought tugged at her mind as she searched for a connection.

"You can take a picture if you want."

Alex averted her gaze, realizing she'd been staring at Salima.

Another puff of cinnamon rolled through the compartment. "What's with the cinnamon?" Alex leaned toward Salima, the scent getting stronger as she moved closer to her. "Most definitely cinnamon. Do you rub sticks over your skin or something?"

Salima faced Alex. "Oh, you are charming. You really don't know anything, do you?" She shook her head. "And you, daughter of Phillip Philothea, the one of the prophecy." She motioned ironic air quotes. "How did your mother manage to keep you so in the dark?"

Her words were like a slap in the face. Who did Salima think she was to stand in judgment? Was her family's baggage common fodder for everyone employed at KHNM? "How dare you? What makes you think you know anything about my mother? Or me for that matter?"

"Right or wrong, being tied to the lineage of prophecy, your family's story is KHNM's story. We know more about all of you than you probably do. No matter what you might think, or how much she might want to deny it, your mother is as much a part of this whole thing as you are."

"Just what do you mean by that?"

"How about the way she sheltered you from everything, like it didn't exist. She had to know one day it would come to this. Yet she kept it from you. Was she in denial? Or just plain selfish? To my mind she did you no favors. But those finer points do nothing for us now."

"Any of that sort of speculation is absolutely none of your business." Alex burned with anger at the insufferable insensitivity of Salima. She was sick and tired of it.

Salima's posture softened. "Sorry, maybe that was out of line. Seeing Medjay opened some old wounds. Let's just start over. Buxton wants us to work together. Let's try and make that happen."

Alex barely knew Salima, but what little of her she did know seemed quite volatile. Alex was under no illusion that they would ever be fast friends. It seemed pointless to try and have anything more than a superficial conversation with her. Time to change the subject. "So?"

"What?"

"Cinnamon?"

The car came to a stop. Salima stepped out of the limo. "You are a treasure." She laughed, then opened the door and headed toward the residency without glancing back.

Once inside, Alex made her way to her room to pack. She was certain it would take no time at all for the agency to secure travel to New Mexico for them, and packing wouldn't take long. All she had were the clothes Salima had ordered for her.

Alex was anxious to touch base with her mother. The conversation with Salima sent her down the twisted path of emotion that always surrounded the subject of her mother. She rooted through her scribe's bag and grabbed her phone. Her mother's phone rang and rang. Alex pulled her watch close to check the time. It was only nine in the evening in Chicago. Certainly her mother would not have already gone to bed. Her anxiety built with each ring. Was something amiss?

Bernadette answered the phone out of breath.

Alex's relief was replaced with alarm bells. What was Bernadette doing at her mother's so late in the evening?

"Alex, I am so glad you've called. You might want to sit down."

"What's wrong?" Alex slumped into the large upholstered chair next to the bed stand.

"It's your mother. I've just returned from admitting her at Bright Dawn Recovery Center."

Alex clenched her jaw. Not again. It couldn't be. She'd been doing so well. And now they were back to square one. Anger flooded through Alex. When would she ever be able to shrug off this strangle hold of her mother's miseries? Her head dropped into her hand, and she closed her eyes against the tsunami of mixed emotions that surged within. Anger, sadness, and hopelessness spilled over and drowned her ability to talk. She knew she should say something to fill the silence, but the words would not come.

"Alex, are you there?"

"Sorry, Bernadette. Do you know what happened?"

"I came in today as normal. But she was nowhere to be found. It was eerie. Everything was in its place but her. I yelled out to her and got no answer. I checked every room, but to no avail. Then I noticed the door that leads to the attic was ajar."

"The attic? What on earth was she doing up there?" Roxanne usually kept it under lock and key. Alex's pulse raced. That dark and dusty space was where her dad's belongings were kept secured away from discovery.

"I didn't know what to expect since I'd never been up there. I brought a flashlight with me. Once I reached the top stair, I saw her leaning against a large opened suitcase, and she was hugging what looked to be an old suit jacket. An empty bottle of vodka was propped against her leg. I couldn't tell if she was still breathing. So, I dialed 9-1-1. They took her in for observation. Once she was conscious, they let me take her to the recovery center."

"You stayed with her the whole time?"

"I couldn't leave her alone. Not like that."

A familiar tug of guilt pulled at Alex. Her mother needed her, and she was not there. She was simultaneously thankful and angry at Bernadette. "Do you know what set her off?"

"Your mother woke up just before I was leaving for the day. I told her about your business trip for KHNM. I knew it would hit her hard. But not like this."

"How do you know about KHNM?" Had mother actually confided in the housemaid but not her own daughter? A hurtful jealousy washed over Alex. These small betrayals had been happening for years, but it was never something Alex could get used to. Her mother always seemed to find a way to make her feel like she was an interloper within her own family.

"I can't say I do, really. A few weeks ago a letter from KHNM arrived via courier. The acronym happened to stick in my mind. Your mother's reaction to it cemented it in for life. When I gave her the letter, your mother blanched and became agitated. When I asked, she attempted to blow it off, like it was nothing. But I could tell something was eating at her. I was dreading telling her about your business trip. It surprised me, though. When I told her, she seemed cool as a cucumber. Only to find her the next morning having fallen completely off the wagon. I am so sorry, Alex. As I am sure you know, there is no contact for the first forty-eight hours."

"Yeah, I know the drill. Thanks, Bernadette. I appreciate everything you've done. I'll give her a call as soon as the staff allows it."

After the phone call Alex packed in a daze, pulling bits and pieces of the conversation out of the fog. One thing was clear. KHNM was the cause of Roxanne's long fall off the wagon.

What was in that letter?

CHAPTER SIXTEEN

Raymond stilled his jittery leg that had been bobbing up and down. He hadn't heard from either of the minions yet. Other nonanimated ushabtis were propped against the wall. Raymond had wanted to keep their numbers minimal, but now he toyed with the idea of creating a couple more. The pit of his stomach twisted and compressed with anxiety. What was taking so long? He had to get out of this place.

Raymond walked toward the laboratory door. He needed to move. Getting out of the lab might help clear his mind.

The clank of his footsteps on the industrial metal stair-case echoed off the rock walls. He breathed in a deep and satisfying breath, relishing the dank organic-metallic smell of wet rock. What excited him so much about being deep inside the earth? Was it a sense of wanton rebellion for Re, solar deity, Ruler of the Sky, to be hemmed in by tons of rock and dirt? A flutter of excitement awoke within him at the thought.

Water droplets tapped in hypnotic repetition as they hit the cavern floor from the upside-down mountain range of stalactites that studded the cave's rocky ceiling.

Raymond paced in front of the lab, lost in thought. Did the Set minion abandon his duty? Had the ancient magic failed? Why hadn't he heard from him yet? The task was straightforward. Kill Horatio. He cursed himself in being so cocksure about his plan. In the end, if his plans were only partially fulfilled, he would have to answer to those in his family who still lived.

Ironically, Raymond's plan to kill his entire family started out as an attempt to cure one of them. All the substances mortals use to dull their pain had little or no effect on the Immortals. Only the sweet nectar of ambrosia let them forget their troubles. Marceline was always the fragile one, pining away for her damaged love. At the time, it seemed to him the key to her heart might lie in a cure.

He exposed his blood to ever higher and higher doses. Until the last time when the ambrosia overtook and destroyed his cells. At the high dose it completely neutral-ized his essence. He couldn't believe it. He'd stumbled on a way to kill the Immortal Ones. Raymond ran the test again and again until he'd just about drained himself, not wanting to believe what he'd discovered.

The knowledge he'd stumbled on scared him a little. Initially, he kept it to himself. But, as time went on, he watched them all become lost in their own hollow, repugnant worlds. That was when it came to him. He would show his ultimate love by ending this cycle of misery. He was the one who got them into this, and he would end it. When the idea first seeded, he contemplated offering it as a voluntary way out of this endless existence. But he knew not all of them would go for it. Horatio was the only one openly dissatisfied. Most of them seemed to revel in their pathetic lives as Immortals. It pained Raymond to the core to see what they'd become. It had to be all or none. It was time he took control and became the Aten. It would be better for everyone.

There was no path back to normal now. He shivered, the damp air seeping into his bones.

How had he become so old? Was it true what the humans said in the texts about him? Had Re become so old and wasted that his bones turned to pure silver? Had his flesh turned to gold? He rubbed his bare chin, his rough fingers scraping against what stubble had sprouted in the last hours of the day. If he grew out his beard, would it grow blue like the darkest lapis?

After his plan was complete, he would wipe away the mortal insects from existence.

Those who plotted against him and tried to thwart his plan had sealed the fate for their kind. None of them could be trusted. How calm and quiet the world would be without them. No more of their shortsighted greed and clambering against each other; no more wars or struggles. It was a crucial flaw in their makeup to never value that which was truly valuable: their short time on earth and their ability to love one another. As long as there were humans, they would climb over each other to get to the top of some imagined heap.

The worst was yet to come, but it took great strength to do what is abhorrent but necessary. Humans proved themselves to be a lost tribe with no direction. Not unlike the Others. They scurried about the earth like rodents blindly chewing through the safe haven provided for them and defiling it with their own excrement. They forgot their responsibilities to the Gods.

Once he had eliminated the Others, he would start on the mortals.

I will enjoy the quiet. An eternity of quiet once they are gone.

He spoke aloud to the vast emptiness before him. "Oh Nun, eldest God of the primordial waters, look, humankind is plotting against me once more." Conviction rang through his words as they echoed through the cavern. "I will do what you ordered me, all those lifetimes ago. Back then, I made my choice to rule and not kill. But I will not repeat that mistake. I shall send my daughter to wipe them from the face of the earth."

A shrill ring from the lab phone resounded through the cavern. Raymond leapt up the staircase two at a time, each footfall in time with the peal of the phone. He stole through the doorway and cut across the lab. Raymond slapped the blinking red speaker button. "Re speaks."

"Oh mighty Re, Rider of the Great Barque across the Daylit Sky. This miserable one must inform you that The

Great One, Lord of the Sky, Horus, has annihilated Neith and escaped."

"Escaped? How do you know this? You were tasked with finding the One of Prophecy." Anger flushed through Raymond. The minions had failed.

"But Master, their paths converged. The great Horus and the one of the prophecy, Daughter of Maat, descendant of—"

"I know damn well who she is descended from." He closed his eyes and pinched the bridge of his nose. "Finish it. And this time don't just watch. You must take the one of the prophecy and bring her to me."

"Yes, Master. This one will follow, Oh Great One."

The light on the speaker blinked off. He grabbed his smiting rod and flung it across the room, shattering one of the large glass windows.

Horatio somehow escaped, and had reached out to Alex. A throbbing pain tore through Raymond's head as he tried to imagine what sort of collateral damage this would inflict on the plan. What was Horatio telling Alex now?

Raymond picked the handset off its cradle.

I must call my daughter.

CHAPTER SEVENTEEN

Alex was amazed how quickly she and Salima were shuttled off to the airport. Destination New Mexico. Buxton had returned from his mission to locate Oscar and Isadore, the last of the Theban Royals, as they were leaving for the airport. His search was unsuccessful. Did Raymond already have them? It seemed safe to assume he didn't. If he had, the game would be over. Raymond would be a hair's breadth away from achieving Aten-hood. Unless, of course, Buxton was wrong, and Raymond needed to kill every Egyptian Immortal and not only the "royal family."

Buxton and Luke would continue to search for Osiris and Isis while Salima and Alex were heading to New Mexico. Alex was skeptical Thoth would be hanging out at the Full Life Awareness Conference, but it was all they had.

It surprised her that Buxton and Salima bought into the idea so easily.

The convention center's decor hit the economically necessary bland point somewhere between elegant and businesslike. It was ready to rent for weddings, insurance conventions, and the occasional new age conference, like the one she and Salima were currently pushing their way through.

At close inspection, the frosted-glass sconces with their delicate flower patterns in the hallway were at odds with the mock linen texture of the creamy beige bulletproof vinyl wallpaper. Convention centers always seemed to have their own special brand of magic that allowed the spaces to morph into what the patrons expected to see. She imagined the businessman who never looked up to notice the cut glass chandeliers in the ballroom, and the wedding reception reveler who was completely unaware of the utilitarian pressboard round underneath the seemingly elegant white polyblend tablecloths. The carpeting was an industrial grade loop carpet with a predictable repeating abstract design in greens and greys. Its sole merit was to cover up the early morning conventioneer's coffee stain or the wine spill caused by the dreaded aunt who always seems to drink too much at weddings. It didn't seem to be a place where the God of Writing and Knowledge would spend quality time.

Alex half-heartedly trailed behind Salima through a loose crowd filtering toward the main ballroom. A man with a gravity-defying, hairspray-shellacked hurricane of a hairdo pushed by Alex. His shoulder knocked against hers. "Jerk," she muttered under her breath.

Salima stopped walking and chuckled. "My oh my, little Miss Milquetoast has a spine under her candy-coated shell. I wondered how long it would take to get to the nut in your center."

"Just because you think you know who I am doesn't mean you do." Alex bristled at having someone assume anything about her no matter how right it might be.

"Well, whoever you are, you just had your brush with greatness." Salima always managed to say enough to make you ask a question, presumably allowing her to feel continually superior.

Okay, I'll bite. "What?"

"The dude who almost knocked you on your ass."

"Again, what?"

"I can't believe you don't recognize greatness when it whirls by you. That is Jorge Trinculo, the king of the ancient-alien theorists." Salima nodded in the direction of the main ballroom where a huge banner with his name and picture were hanging. "Probably late for a press conference or possibly a call from the mother ship. If you want to see him flip his wig, which I am sure is quite a spectacular sight, be sure to pronounce his first name with the Spanish *H* sound. He prefers the Portuguese *G* for George."

It took a couple of clicks to recognize him. She'd seen him as a talking head on a show asserting that aliens influenced earth's ancient cultures. She'd only caught it a couple of times and assumed it was a mockumentary à la Christopher Guest.

Salima continued her tirade. "This convention center is full of them. What some of us like to call Pyramidiots, those who are willing to believe any far-fetched idea so long as it is conceptually attached to a pyramid, sphinx, or pharaoh. A few years ago I suggested for the betterment of the human race that KHNM should torch this place one year and be rid of the whole lot of them." Salima shook her head. "But I could not get any takers."

"That's pretty harsh."

"I guess you could see it that way. I don't see why they are compelled to bring aliens to the party. It gets under my goat when they can't attribute the ancient monuments to the people who built them."

Alex laughed at Salima's allusion mash-up. "You've got a goat in there somewhere?" Alex motioned to Salima's skintight jeans and T-shirt combo.

"Ha ha. Very funny. You know what I mean. I take it a little personally. The temples of ancient Egypt were built as places to worship the Great Gods, and . . . well . . . it's beyond insulting."

"I don't know. You are okay with the ancient Gods walking among us, why not aliens?"

Salima gave Alex a searing look. "Because I was there."

Alex stopped walking, as if she'd forgotten how to work her limbs. Salima marched on.

After getting a few long, leggy strides away she stopped and turned, quickly closing the gap between them. She edged close to Alex, locking eyes with her. "You mean you really have no idea who I am?"

Alex knew Salima had been an agent for KHNM for quite some time, but did it make her immortal? Did the agency use ancient magic to give them superlong lives? Even if that were the case, Alex doubted they could extend it all the way back to when the pyramids were built. And the agency wasn't that old, anyway. Maybe she was a—

"Holy crap" was all Alex could say as she gazed into Salima's fiery green eyes. For the first time she noted a golden ring of fire hugging her brilliant irises.

"You at least got the holy part right." Salima smiled.

"So you are a Goddess?"

"To be more precise, I am an Immortal. None of us are Gods anymore."

"Mighty Isis, Great Enchantress, and beloved of Osiris?"

Salima laughed. "God no, not that prima donna. I am a high-value combo deal. With me you get three for the price of one."

"So it's true." Alex, overwhelmed, wished for a place to sit down. However, the stream of conventioneers passed by them like river water around a rock.

Salima's face pinched. "True? What do you mean?"

"Sekhmet, Hathor, and Bastet are elements of the same Goddess." Alex had a professor who asserted these three female Goddesses were actually different aspects of one. The idea always seemed to make sense to Alex. However, the professor had never found enough evidence to publish this concept.

"Nothin' but."

Alex's mouth gaped open, and she was filled with an awestruck reverence. "So when you are contented you are Bastet, when you feel like warring you are Sekhmet, and—"

"And when I feel like whoring I am Hathor."

Alex grimaced. The awe-filled joy of finding herself in the presence of the Goddess of war, love, and home vanished like a fraudulent wish.

Salima sighed. "Sorry to burst your little idealized dream bubble, but I call them like I see them. In my long life, I sure have seen a lot. Propriety is something particularly unique to you humans. It's not something we tend to bother with. If we worried over every shocking thing we'd done, well, let's say it would be a long and dreadful life indeed."

Alex stared dumbstruck at Salima.

"Okay, if it makes you feel better, how about this? I feel amorous while I embody Hathor. How is that? Is that G-rated or Godlike enough for you?" Salima walked away, then turned around. "Quit standing there like an ugly old possum. Let's find what we came here for. You are on the clock for KHNM now. You can process your feelings on your own time."

Alex followed Salima in a trancelike stupor into the grand ballroom. The noisy din created by hundreds of people packed in the small space was incredible.

It was all coming together now. The broad strokes she witnessed of the many shades of Salima were starting to form a pattern. She was partnered with a pissed-off Immortal whose emotions could turn on a dime. Great.

Salima redirected her quick stride to the black curtain that lined the rear wall of the ballroom, where Jorge and his gravity defying updo had disappeared. She grabbed at the heavy fabric, attempting to find a way through. By the time Alex caught up to her, Salima had parted overlapping layers. Her hands stretched out as she twisted her neck to look at Alex. "You stay here. I am gonna see where Mr. Swirls is running to. I'll be back in two shakes."

The curtain flashed closed, leaving Alex in a cloud of dust motes that glistened against the curtain's dark fabric, illuminated by the intense ballroom lighting. Dead skin masquerading as fairy dust.

A dull warning light sparked in Alex's mind. Salima's sudden insistence on singularity seemed suspicious. Then it hit her.

Salima is Hathor. She is Raymond's—Re's—daughter.

Alex ducked behind the curtain and double-stepped to catch up to Salima. "I'm coming with you. I don't think Buxton would like us parting." She was glad she hadn't shared more than the minimum about her interaction with Horatio. She should keep Salima at arm's length, given her family connections. She could be the mole Horatio mentioned.

"Suit yourself," said Salima as she charged forward. She didn't glance back at Alex. It struck Alex odd that this Jorge guy pulled Salima away from their mission. They were here to find Thoth, not to hunt down an ancient-alien theorist.

The space behind the curtain was in dark shadow. It was obviously not intended for conventioneers. The bright lights of the ballroom on the other side of the drapery spilled in through a gap between the curtain and the ceiling. It cast a dull light in the corridor. As Alex's eyes slowly adjusted, she could make out a faint shape of a door at the opposite end. Salima was pulled toward it like a metallic body at a rare-earth magnet.

A puff of movement ahead activated the drape. Alex squinted along the waves of fabric moving toward her. The movement seemed out of place. She slowed her pace and called to Salima.

Salima turned around. Alex pointed toward the moving curtain. Salima's eyes grew large. "Minions!"

Something bumped into Alex as it ran by, knocking her off balance. The minion charged toward Salima.

Suddenly, Alex's arms were jerked behind her. She shoved her shoulders forward to try to force separation from the tight hold. The more she struggled, the tighter the grip became. She blocked the pain as she concentrated on trying to get free. Her captor pulled her wrists together. Realizing she couldn't pull free, Alex leaned into the minion's chest and kicked her heel into its knees. A searing pain shot up her leg as she made contact. The minion's grip loosened ever so slightly. She shifted her weight, and her scribe's bag slipped into the gap between them. If only she could get her hands free. She glanced up the corridor. Salima was fully engaged in fighting the other minion.

An electronic buzzing rang in Alex's ear. The minion

released her left hand and immediately swung its arm around her neck in a choke hold. It slapped its free hand against its chest and spoke. "Oh mighty master, this simple servant has completed its task. I have the One of Prophecy in hand."

Alex swung wildly to free herself. The minion's grip tightened around her windpipe.

A voice emanated from the symbol in the ushabti's chest. "What about the other?"

"The She-Beast ran, but my twin has gone after her."

"You have completed your duty. Return her to me." The disembodied voice had a hard edge.

"Yes, Master," the minion droned.

Alex clawed at the minion's arm. She had to get free. The urgency conflicted with the lack of oxygen to her brain. The world became hazy like a distant mirage. Her body slackened.

Pinpricks of light clouded her sight. A hard shove sent her to the cement floor. Her head knocked against it with a hurtful thud. Cold, pure air filled her lungs. She could breathe again. She opened her eyes to see a male form battling the minion who had held her captive.

Alex peeled herself from the floor and limped away from the action. There was something familiar about the man in combat with the minion. Niles? Mister part-time life coach from Chicago O'Hare? What was he doing here?

"Run!" he shouted.

As her awareness cleared, she noticed her attacker for the first time. The likeness was uncanny. Horatio?

Raymond must have created this minion from Horatio's remaining bodily fluids. The creature's eyes were a matched steely blue.

"Snap out of it, Alex!" Niles ducked from side to side, deftly avoiding the meaty punches from the minion. "I know my handsomeness can be hard to take in all at once." His voice was jaunty, but he grimaced as the minion landed a hard hit to his gut.

"What are you waiting for, Alex? Run," Salima yelled. She punched the minion with a force that would spin the head off a human. The unaffected minion shoved Salima backward and slammed her to the floor.

She wasn't going to run. That meant one thing. She had to think quickly. Niles and Salima could only hold them for so long.

If the minions were created from Horatio's essence, maybe his raw juices might incapacitate them like a poison. Or make them more powerful? Either way she had to try.

Alex pushed her hand into her bag and grabbed the syringe. As she lifted it out, the plunger end caught on the zipper. It flung into the air in a slow arc. Her hand whipped up with the quickness of a cobra strike and grabbed the vial with the sharp side out.

Alex ran to the minion who straddled Salima's chest. Its hands throttled her throat. Alex jumped on the minion's back, jamming the syringe into its neck. The minion shifted its grip on Salima and swung at Alex. She ducked. The meaty fist barely grazed the top of her head.

Salima took advantage of the distraction and landed a

solid blow to its face. Alex pushed down on the plunger, releasing Horatio's essence into the minion.

The creature stopped moving as if its magical circuits shorted. Its flesh turned from hues of living tissue to what appeared to be a deep-grey stone. Salima heaved off the heavy mass as it crumbled to pieces. Her face broke into a broad smile. A thud sounded nearby, drawing their attention to the continuing fight. "It looks like Thoth needs help."

"Thoth?"

"Niles, Thoth . . . whatever name works."

"You mean—"

"You are priceless. Let's get over there before that minion manages to ruin his pretty face."

Niles had the minion pinned against the concrete wall, struggling greatly to control it. His body shook as he pressed the minion with a great force, as if trying to fuse the creature's atoms with the structure of the convention center.

"Hold it still," shouted Salima.

"Trying to," Niles said through clenched teeth. His upper body jerked violently against the minion's attempts at freedom.

Salima reached past Niles and grabbed the minion's head. As she struggled to twist it back and forth, the corridor resounded with the sound of grinding stone. A sharp crack echoed through the space as the minion's head separated from his shoulders. Salima held it up, then unceremoniously pitched it to the side.

Niles knocked the minion to the floor, revealing a minion-shaped impression in the wall.

His eyes locked with Alex's. "What the hell are you doing here?"

"For once it was a good thing she did not listen," said Salima. "She actually saved both our skins."

"How does *that human* expect us to protect her if she won't listen?"

Salima stood with her fists planted on her hips. "We? Admittedly I'm not thrilled about it, Bird Boy, but this is the Salima show. You aren't active anymore. Buxton assigned me to nursery detail."

Rage boiled up within Alex. "Why are you both talking about me as if I weren't here?" Who did these assholes think they were dealing with? "Nursery detail?"

Niles and Salima started as if they somehow managed to forget Alex was standing three feet away.

"So how does it feel to be saved by a supposed baby?"

Niles opened his mouth as if to say something, then closed it. Alex turned to walk away. She had no idea where she was going. All that mattered in the moment was to get some space of her own.

Niles shouted. "If you'd done what I'd asked, you wouldn't have been here in the first place."

"I believe it has been established that, had I left like you ordered—and by the way, I will be perfectly clear, you have absolutely no authority over me whatsoever—you would more than likely be dead." She balled her hands into fists. "So, I guess, you're welcome." Her angry gaze migrated from Niles to Salima. "So, what is this about protecting me?"

"Do you think I've been hanging around you because I like your company?" asked Salima.

"So, why don't you take a moment and explain it to me, Salima. She-Beast of the Three-Beasts."

"Three-Beasts." Niles laughed heartily. "Love it, actually. Now I have some ammo against Bird Boy."

"Where'd you hear that?" Salima spoke through clenched teeth.

"Maybe I made it up?" Alex blinked with put-on wide-eyed innocence.

Niles pushed himself between them. "Hey ladies, as much as I do love to watch a girl-on-girl fight, I think it is best that we get out of Dodge. The posse might be hot on our tail soon."

Salima glanced at Niles. "When did you become a cowboy, Thoth?"

"Not exactly sure ma'am," Niles said in a slow western drawl and mimed tipping a nonexistent ten-gallon hat. "Sorry, I mean, She-Beast." He ducked as she swatted her hand at him.

Salima's eyes sparkled bright.

Niles swept his hand out and flicked his wrist toward the door. "Onward and outward, ladies." He linked his arms with Salima, then Alex. "I know the best way out of this concrete maze."

Salima stripped her arm away from Niles and charged ahead.

Alex startled at the warm pulse from his arm, making her think of when they met before at the airport bar.

He glanced at her sideways. "Don't mind her. Salima's bark is worse than her bite. It may be hard to conceive, but underneath that bluster is a caring heart."

"That's what Buxton says, but I have yet to see the evidence. Does she know where the exit is?"

"Maybe. I think she might want some space. Right now she is using a tried-but-true stalking tactic of hers: following from the front. It allows the prey to drop their guard."

"So now we are prey?"

"Old habits are hard to break. Especially for ancient She-Beasts."

He tugged her arm closer, pulling her near, and whispered in her ear. His warm breath tickled her skin, making a shiver run up her neck. "You and I need to talk."

"What?"

"Later."

They moved beyond the black-curtained corridor to the convention center's loading dock.

Up ahead Salima passed an open door and stopped in her tracks. She'd spread her arms and rested her palms on the door jambs. "Well I'll be." Her head swiveled in Niles and Alex's direction. "Look who's here. Niles, you're gonna love this one."

Alex peered into the small janitorial closet. The weirdly sweet chemical smell of industrial cleaner overwhelmed her. In the dim light she picked out strange brown tendrils swirling up from behind a massive professional floor polisher.

Salima shifted her weight from one foot to the other and cocked her head. "You can stand up now. I know you are behind that big silver thing." The room was filled with a tense silence. "Don't make me come in there and get you."

A body rose slowly. It was Jorge Trinculo, the ancient-alien theorist.

"Ah shit." Niles breathed a heavy sigh. "Not him again. How does he always manage to show up at precisely the wrong time?"

Salima shook her head. "Beats me. But I say we squeeze all the juice we can out of this lemon."

"When life gives you scurvy, make lemonade?" Niles interjected.

"Exactly. No such thing as a problem, only opportunities in disguise."

"So Salima, what are you proposing? That we shake him down?" asked Niles.

A bottle of bleach thunked onto the floor as Jorge tried to steady himself against the chrome shelving unit. "Please don't. I don't know anything." His body trembled like a cowering dog.

Niles laughed. "Surprised to hear you actually admit it. Last time I caught one of your so-called documentaries," said Niles, making exaggerated air quotes with both hands, "you seemed to think you knew a lot."

Salima moved closer to Jorge. "I don't know. I think this

time he might actually know something. Why did you run from me?" Jorge's eyes grew big. "Usually, we can't shake you."

"As much as I would love to spend quality time trying to get some sense out of him, we don't have the time," said Niles.

The color returned to Jorge's face and his expression eased.

Salima stepped forward, her eyes wide and directed at the space behind Jorge. "What the hell is that?" Jorge's head swiveled to look. Salima's fist swung up and punched Jorge squarely across his jaw. His eyes rolled back, and he slumped to the floor, knocked out cold. She grabbed his body, flipped it into a canvas bin with wheels, and made her way to the rental car.

Niles matched her pace. "I forgot what it is like being around you. Bodies dropping like flies."

Alex trotted to catch up to them. "So, last time I checked, having an unconscious semi-famous person propped up against your backseat window isn't exactly flying under the radar."

Salima pressed the cart against the trunk as she dug out the car keys and tossed them at Niles. "Pop the trunk for me, Bird Boy."

Niles's playful smile vanished. "I don't see what we will get out of dragging him around."

Alex couldn't understand why either. It made absolutely no sense. "Shouldn't we be trying to track Raymond down, not questioning a random alien geek?"

Salima put her hands on her hips. "I think Jorge has something to tell us, and right now that is all that matters. Buxton put me in charge. What I say goes. And Niles, you gave up your agency card some time ago. You used to have some sense in you, until your judgment started to falter. You cost a good agent his life." Salima's gaze turned from Niles to Alex.

Niles threw the keys back at her. "Open it yourself." He slipped into the car and slammed the door shut.

The world shifted under Alex. Did Niles have something to do with her father's death? Was that what Salima was implying? Why did that suggestion seem so impossible to her? She barely knew Niles, but somehow it felt like she did.

Salima opened the trunk. A broad smile pulled across Salima's face. "Lucky for him, we got stuck with a sedan." Salima unceremoniously tossed Jorge in and slammed the trunk shut.

CHAPTER EIGHTEEN

Salima peeled out of their parking space and raced the rental car through the parking garage, weaving around vehicles and pedestrians with a careless precision. The squeal of rubber accentuated the deafening silence within, the atmosphere thick with things left unsaid. As the hell ride of awkward silences lengthened, it became a mental game of chicken; whoever spoke first would lose. Alex certainly wasn't about to be the first. She took in a deep breath and relaxed her clawlike grip on the pleather armrest.

After they put the city limits behind them, the long stretch of highway was sparsely populated with a loose collection of cars. The rental clipped along at a swift pace through the endless New Mexico desert lands.

The monotony of the beige-brown hills and dusty dark-green scrub cast a drowsy spell on Alex. She closed her eyes and basked in the sunlight that streamed in. The tension in her back and shoulders started to melt away as she rested her head on the warm window. The lazy hand of sleep gently tugged at her mind. She slipped into the hazy world of half awareness.

The strong rays that penetrated the glass spurred a vague recollection of Niles touching her arm, and the warmth that pulsed through him. The soft heat of the sun wrapped her in its comforting arms. Alex slipped deeper into her dream haze, and she found herself in a warm embrace with Niles's arms protectively around her. His deep blue eyes searched hers as if asking for an unspoken permission. A sense of belonging and longing welled up within her. He leaned in, and his soft lips brushed against hers as his fingers trailed lightly down her neck. Her flesh tingled like a thousand minuscule sparks of lightning wherever his hungry hands traveled . . .

Alex's head knocked against the window. Her eyes blinked away her imaginings as the bright daylight burned through her squinted, sleep-filled eyes. A deep flush swept through her as she contemplated the back of Niles's unknowing head. The pulsing hot burn of embarrassment singed her skin, growing deeper as his unmistakable words came back to her. *That human.*

It surprised Alex that she felt a twinge of disappointment at having disappeared from Salima's torment radar, now that the abuse had shifted in Niles's direction. How could she miss the almost nonstop barrage of insults? Was it a deeply hidden yearning of an only child to have a sibling?

Alex could count her close friends on one hand. She knew it was pathetic, but she never wanted to be encumbered by relationships that required much tending. In moments of self-reflection, she'd seen her mom was the logical scapegoat. She would tell herself the sad story of how she never had a childhood because she became her mother's keeper when her father died. However, as she got older, that story she was used to telling herself seemed more like a cop-out.

As she sat in the silent car with Salima and Niles, both virtual strangers, it was a little sad to claim a grudging and dysfunctional friendship with one and an inexplicable and almost juvenile attraction to another. How was it she'd come to be in her midtwenties and this was the extent of her emotional investment? Once again, she was relegated to her natural state of third wheel, outcast.

Alex stared at the back of her companions' heads as they pointedly ignored each other. She found her gaze lingering on Niles as he sat, oblivious to her contemplation. His change in attitude from when she last saw him at the airport was a complete reversal.

A fresh wave of embarrassment rolled over her as she recalled their first meeting. In reflection she must have completely misunderstood the moment or been oblivious to his ironic flirting, if that was what it was. Maybe any connection was a misinterpretation of misunderstood technologies, as the ancient-alien theorist would speculate. Was there a romantic tie between Niles and Salima? Were they ever old-time God-flames? Regardless, if he thought of her as *that human*, he must have been toying with her.

A dull and persistent thud was coming from the trunk. Jorge must have awakened from his fist-induced coma.

Niles's voice cut through the thick silence, abdicating the win. "I believe your guest has realized he's locked up."

Salima remained silent.

"Issues of hospitality aren't high on your list, apparently." The thumps continued. Niles cleared his throat. "So, assuming he survives trying to beat his way out, where are you taking him? And by proximity, us?"

"To Santa Fe to visit my little friend." Salima's voice was peppered with mischief.

Alex caught sight of Salima's reflection in the rearview mirror. The familiar expression made her cringe inside. It was a look Alex classified in her mind as the honey badger. Salima pulled it out of her bag of tricks when she was certain she just told you exactly what you did not want to hear, and was enjoying the hell out of it.

"Great." Niles's tone suggested it was anything but. "Then I guess at least Jorge won't feel lonely; there will be another loser to keep him company."

"Oh, I wouldn't be so hard on yourself, Bird Boy." Salima's voice had a laser-sharp edge to it.

"Funny, She-Beast of the Three-Beasts. You know exactly what I meant," Niles said. The thumping was insistent and continuous. Alex wondered if Jorge was going to do actual damage to the rental car's trunk.

"How long do we have to listen to that?" Alex asked. "Maybe we should pull over and do something about him?"

"Best idea you've had in a long time." Salima skidded to a stop on the deserted roadway, kicking up a cloud of dust. "You two stay here. I'll be back in two shakes." She stepped out of the car and onto the asphalt.

The trunk popped open. She strained to listen to what Salima and Jorge were arguing about, but couldn't quite make it out. There was a dull thud, and the trunk slammed shut. Salima returned alone to the driver's side and opened the door.

She slapped her hands on her pant legs as if brushing off a layer of grime. "I chatted with our detainee. He decided he preferred his table for one." Salima slid in the car and blazed it back onto the deserted desert road and sang, "We're off to see the wizard—"

"The wonderful wizard of weird," Niles cut in.

Salima pulled the car onto a dusty dirt road with a nondescript mile marker. In the far distance Alex picked out a small building. It had a large unlit neon sign that read Bes's Cafe. It was miles outside of any urban, suburban, or agricultural town. It stood alone, amongst a sea of scrub, dirt, and rocks.

"Are we stopping for lunch?" She was certainly hungry. The parking lot was empty.

"No. Although, I do hear they have the best twelve-egg omelet in New Mexico," said Salima.

Niles chuckled. "You've gotta really like eggs to eat one of those."

A man walked across the parking lot with a fairly large duffel bag. Niles pointed at it. "Gym bag or massive omelet carry out?"

Alex's stomach chimed in with an audible grumble.

"Later," Salima said, presumably in response to Alex's empty stomach. "Food will have to wait. This is where we take care of Jorge."

"In such a public place?" asked Niles.

"Take care of him? What do you mean?" Alex had no idea what Salima had in mind for Jorge, but if it was something that needed to be done behind closed doors, she didn't particularly want to be involved.

Salima pulled the car to a stop and let the engine idle. "Things aren't always how they appear." Salima spoke in a loud voice without turning her head toward the backseat. She directed her glance in Niles's direction. "Why don't you take little missy in with you? Introduce her to the old man. Let him know I've got a delivery for him out back."

Niles opened his door and leaned out of the car. Salima yelled toward his departing form. "Behave, Bird Boy. I know you think you are quite the lady-killer. But there's no time for that."

Grimacing, Niles thrust his head through the open window. "Come on, Alex, let's get this over with."

Alex stepped out of the car. As soon as she released the

handle, Salima gunned the engine and sped away in a cloud of dust toward the back of the restaurant.

Alex caught up to Niles. When she reached his side, he stopped walking and turned to her. His expression held a warning. He placed his hand on her shoulder. A shiver ran through her. The familiar and pleasant warm throb penetrated her cotton shirt. "Whatever you do," Niles said as he nodded in Salima's direction, "don't let Salima know about Chicago." He squinted and then paused as if he were trying to find the right words. "She can't know we've met before. No one can, I don't—"

He was cut off by a disembodied voice in the distance. "What the hell are you doing around here, Bird Boy?"

Niles jerked around in the direction of the voice.

Alex couldn't see a soul. Was this old man Salima referred to a spirit, or specter? Nothing would surprise her after the past couple of days.

A short, stocky man whose wide bald head rose just below trunk level emerged from behind an old white Dodge Dart. He had the appearance of a double-wide demon who'd been compressed in a way that pushed his girth outward horizontally. His mouth curled up at the edges in a wicked grin, exposing his sharply pointed teeth.

Of course, Bes's Cafe . . . The odd-looking man was Bes, the God and protector of home and hearth. It struck Alex as odd that average Egyptians had worshipped this stumpy and frightening-looking God as their household protector.

A flash of annoyance on Niles's face quickly morphed into a plastered-on smile as the short man approached.

"You and Salima can't let the Bird Boy thing die. It stopped being cute about ten centuries ago."

"Oh, I guess it's all a matter of perspective. From mine it is still fresh and new like a spring breeze. It's the gift that keeps on giving." The little man laughed and looked Alex up and down as if appraising livestock. "So who is your little human friend?"

"Little? You're one to talk," Niles answered.

"I was speaking entirely of little in the mortal sense. God, man, stop being so literal."

"If only I could," Niles mumbled.

The short man grabbed Alex's hand. "I guess your rude friend is not going to introduce us. Gormund is the name. Protecting humanity is my game."

"When you aren't being a lecherous beast," Niles chimed in.

"Takes one to know one." Gormund winked at Alex.

As soon as Alex clasped Gormund's hand she almost immediately released it. There was an odd unpleasant sensation from touching him. Was it the soft skin or its wetness? He broke contact with Alex as if sensing her discomfort.

"Hmm, that explains a number of things." Gormund's sly tone and knowing smile implied an unknown universe. Alex guessed the little man knew many secrets.

"Enough chat," said Niles. "We've got a problem for the solver."

Gormund leaned into Alex's space and sniffed around her. "This one?" His smile turned into a leer as his toad-like stumpy hand rubbed her forearm. "I sure hope so." The small man purred. "I bet this one has a lot of tales to tell."

Niles's expression pinched as if he'd smelled something bad. "No. Not this one. I assure you, though, who it is will make you happy. Very happy."

"Spill the beans," said Gormund, his expression aglow with anticipation.

"Jorge Trinculo."

A wide smile spread across Gormund's face, exposing his sharp, pointy teeth. He rubbed his hands together. "Let's not keep Salima waiting." The small man charged forward and then stopped about ten paces out. He turned, hands on hips, and yelled back at them. "What are you waiting for? We've got work to do."

Alex and Niles followed in Gormund's low but wide wake. They traveled a well-worn path that snaked through the rocky scrub toward the back of the restaurant. The trail wasn't overly large, making it hard for Alex not to knock elbows with Niles.

With Gormund up ahead would she be in the clear to talk now? Maybe it would be best to stick with a safe topic. Maybe the little man possessed supersensitive hearing abilities. "So, what's the deal with Jorge? He seems harmless enough." The words tumbled out in an ungraceful hurry from Alex's mouth.

Niles turned his head toward the vast expanse of empty that stretched out before them. Alex almost convinced herself he hadn't heard her as long seconds of silence ticked away. But they were so close, the idea was ludicrous. Maybe he was flat-out ignoring her. Or he was letting her know that they shouldn't talk at all.

Niles cleared his throat and looked at Alex. His eyes were tired and weary, as if he carried an unbearable burden. "He is, at the crux of the issue, a compounded mistake. KHMN has . . . tried to do what they thought would be best for him. Some, including myself, find their actions to be troubling at best, deadly at worst. They decided that, for the greater good of the agency, they should not have his blood on their hands, no matter what the cost. However, over time they've mitigated the sense right out of that poor man. How many times can you erase data before the recording material becomes compromised?"

"KHNM erased his memories?"

"More or less. Jorge had the misfortune of stumbling onto sensitive information back when he first started investigating his theories of alien intervention with the human species. Lucky for KHNM, he tracked down leadership to inform them he intended to expose them to the media. To this day they are not certain of his motives for contacting the agency. Were they altruistic, or did he just want to get an interview with the director to document what he found out? But, whatever the case, he was going to expose us."

"Us?"

"I was an agent at the time. And specifically, I worked on the case that exposed us to him. And believe me, there isn't a day that goes by that I don't wonder what I could have done differently. Of course, erasing his memories isn't the most reliable of magical practices. Sometimes he has unfortunate recollections, and that can get messy, so they had to make sure he was indebted to them." Niles kicked a rock from the perimeter of the path, and it skittered across the dusty ground.

"How did they buy him off? His agenda seems more focused on chasing after his alternate reality and not money."

"You familiar with the TV show he does?"

"Yeah."

"That's it."

Her mind reeled at the thought of KHNM bankrolling Jorge's television series. "And that keeps him quiet?"

"For now. Those who think they have something to say always love an audience."

"But why bring him here?"

"Usually Jorge is running toward us like a strange sort of paparazzi. Maybe Salima thinks it is worth the trip. That possibly he knows something about Raymond. She doesn't share much."

Gormund was standing in the distance, waving them toward a plain, sun-bleached door at the back of the restaurant. Stacked around it were green industrial-sized dumpsters. The rotting, fetid smell of the trash made Alex's empty stomach flip. Maybe it was a good thing she hadn't eaten in a while. She pinched her nose in an attempt to keep the aroma at bay.

"Out here in the middle of nowhere, trash pickup is fairly sporadic." Gormund opened the rickety door and pulled on a long metal chain. A bare lightbulb came to life. Gormund swept his hand dramatically across the now-illuminated threshold. The small space had all the glamour and excitement of an everyday basement, with a staircase leading downward. "Ladies first."

Alex made her way down the steep concrete stairs. While descending, she noticed a change in building materials. The steps and passageway moved from concrete to a soft beige limestone. The kind of rock Egyptian tombs were made of. Had her world magically shifted? Had they somehow descended out of New Mexico and into a Luxorian tomb hewn from the desert cliff face?

A light flickered at the base of the stairway. As Alex descended to the last step, her jaw dropped. A great domed burial chamber lay before her, and at its center lay a grand sarcophagus. A deep lapis-blue night sky was painted on the arc of the ceiling, along with a depiction of the sky Goddess Nut, who swallowed the sun in the evening and gave birth to it every morning. Her sinuous heavenly body stretched over the length of the tomb, surrounded by countless stars that glimmered gold, serving as her eternal companions.

Niles crashed into Alex. As she teetered forward, he grabbed her hips to steady them both, adding momentum to the unbalanced equation. They tumbled onto the rock-cut floor in a tangled mess.

Alex gazed at the majesty and beauty above her . . . and the room too. *God, stop acting like a lovesick schoolgirl.*

As she untwined herself from Niles, Alex glanced to the other end of the vaulted room.

Her heart sank. Great. Salima witnessed the graceless fall. Alex brushed the dust from her backside, wishing she could do the same to her dignity.

Gormund perched on the last stair with his arms crossed over his chest. His eyes glinted with amusement, apparently enjoying the show.

Salima's voice echoed from the other end. "Smooth move, you two." She gracefully made her way to Gormund. "Long time no see." She bent over and hugged him.

"So where is Jorge?" Gormund rubbed his hands together.

Salima pointed away from the granite sarcophagus. "I laid him down over there." Jorge's body was propped up in a sitting position in a far corner.

"What is this place?" The tomb walls were covered in bright jewel-toned depictions of the afterlife. Whoever painted the scenes composed them on a white background, making them visually leap from the wall. The flickering light gave the painted figures an illusion of movement. Alex wondered at the expansive beauty surrounding her. It was as if she'd stepped back in time or was visiting a tomb of a great Pharaoh. It seemed impossible this was located smack-dab in the middle of rural scrubland, USA.

Gormund held his arms out. "This is the resting place of High Priestess, Adorer of Maat, Lady of Justice, Seer into the Heart of Man . . . our lovely Meyret." His normally gruff voice was soft and reverent.

"But why here?" asked Alex. "And is she resting as in a short nap? Or resting as in dead?"

Alex couldn't believe someone was sleeping within this massive stone box. The top of the sarcophagus rose above her head. She leaned in to examine the deeply yet delicately carved hieroglyphs that embellished the stone coffin up close.

"She is under a deep sleeping spell. When she was a priestess at the Temple of Maat, she studied ancient spells and magic. The scrolls she had access to were created before the time of Pharaoh Sneferu and his first attempts at pyramids, before Narmer united the two lands of Upper and Lower Egypt. This archaic knowledge, now lost to time, taught her the craft of opening someone's mind to learn their intentions. The spell she is under allows her, born to this earth a mortal, to cope with the prospect of life everlasting. Humans don't do too well when facing eternity."

"Nor do the Immortals for that matter," said Niles.

"True." Gormund sighed. "Sad, but true. How different are Gods and man? Excepting, of course, span of life, we Immortals have proved the difference is not much."

"So if she is Immortal, why does she sleep?" asked Alex.

"As I said earlier, Meyret was born mortal and, therefore, had a hard time dealing with immortality. Her heart broke a multitude of times as she watched each generation of humans grow old and die. Eventually she climbed into the mountains and lived as a hermit. Some called her the

Mad One of the Red Land. People would come to her looking for answers."

"So let me get this straight. We are awaking a maddened Immortal? What can you expect to gain from that?" asked Alex.

"Meyret is anything but crazy." Niles smiled at Alex.

Gormund continued on. "The spell she is under helps keep her sane. A magician from a distant land who searched her out to solve a deadly problem plaguing his kingdom contrived the spell. At first sight of her he fell in love. He returned to his land and spent the remainder of his life working on a binding sleeping spell to lessen her immortal doldrums. As an old man he traveled back to her cave. The magician drank the potion for his beloved and breathed the spell into her with his dying breath. Meyret is magicked to rest peacefully, only breaking the veil of sleep when her visions are needed. I am tasked with watching over her in the meantime."

Alex pushed onto the balls of her feet to peer over the top. Inside the massive granite box an enchantingly beautiful woman slumbered. It felt voyeuristic to watch Meyret sleep, but Alex couldn't resist. The priestess's skin radiated like creamy alabaster, her lovely face like the moon against a midnight-black curtain of silken hair. She wore a fine linen shift. Her body was adorned with massive and yet delicately crafted jewels. The rich glint of gold, the deep blue of lapis lazuli, and the radiant rust-orange of carnelian dazzled Alex's eyes. Her legs quivered as she strained to stay elevated, not wanting to tear her eyes away from the vision that lay before her.

An image flashed in her mind as she lowered herself down. One she'd seen many times.

It was a photo taken inside the tomb of Queen Nefertari, Beloved of Ramses the Great. So enamored was the great king of his wife that he built her a temple alongside his at Abu Simbel. Hewn for eternity in the limestone lintel above the entrance were his words of love for her: *She for whom the sun doth shine.* It was as if an incarnation of that great queen lay before Alex in all her splendor.

Gormund continued. "As you can see, we gave her a convertible model and lovingly rendered the night sky above her so she may gaze upon its beauty in her eternity of dreams." A shadow of sadness haunted his words.

"And we're going to the trouble of waking Meyret for Jorge?" Niles expression crumpled with disapproval.

"We need more info." Salima's voice had a defensive edge to it. "We need to know what he knows. My instincts are usually spot-on. If you two don't want to be a part of this, go upstairs and get yourselves an omelet."

Gormund grabbed a remote control from a nook at the base of the sarcophagus and dimmed the lights. "After a long sleep, she doesn't like the lights up. Can't blame her, really."

"Does that control the amount of gas pumped into the torches?" asked Alex.

Gormund's chest puffed up proudly. "LEDs, baby. Programmed for flicker mode. This is a twenty-first century resting place. We replaced the torches a while back. Getting rid of the soot buildup took ages." He replaced the control and grabbed a large papyrus scroll. "Now, I need you to be completely silent and stand at the cardinal points. Jorge can stay where he is. Meyret will make her way over to the subject when she wakes. Alex, I want you on the east corner of the coffin. I will take the west end, and you two are left with the remainders. When you get to your places, press your body against the stone edge, then stretch your arms out toward the others near you, as if we were trying to reach out and touch each other's fingertips."

As they located themselves, Gormund added, "Remember, complete silence."

The cold stone corner pressed into Alex's chest as she stretched her hands out to each side, reaching as far as they could go.

Gormund made humming, mumbling noises. Alex focused her hearing; she could make out snippets of a language which was unidentifiable but somehow not completely unfamiliar. His voice grew louder with each repetition. Alex concentrated on the rhythms. They became like a warm presence as her body relaxed into the stone. She was pulled by the gentle tug of a force that drew her ever closer to its cool, smooth surface.

Her closed eyes sensed a bright flash of light as a thunderous clap of noise cut through the large space. Alex's gravity shifted, and her stomach sank as she fell backwards onto the limestone floor, like a tree cut from its base, cleaved from the stone sarcophagus's magnetic hold on her.

She landed flat on her back and mentally scanned her body for damage. Surprisingly, there was none. She turned her gaze to the painted night sky above and blinked away the trance-fog that hovered over her mind.

Something was different with the ceiling. Alex squinted. The head of the Goddess Nut was leaning over her. Her large almond eyes filled with concern. Alex shook her head. It wasn't the Goddess staring down at her. It was the priestess Meyret, now fully awake.

So you came. Meyret's voice danced through Alex's mind, although the priestess hadn't opened her mouth. *I'm glad to see you. I have waited so long to meet you.* The priestess smiled as she knelt and placed Alex's head in her lap, stroking her forehead. *Dear One.*

The others gathered around and were standing above her, staring at her.

Gormund moved close to Meyret and touched her forearm. "Oh Great Priestess, this is not your subject for waking." He pointed toward Jorge. "We need to hear what is in the heart of that man."

"Lead me to him, my dear guardian." She stood and hooked her arm with Gormund's, allowing herself to be drawn away. Her voice had sounded sweet and clear like a playful wind chime teasing the summer wind with its music.

Alex lay on the ground, feeling its solid coolness as she contemplated what happened between herself and the priestess. Was it possible Meyret could speak directly into her head? Or had she imagined it all? Did the jolt of electricity that shot through her when Meyret awoke clean her mental clockwork?

Alex and Niles followed the others to where Jorge lay. Salima and Gormund were attending to a multitude of knots that bound his entire body. The golden rope shimmered. It was not chain-like, nor was it woven. It had a fluid nature, as if it were caught between a liquid and a solid state. Alex wondered at the weblike quality of their work. Their efforts seemed a little over the top for one harmless human. "How many knots can you need? I can't imagine Jorge would be much of a flight risk?"

"Magical," Salima said in a matter-of-fact voice as she pulled a knot as tight as possible. "Jorge has magical powers?" Alex wondered if his exposure to the Others had changed him somehow from a standard-issue human.

Salima shot a sly look at Gormund and rolled her eyes, but offered no explanation as she maneuvered around Jorge, tugging at the other knots.

"I can't imagine he could hurt a fly. Do they have to be that tight? I think you might be hindering blood flow to his head," said Alex.

Salima looked up from her task with an inspired smile. "You think?"

Gormund unwound a thicker banding of gold. As he wrapped it around Jorge's head, Gormund spoke with a slow intention that matched the pace of his work. "The knots are magical. They provide a grid of sorts for Meyret to travel into his mind, or what is left of it." He shoved one of the ends into Jorge's ear. "And believe it or not, this is his USB port, of sorts." Once the magicked material entered the ear, Gormund pulled his hands back. The golden material liquefied and then swirled around Jorge's head like twin rivers, touching but still separate as the gold mercury-like substance twined around his head.

Gormund grabbed the remaining end and handed it to Meyret. She knelt down and cradled Jorge's head with her hands. Meyret closed her eyes and chanted. She swayed like a cobra to an unseen charmer. Her sweet voice slowly became louder and louder as the chant grew. Her angelic voice filled the space. As the volume increased, it reverberated through the tomb in an eerie call and response.

Alex peered down at Jorge, his head still cradled by the long, slender hands of the priestess. His eyes flickered open, his fear apparent in a wide stare that darted around like a trapped animal searching for escape. His body jerked and twitched as he struggled to break the magical bindings.

Meyret shifted Jorge's head to her left hand and placed her right hand on his chest above his heart. His breath was shallow. Meyret spoke in a low, soothing voice. "Maat, Goddess of Truth and Justice, show us what is in this man's heart. Tell us the truths he knows but does not want us to know, truths that might harm our beloveds."

Jorge's body stilled as if in a trance, his eyes staring blankly up at the painted night sky above.

"I think he is ready for your questions," said Meyret. Four sets of expectant eyes were directed at Alex. "Me?"

Niles coughed to conceal a laugh. "I think your questions might end up being more concise than ours. You don't know him like we do. Our past experiences with him might muddy the conversation."

"Or maybe, like Buxton, you misguidedly believe she is the One of Prophecy." Salima sneered.

Niles shot Salima a knowing look. "Why don't you relax and focus on locating your calmer inner Bastet. I, for one, would find that to be far more palatable if we are all going to be stuck with each other until this gets sorted out." Niles glanced in Alex's direction.

Gormund's body winced and twitched like a dog tired of waiting for its treat. He rubbed his rough and stubby hands together. "Come on. Time's a wasting. These magical spells do have a shelf life, you know."

They were all looking at her expectantly. Alex hated being put on the spot. Jorge appeared to be under a heavy trance. She wasn't certain if he could hear her. "What was your purpose at the Full Life Awareness Conference?"

"Aliens," Jorge whispered, then giggled like a child who took glee in sharing secret information.

Gormund let out an exasperated sigh. "Aliens. Really? That's his answer for everything. Any mystery in the world, it always boils down to aliens somehow or another. I think I might be well within reason to suggest some degree of torture." Gormund beamed a brilliant smile to Meyret, exposing his fine and sharp choppers. "I mean just in this case, of course. It is a matter of urgent and expedient need."

"Does this spell somehow hinder his ability to communicate? Or does he normally only speak in monosyllables?" asked Salima.

"'Aliens' has more than one syllable," Niles quipped.

"Whatever," said Salima.

Alex cleared her throat; the others gazed expectantly at her. The pressure was on. She had no idea what to say. She leaned in toward Jorge and spoke slowly, looking directly into his upturned face. "Why did you run from Salima?"

His breathing became erratic, like a sleeping poodle dreaming of being chased by the hounds of hell. Jorge's head jerked slightly from side to side as he became agitated. "Was told to avoid—"

"Who told you to avoid the Immortals?" Salima interjected. Apparently she didn't enjoy playing second fiddle. Or was there another reason why she'd cut him off?

"The great one."

"You are taking too long. We don't have time for this." Salima thrust her face a hair's breadth away from Jorge's. "Do you know where Raymond is?"

Jorge droned, "The Red Lands."

Niles's expression hardened. "Damn it. He is much further along than we thought. He's gone home to Egypt. We better hit the next flight out."

Alex felt a tinge of concern as she took in the bland and inanimate expression of their captive. "What about Jorge?"

Gormund's face widened with glee. "Don't worry about him. I have planned an enjoyable end for him."

"End? You can't mean . . ." For the second time in the past hour the innuendo implied Jorge's final day.

"Oh, god no, what do you take me for? A little beast?" He shook his head. "Have you ever heard of the Star Axis artwork?"

Alex shook her head.

"Most people never have. It's not far from here. It's a massive concrete pyramidal structure." The small man's face opened with a look of pure rapture.

"Well? Spill the beans, Gormund. What are you going to do to him?" Niles said. His patience seemed to be wearing thin.

"I am going to have Meyret cast a forgetting spell and then layer on an abduction spell in which each of us will be represented by little green stand-ins. This will completely change his cognitive map of what has happened to him. Then I take a little drive out into the desert and leave him there to meditate for a while with a throwaway cell phone and some water. Perfectly rewritten experience for dear Jorge. If you are around a TV when his next episode airs, you should check it out. I am willing to guess his latest experience will make great fodder."

"Nice one, Gormund," Salima said as she slapped him on the back. "Good to see you." She hugged Gormund and Meyret and made her way toward the staircase. She turned to address Niles and Alex. "Come on, you two. I'm gonna let the boss know we are headed to Egypt."

Alex wondered if she'd meant Buxton or Raymond. Or both?

"Did you happen to bring your passport with you when you left Chicago?" asked Salima.

"Well, no I—"

"Doesn't surprise me. I'll let him know that will be another thing they will have to finagle." She turned toward Gormund and Meyret. "Good seeing you two."

"Thanks. To you both." Niles touched his forehead in salute and sauntered off to follow Salima up the stairs.

Alex felt awkward standing alone with these two strangers. She meagerly offered her thanks and headed toward the stairs. With her back to Gormund and Meyret, Alex felt a tickle- like sensation in her mind. She turned around. Her gaze was drawn to Meyret. The priestess's eyes held a sense of longing. Alex heard Meyret's voice in her head. *I hope to see you again, Dear One. You and I are of one blood.* The priestess smiled a weary smile and then turned to walk alongside Gormund, her long and graceful strides somehow in time with his short loping steps.

CHAPTER NINETEEN

Warm sunlight streamed across Alex's face. Her eyes opened to unfamiliar walls. A rich tapestry of street noise filtered in through the window above. Judging by the bright light and the sounds on the street below, the day was well underway. There were vendors yelling, engines whirring, drivers honking, and donkeys braying. A steady aroma of exhaust wafted up from the busy boulevard to her second-story room.

The thin coverlet she'd thrown over herself in the cool of the evening was now overly warm and slightly damp with sweat. She tossed it aside and sat on the edge of the bed as she worked at reconstructing the hazy activities of the previous night.

It all began with the mad dash to the airport in the hopes of making the next flight to London and then on to

Egypt. When they arrived at the departure gate, both Salima and Niles took off on a personal mission. Presumably both of her self-appointed guardians didn't feel the threat level was too high behind the lines of airport security.

Salima returned to board the aircraft insanely early with the first-class pre-board. She must have upgraded herself. At the time Alex had felt a twinge of jealousy. How nice it would be to recline in a roomy, plush leather seat while sipping champagne? Would Salima be making happy wishes on the bubbles? Alex doubted it.

Niles had plopped down on the coach seat next to Alex moments before the flight was about to push back, smelling suspiciously of scotch.

As Alex tried to wake, she kneeled on her bed and peered out the window. Last night, when they had arrived in Luxor, it was during that eerie and undefinable time between night and dawn where nothing belongs to either. The empty streets were simultaneously shrouded in deep night shadow and the crisp clarity of a new day's dawn. She'd imagined at any moment bakers and street cleaners and all other early risers would be emerging into the silent city to start their workday as Alex, Niles, and Salima made their way to the unassuming two-story sand-colored building that was Chicago House.

KHNM's Luxor headquarters was located within the indomitable and hallowed walls of Chicago House, where season after season it was the residence for the archaeologists, researchers, epigraphers, librarians, and artists who worked on the various archaeological sites held by the Oriental Institute in Luxor. In hindsight, it made perfect sense that KHNM's Luxor branch would be at Chicago House since it was a satellite of the Oriental Institute.

From her window, she could see the river Nile and the newly expanded Corniche that ran the length of the Luxorian riverbanks. Far away, palm fronds danced in the midmorning breeze, their spiky tendrils interlacing with one another. Alex had a hard time believing she'd actually made it to Egypt.

She closed her eyes, attempting to forget the excruciating moment when the plane touched down and she was jostled awake, only to realize she'd somehow fallen asleep nestled on Niles's broad chest. If that wasn't bad enough, she had twined her fingers around his. He looked oddly startled as she lifted her drowsy head away from him and mumbled how sorry she was, wishing there was a way she could crawl under the seat and disappear. She cringed at the memory. It could have been worse, she could have drooled all over his crisp oxford shirt as she slept like the dead. At least she had that to be thankful for.

Her stomach made a long yawning growl. Alex glanced at the alarm clock resting on the bedside table. It was hard to believe it was already ten in the morning. Alex slid off the bed and went to her meager carry-on bag, which lay open and violated in her rush to collapse into a deep sleep. She rooted around in its limited offerings. She hoped there might be options available for purchase other than the run-of-the-mill tourist fare; she couldn't imagine facing off against Raymond in a King Tut T-shirt.

The inviting savory smell of eggs and bacon filled the small room.

The elegantly understated dining room had a distinctly art deco feel to it. Alex was surprised to see Buxton at the breakfast buffet so late in the morning. Even though he'd met them upon their arrival, she'd assumed he was a consistent early riser.

Buxton was impeccably dressed. Today he sported a bow tie with a blocky Mondrian print in primary colors. His aesthetic— a delightful blend of a classic tweedy scholar and chic modernist—was caught in a lovely place between smart and smarter. The room and its antique yet sleek furnishings were the perfect habitat for him.

"Good morning, sunshine. Getting a late start today, are we?" His eyes sparkled with mischief.

Alex turned toward the food and responded playfully, "Whatever happened to 'How have you been? It's been such a long time since I've seen you'? Or even an old favorite, 'so glad to see you'?" She scooped a pile of hot scrambled eggs onto her plate, then grabbed the silver tongs and artfully curated the choice bacon slices in the chafing dish, being sure to select only those that were in that sweet spot of just done and crispy. "As you know, we arrived sometime around O-dark-thirty." She sat at the table and grinned at him, flipping her hair with the back of her hand. "We girls need our beauty sleep."

Buxton was fiddling with a butter knife, turning it end over end. The thump became persistent in the silence of the room. He seemed to be weighing how to say something he had on his mind.

Alex bit into a slice of bacon. "So where are my two companions? Did they both upstage me by being up and at 'em at the crack of dawn?"

"Niles had some personal business to take care of. Should be back sometime before lunch." He stared at the knife he was worrying.

"And Salima?"

The heavy end of the knife thunked and clattered to the floor. "I had to send her away for a while. I am not sure when she will be back." His voice had a strange edge as he reached to retrieve the lost knife.

"Where'd she go?"

"I needed her to locate someone for me." His tone had the sort of finality that did not welcome further questioning. "I would assume you would be glad to see the back of her. It didn't appear you two were exactly peas in a pod." A spark of humor returned to his voice.

Alex chewed on the bacon as she considered the old man across from her. His careworn face was drawn forward in a frown, and his normally clear, bright eyes were heavy lidded.

"How about you and I take a stroll around the compound?"

"Sounds delightful." Alex shoveled in some eggs and headed off with Buxton.

As they made their way through the compound, Buxton introduced her to the staff. Their regard for him was apparent, their expressions softening when they spotted him. Alex could relate. Buxton was easy company. In the short time she'd known him, she recognized how their conversations had a natural ebb and flow, like a river rolling gently from bank to bank. Silences between them were companionable and unstrained. Alex imagined this would be what her relationship with her father would be, if he were still alive.

Buxton opened a large wooden door, revealing the library. She imagined she felt the way the children did when they first saw Willy Wonka's chocolate mixing room. She nearly broke into the old-school version of Gene Wilder singing "Pure Imagination" as she entered the room.

"Explore as you like. You have an unusual amount of freedom. Our librarian Gini is out of town. So you basically have free rein."

Alex inhaled the familiar musty-dusty smell of old paper. The antique mahogany shelves lining the room were filled with books standing at attention like silent border guards to new worlds of knowledge. Their gold-embossed spines gleamed, each vying for her attention, calling her to visit their undiscovered territories. She could spend a happy existence randomly perusing the library's offerings and yet not making a dent in its riches.

The books created a dun-colored rainbow containing erratic clusters of washed-out rust- browns, age-weathered mint greens, and the faded-denim blues of bound academic studies. Broad work tables dotted the room's interior along with horizontal file cabinets holding maps and illustrations. Near the entryway stood an olive-green card catalog, circa 1920, containing small, yellowed rectangular cards to guide one through this archipelago of knowledge. She wandered toward the back of the room, running her finger along the books' spines, catching the merest glimpses of their titles and subjects. The conservator inside her cringed as the suppressed seven-year-old leapt with a naughty glee.

Buxton followed Alex to the farthest horizontal file as she pulled out the top drawer. He leaned against its cabinet and silently witnessed her exploration. She marveled at the manically detailed drawings. Chicago House Institute was renowned for its many-layered approach to ensure accuracy when recording temple inscriptions and artworks. The process always struck her as being equal parts thorough and insane. It was as if they were trying to capture the immense desert one grain of sand at a time. However, she was glad they were unhinged enough to attempt it. She was fixated on an intricate drawing from 1967 of Medinet Habu temple.

He peered down at the pulled-out drawer. "I see you have good taste. The process for recording hasn't changed at Chicago House for decades, but somehow, the recordings from that time period leap off the page. I must admit I have fallen down that same rabbit hole myself a number of times." Buxton lowered his hand toward the old drawing, fanning his fingers above the surface without touching it. His hand then gently moved to Alex's forearm. The usual twinkle in his eyes was replaced with an expression that landed somewhere between concern and regret. It reminded Alex of her mother's face all those years ago, when she sat on Alex's ruffled and brightly hued butterfly-patterned bedspread and told her that her father was never coming back.

"What's up?" Her voice cracked, afraid of what was to come next.

Buxton nodded toward the opposite wall. "Come this way."

Alex followed him to an old, weathered bookcase. His knees popped and cracked as he squatted and extracted a slim book from the lowest shelf and handed it to Alex. She held the antique book in her hand; its cloth cover was of a worn deep blue. It was finely decorated with a chain of golden Nile lotus blossoms forming a decorative border around the title. Resting atop the title text was a gold-embossed emblem of a solar disc with unfurled wings emerging from its center. *Translation of the Brown Siwa Papyrus,* by M. M. Brier. The title page had a publish date of 1934.

Alex whistled. "Shouldn't I be wearing gloves or something?"

"This book ultimately is yours. It is a translation of a papyrus written in the first century BCE. An English traveler named William George Browne found it stowed away in a clay canister in 1792 during his search for the ancient oracle's temple in Siwa. M. M. Brier found it in an antiquities shop sometime in the 1930s and took on the task of translating it."

Alex placed the book on the worktable behind her, gently turning the aged yellow pages. "So how is it mine?"

"It holds answers for you, Alex. About the prophecy. We can guess now that Raymond intends to kill them and take the powers for himself. Basically, to become the Aten, The One True God, and use the powers to enslave humanity or quite possibly annihilate us. If all goes well, you will battle against him."

"Battle? What do you mean, 'battle'?" Before the past couple of minion incursions, the only thing close to fighting she'd ever done was take a weekly course in kung fu her dad enrolled her in. After he died, her mother saw no sense in her continuing. How would she battle this all-powerful God? So far he'd killed three Immortals. Had he absorbed their powers into his magical weaponry?

"This book will at least give you a context for your family's hereditary connection to the agency." Buxton's gaze softened as he looked at Alex. "It's a shame, I always thought . . . Well, I hoped I would have been able to share this with you earlier on in your life, but your mother would have none of it. But that's in the past, and we can only deal with the present."

"Speaking of my mother, do you know anything about a letter that was sent to her before I was called to duty?"

"I stopped trying to contact her years ago." Buxton squinted.

"It was from KHNM."

"Peculiar. I am the only one authorized to communicate with Roxanne. I wonder who—"

"That's exactly what I aim to find out. Apparently, all of this KHNM business landed her back in rehab."

Buxton grasped her arm. Concern washed over his face. "Oh, Alex. I am so sorry. What a sad mess this is."

CHAPTER TWENTY

W hen Alex got to her room, she tried to call her mother at home just in case she'd gotten out on good behavior. It rang into infinity due to Roxanne's inability to move into the realm of message recorders. She would burst into bemused laughter at the merest suggestion of a cell phone. Roxanne didn't want to be available to the world at a whim, and did not think the responsibility should rest on the receiver of the call. If someone wanted to get a hold of her badly enough, eventually they would. The sad outcome of this telecommunication philosophy was that most of Roxanne's friends eventually dropped off, making her even more dependent on Alex.

Alex came to realize that her mother's shrinking world was tightening the tether she had on her daughter. After being on the verge of a mental breakdown when she tried to balance her master's dissertation alongside being her mother's full-time keeper, Alex realized she needed to slowly wean Roxanne off her dependency on Alex. They'd made slow progress.

But now this. Rehab again.

Her mother was trying once more to reel her into her drama and sickness. She knew she had to stay resolved. The codependency of their relationship did neither of them any good.

Alex finally got somewhere when she called the rehab center. The nurse on duty informed her Roxanne was still sleeping. *"It is only five in the morning,"* the nurse added in a brusque tone. No wonder her mother always stayed there during recovery. The passive-aggressive culture must make her feel right at home.

The small room began to feel like a human-sized cage. She slipped the book Buxton gave her into her scribe's bag and headed out. She would need to be bright eyed and observant of her surroundings. Knowing she was a person of interest to Raymond did give her pause, but the area around the Nile had throngs of tourists. She doubted he would be bold enough to try anything in broad daylight.

Alex strode through the outer gate of Chicago House and onto the busy Corniche that ran alongside the Nile through Luxor. It bustled with the hectic circus of Egyptian midday traffic.

Tour buses and taxi cabs kicked up dust as they whizzed by. Beyond the busy roadway lay the promenade that was dotted with benches and street vendors. Further in the distance, Alex could make out the great and mighty Nile.

She darted through the vehicles as their drivers vigorously honked at her. Once on the promenade she took advantage of one of the benches to catch her breath. She underestimated the lack of concern the Luxorian drivers would have for a pedestrian crossing. The sun-soaked stone bench radiated a pleasant burn against her legs as she basked in the brilliant and hot sunlight that rained down. She closed her eyes and listened to the sounds of nearby river birds calling to one another as they flew by, people shouting, and the water lapping against the shore.

Alex took a deep breath and opened her eyes. A spark of excitement passed through her.

She made it to Egypt, the land of her dreams. It was the subject of her college days and encompassed both her professional and personal life. It was intimately familiar and yet alien.

She picked up a stray pebble on the ground. Its red color stood out against the sand-beige color around her. She clasped it in her hand, feeling its sun-beaten warmth as she gazed west across the river. The red land, the place where dead kings and queens were laid to rest for eternity in their valley of tombs. The ancients called it the red land because nothing lived there and only death prevailed. Her breath caught in her throat. This was the land that took her father from her. Tears welled up in her eyes.

Westerners, that was what the ancient Egyptians called their dead. Had her father's soul gone West? Was it still hovering over the land he loved so dearly? So much so that he was willing to die for it. The thought of him or some small essence of him existing in the far-off cliffs or the majestic Nile gave her comfort.

She unhinged her scribe's bag and dropped the stone inside. It made a clinking sound. It must have landed on Niles's fancy pen. She'd have to try to remember to return it to him. It was one of those things that she kept remembering at exactly the wrong time. Like now, when he was nowhere in sight.

Alex left the bench and slowly wandered down the promenade. A trinket stand selling odd bits of cheap jewelry caught her eye. Some resembled ancient artifacts, and others were more modern renditions of Egyptomania. There was a locket in the shape of a small coffin. A latch pin was located at the foot of the coffin. She pulled the pin out and exposed a tiny metal mummy nested within.

She had to have it. This would be the one rare purchased memento. Not one of her usual, and oftentimes ridiculed, pocketful of found treasures. As she handed the elderly cart owner the money, she realized she would have something funny to tell her mom, once they got past the usual dysfunctional garbage. Roxanne would get a kick out of hearing about her little magpie actually buying an honest-to-goodness souvenir.

Alex retrieved the pendant from its small felt bag and strung it alongside the djed pillar. After locking the clasp, she swung her body backward to avoid a bird as it flew by her face. The tip of its wing swooped by, nearly brushing her nose.

The little songbird landed on the nearby cart handle and stared at her. To the ancient Egyptians, the Ba was part of the dead one's soul. It allowed them to wander the land of the living, and was usually represented in the form of a bird. Alex smiled at the fanciful thought that maybe this bird was her father's Ba-soul looking out for her. The bird trilled and flew away. She shivered against the heat of the day. Alex couldn't shake the feeling someone was watching over her, or just plain watching her.

A small boat that was docked next to one of the innumerable boxlike Nile cruise ships piqued her interest. She'd heard of these boats for hire from colleagues who worked in the field during the excavation season. You could hire them for an hour or two and lazily sail about the Nile, more often than not without any particular destination in mind. Caught up in her newfound independence, she hired the small felucca. It had a majestic white sail and was captained by an old man with a warm smile. At just thirty Egyptian pounds for an hour, she couldn't pass it up.

Alex sat down and leaned against the wooden edge of the felucca as the captain pushed off. She tilted her head up at the colorful empty soda-pop cans strung together on the boat's sunshade above her. The breeze caused the cans to bump against each other, creating a pleasantly loose-sounding wind chime. She was enchanted by the visual symphony of the other sailed boats as they skimmed across the smooth river. Waterfowl and river birds flew in open, swooping patterns against the dusky-pink sky. Her heart soared with them in a joyful kinship of wild freedom.

This was the black land, the silt-rich banks that supported Egypt's agriculture and cotton trade. Out beyond the narrow emerald strip lay the dreaded red land of death and the afterlife.

Alex gazed wistfully across the landscape, taking in both red and black as she tried to envision what it might have been like when the great Pharaohs ruled. It boggled her mind to contemplate all that this river of rivers had witnessed and influenced.

She pulled out the old book Buxton had given her and rubbed her fingers over its rough canvas cloth. Alex drew it close and inhaled its delightful musty smell. Pulling it away, she noticed the pages jutted out unevenly, the mark of a fine publication.

The introduction by M. M. Brier was typical of a text from the 1900s. The language was dry and overwrought. Alex couldn't fathom why Buxton was so anxious for her to read it. She struggled to stay focused on the antiquated academic tome as the wondrous landscape of Egypt rolled by.

She fanned through the book and stumbled upon something unusual for a scholarly text. In the center of the book was a replica of the ancient scroll. A centerfold for geeks. She unfolded it gently. The hieroglyph alphabet was something she'd learned in her undergrad days, but reading hieroglyphs was never her strong suit, although she delighted in their shapes. The translation of the scroll would be her best bet for information.

The felucca captain whistled, then smiled, and pointed to his watch. Her time must be half over. Her heart sank as the boat turned around. Her freedom was most certainly coming to an end.

Alex returned to the hieroglyphs and was about to fold up the pullout when a pattern of hieroglyphs jumped out at her. They appeared to be stacked in a name format. An owl, mouth, and loaf of bread hieroglyphs combined with a feather of Maat at the end spelled M-R-T. She knew the ancient Egyptians never used vowels, so this scroll was written by someone named Meyret. The symbol of the feather could well mean this Meyret was a priestess of Maat. Could this be the same Meyret who lived in the basement of Bes's Cafe? Alex dove into the translation of the text with a new vigor.

She read about a high priestess of Maat who lived in the Siwa Oasis, located about seven hundred miles west of modern-day Cairo. The translation was from a narrative written by a priestess sometime around 100 BCE. It told of a warrior who came to Egypt from across the Great Green Sea. He ruled the heart of the priestess and eventually the entire world. He was a foreigner, but was descended from the Great God Amun. The priestess and the warrior swore to love and live forever. But conquest called to him. It was his destiny to conquer all. As he battled in foreign lands, she searched high and low for a spell of immortality, to bring their dream to life. She drank from the cup of eternity, but he died on a faraway campaign before she could share it with him, leaving her with immortality and a child.

After generations of her line had passed to the Field of Reeds, she came upon a prophecy written on the day her beloved was born. The priestess Meyret who penned the narrative credited a Priestess of Artemis in the far-off land of Ephesus.

Amun envisioned as a snake the northern
lady's bed doth take

Amun clothed as the great mythic viper lies
upon the bed of the northern queen

A fiery blaze across the vast Green Sea
consumes the temple and signals
prophecy

A western lion stalks the eastern lady's love
in a holy alcove

A passion frozen in time and one from this
love's bloodline

Fights to save the cause divine

May you banish the God's abomination and
ensure man's salvation

So what did this mean? How did this relate to Alex? She slowly read the verse aloud.

Something about it felt so familiar. It rang a bell but seemed more related to ancient Macedonian or Greek history than Egyptian.

> *Amun envisioned as a snake the northern*
> *lady's bed doth take*
>
> *Amun clothed as the great mythic viper lies*
> *upon the bed of the northern queen*

The first two lines of text had parallels to the conception myth of Alexander the Great. In that myth, the Egyptian God Amun visited the bed of the Macedonian Queen Olympias. That union conceived Alexander, making him born of the Gods and not simply a human ruler of Egypt. Alex had always thought this myth was merely propaganda to get buy-in from the conquered. She had a vague memory that Alexander's birth was associated with a great temple burning down in Ephesus. However, she wasn't certain if it was something she'd learned in her undergrad years or was something Buxton told her.

> *A western lion stalks the eastern lady's love*
> *in a holy alcove*

A passion frozen in time and one from this
love's bloodline

Alex had seen representations from Alexander's life associating him with a lion. *Eastern lady's love in a holy—* Alex jolted to attention as the boat bumped against the dock. She slammed the book shut. If her interpretation of the text was correct, she, Alex Philothea, was a direct descendant of not only the beautiful priestess Meyret, but Alexander the Great.

CHAPTER TWENTY-ONE

R aymond smiled with satisfaction into the bright sunlight as he let the intense white heat cascade over him. The sun's rays reached down from the heavens and caressed him like a long-pined-for lover. He breathed in the heady scent of Egypt, the arid desert and damp marshland.

The Nile gently lapped against the hull of his boat, filling him with an easy joy.

He opened his eyes, taking in the timeless dichotomy of Egypt. The vibrant, razor-thin strip of green allowed life and culture to flourish, and beyond lay the desolate and deadly sand-colored cliffs. A crane swooped in and stood amid the swaying river grass, its long, skinny legs submerged in the cool, rich river silt, patiently waiting for its hapless prey to shimmy by.

Not unlike Raymond.

He wanted to burn this moment into his memory, so he would remember how it felt to be surrounded by perfection and balance. Thankfully, the humans would soon have a strong hand to guide them. Then they would understand perfection like this. Raymond was familiar with their willful ways and assumed they would initially put up a fight against his imposed yoke. But that wouldn't last long. They should be grateful he chose to rule and not exterminate them. How could fragile mortals ever expect to best a God?

His thoughts rolled back to the ridiculous celebration the city officials had given him in honor of the indecently large cash contribution he'd made to their "conservation fund." Raymond was certain that by giving him their prized hovercraft they were showing him a deep respect. His gaze wandered over to the sand-colored hulking machine parked in the distance. Raymond wasn't exactly sure what he was going to do with the craft, but he couldn't refuse it once the gift was offered. One thing Raymond was sure of, his "donation" wasn't going to restore any temples or tombs. That suited him just fine. All he wanted was to be left alone, and in Egypt cash could buy solitude.

What did he care about the temples of humans anyway? No one worshipped or made offerings to the Gods any longer. The crumbling stones did his kind no good. If they had, he and his family wouldn't be stuck in this unbearable situation. The humans would soon have a leader who would pull in the reins and save them from themselves.

The sound of a minion's heavy and determined foot-steps slamming against the teak deck broke his contemplative mood. The minions' performance was disappointing. As soon as he had full command of the power source, they would be eliminated. Once he had limitless powers he would be able to create much more dependable servants.

"Great Master, we are at your command. The captive will not awake from the severing spell until after we are scheduled to sail tonight. What will you have us do with him?"

Raymond sighed. That idiot Jorge had turned up again. Hadn't he warned the man to stay away from himself and Others? He'd been useful in the past in gathering information. But in this instance he was useless.

These minions were not much better at orders than that mortal, Jorge.

They needed everything completely spelled out for them. They were pretty close to useless. Was it the many centuries of waiting to be called to duty that had greatly diminished their abilities? "Take him away. Leave him where he will be easily found."

"Yes, Oh Golden One. We will take him right away." The minion turned and walked away.

Raymond shook his head with disgust. "After dark, you imbecile," he yelled at the retreating minion.

It spun around and faced Raymond. "Yes, Light of the World. After dark it will be." It turned and made its way below decks.

Raymond cringed at the god-awful monikers they were compelled to call him. Yet another reason to toss them in the trash heap. If they were worth their salt, he would have already had this Alex Philothea in his grasp.

She probably had no idea what it was she was up against. Probably those idiots at KHNM were bungling their side of things. She probably wouldn't be pursuing him so hard if she knew everything. He chuckled to himself. The pathetic futility of it all. The date doesn't fall far from the tree. He'd killed her father all those years ago, over the artifact, and now he was eager to coat his hands in the blood of Phillip's daughter. Put an end to that balderdash of a prophecy.

At least Raymond knew his quarry was heading toward him. It didn't take much interrogation to get the information out of the pathetic creature his daughter had dragged on board last night. She'd found him sniffing around Raymond's boat. Witnessing a severing spell was never pleasant, even when it was spun by as skilled a practitioner as she. Besides all the screaming and pleading, listening to Jorge rant on about aliens and some stargate pushed the limits of Raymond's patience.

Jorge turned out to be a special case. Each severing spell cast on him pulled his personal orbit ever closer to the Others, the magical residue within him putting him on a tragic trajectory. The mortal mind can only handle so much. He'd had so many severing spells the synaptic connections between what he experienced and the memory implants must have become indecipherable and distorted like an old, over-played cassette tape. No wonder he had fixated on aliens. Over the years Jorge became like a sick mongrel dog the family couldn't quite ignore or put out of its misery. Did it stem from a grudging affection or sheer entertainment value?

Raymond guessed the latter.

His chest tightened as he thought of the sad cargo stored below decks. Nearly the entire set of his family's sacrificial essences were encased in sterile delicate glass tubes. Anxiety snaked its way through him. Dead. They were dead. By his hand. Only two more of the required were left to find.

He must get to his sacred space.

Where was his daughter? She should be there by now. The task just involved a little light stalking. She should be able to handle that.

Raymond reached for his binoculars, surveying the surrounding marshland. As he searched for his daughter's small craft, a felucca in the distance caught his eye. He zoomed in. The vision came into focus. He spotted a plain-looking brunette with glasses reading a book, all alone.

His smile returned.

CHAPTER TWENTY-TWO

The old sailor climbed out onto the wooden dock and reached down to help Alex up.

His weathered, mahogany-colored skin scratched her as he clasped her hand. The boat rocked with the shift in weight, making her grateful for his steady grip. After handing him the fare, she sauntered down the pier to the promenade, breathing in the strange fragrance of Egypt, a peculiar mix of dry and wet.

Her feeling of well-being faded when she reached the promenade. The odd sensation of being watched returned. As she surveyed her surroundings, her pulse quickened with a disturbing realization. Her intuition had been spot-on as of late.

A large flock of pigeons flew overhead and landed on the wall directly above her. Near the birds, she spotted two people that seemed to be looking at her. They quickly jerked away from her line of sight. Alex pressed herself flat against the wall. Was she being paranoid? Maybe her imagination was getting the better of her. She raced up the stairs. Chicago House should be on the other side of the roadway.

At the top of the stairs, Alex checked in the direction of the disappearing heads. Their vacation-wear-clad bodies were moving toward her with a determined air. Minions. Alex glanced at the roadway. It was heavy with the late-day commuting cars and lorries. She couldn't see a clear break in sight. She would have to dance an agile jig to avoid becoming road paint. Adrenaline coursed through her body as she jumped into the street. She wove in between the oncoming traffic as drivers blared their horns.

She reached the curb outside Chicago House panting and out of breath. Her pursuers were cut off by the constant stream of traffic. They stood side by side staring across at Alex with cold, dead eyes. She ducked through the broad gate of the compound and turned around for one last look to see if they'd followed.

They'd vanished. A chill ran down her spine. Raymond must be tracking her. Why hadn't they continued to follow her? Alex bent over and placed her hands on her thighs and tried to catch her breath. Maybe Chicago House was for minions what a churchyard would be for the undead. The thought made her laugh, but at the same time seemed like it could hold true. Maybe on second thought, it wasn't a good idea to go out alone.

"Where on earth have you been?" Buxton's agitated voice boomed in the courtyard.

The tone of his voice made Alex bristle. Alex swung around to face him. His face was dangerously red.

"I just . . ."

"Have you no idea the danger you are in?"

"You're damn right I have no idea. And do you want to know why?" Years of pent-up anger and frustration welled up within her and exploded out of her mouth. "Because all my life everyone has done their best to keep me in the dark." She stomped past Buxton and into the foyer. She spun around and walked back to face Buxton. "And to be crystal clear, that includes you."

Once in her room, Alex sat on the bed and grabbed the weighty receiver out of its cradle. Instinctively, she knew better than to recline when talking to Roxanne. The mere thought of it made her empathize with Prometheus, belly exposed while awaiting the return of the eagle.

She dialed the Bright Dawn Recovery Center. With each unanswered ring to Roxanne's room, Alex felt a small glow of hope spark. Maybe she lucked out and was still out of sync with Roxanne's recovery regime. She had braced herself for Roxanne's fallback mode of high-octane bitchy-cranky whenever she tried to kick her addictions.

The ringtone stopped. Alex's heart sank when her mother's sharp voice cut into the silence. "The nurse told me my daughter called this morning. I told her I didn't know I had a daughter, because if I did have one, she would have most certainly called me sooner than now." The line went silent. "So who are you?"

Nothing like starting out with a solid passive-aggressive layer of guilt. "I would have tried to call you earlier than today, but Bernadette said you were on a forty-eight-hour communication lockdown."

"After all my sacrifices and work to keep you away from those bastards at KHNM, you get mixed up with them anyway."

"It seems to me all your secrecy hasn't done me any good. You shielded me from things you don't want to face. Possibly putting my life and the whole of humanity in jeopardy."

"Give me a break." Her mother produced a heavy sigh. "You believe that claptrap? It sounds like they're feeding you all those lies about Gods and whatnot. Probably Buxton and Niles are filling your mind with trash. Wouldn't trust either one of them. Niles thinks he is clever with that silly name of his. You know, if I ever see him, I will give him a piece of my mind. If you run across him, tell him that Roxanne will never forgive him. That bastard ruined my . . . ," she said, her voice cracking, "our lives."

Niles? Ruined our lives? Her mind spun. Alex brushed the idea off when Salima hinted at it in New Mexico, but now her mom was insinuating the same thing. That he had something to do with her father's death all those years ago. Alex's heart raced. "How?"

"You have that son of a bitch tell you himself. I am focused on getting better right now, not mucking up the past. I'm not about to sit here and replay a story I'd rather forget. Why do you think I am here at Happy Villages?"

"Bright Dawn," Alex mumbled.

"What?"

"Never mind, Mom." It seemed strange to Alex. If her mother didn't believe all of this was true, why had she gone out of her way to lock it all up and throw away the key? The way this conversation was headed, Alex figured it was another topic for another day. She and Roxanne had to move on from this or they would get nowhere.

"Now, Alex, why are you dredging this crap up? I am checked into a health spa trying to get better, and all you can do is call me and stir up the past."

"Okay, Ma, I called to see how you were. As soon as I realized I could, I did . . . Look, I'm glad to hear you are working to get healthier." It took Alex her entire youth to learn the code words needed to pacify the wild beast that lurked within Roxanne during the recovery process.

Her mother could be as gentle and docile as a spring doe when she was happy and medicated. Otherwise, it was as pleasant as trying to emotionally bare-knuckle fight a dancing kangaroo.

There was a long silence on the line. "So is Buxton there?" Roxanne asked in a small voice.

"I thought you didn't want to talk about it."

"Well, I don't. But I am worried." Uncertainty tainted her mother's voice. "I have spent your entire life doing my best to keep you from those KHNM people. And there you are, tiptoeing through the tulips with them. I don't understand how it has come to this." Her mother was winding herself up.

"They came to me. I had nothing to do with it, Ma."

"No use in crying over it now. Your father used to go on and on about things to come, and I did my best to keep you from it. But, you're there . . . and everyone is running around like Chicken Little."

"I never said that." Alex could feel herself softening a little. Her hard protective coating was starting to slowly wear away. "Did you know for all these years that I am related to Alexander the Great? Is that what you were sheltering me from? And why the lie about how Dad died? Buxton told me his death wasn't an accident."

"There's more to it than that."

"I've got time."

Roxanne must have covered the receiver with her hand. All Alex could hear was a muffled conversation. "Mom, what's up?"

"Sorry, dear. Nurse just came in. She's livid because I am late for a session."

"So I guess we're not going to talk about it now." It seemed a little too convenient. Did her mother make up the bit about the nurse to get out of dredging up the past?

"Hey, sweetie?" Roxanne's sugary voice began filling Alex with dread. It was always a portent for bad. Usually really bad.

"Yes, Mom." Alex hunched over and leaned onto her thighs, bracing herself for what was to come.

"There is something your father told me to tell you years ago. That if you were ever in a bind, you should find . . . Oh, what was her name? It was a strange one. She is an old bird who thinks she is the reincarnated lover of some pharaoh . . . Isn't it funny?"

"What's that?"

"Why does everyone get reincarnated as a high priestess or a pharaoh? What happens to the latrine muckers?"

Alex rolled her eyes. "I thought you were in a rush to get to therapy."

"Oh, yeah, I gotta run, darling."

"So what was the woman's name?"

"I don't remember exactly, but it sounded a little like a sneeze."

"Sneeze?"

"Ah-choo or something like that. Ask one of your KHNM friends. Hey, I got to go. Stay out of trouble. I can't take worrying about you when I am trying my best to get better. Love you."

The line disconnected. "Love you too, Mom," Alex said to the empty room.

CHAPTER TWENTY-THREE

After the call with her mother, Alex's state of mind was a numb mess. She glanced at her watch and realized it was the pre-dinner communal cocktail hour for the excavation staff at Chicago House. Every once in a while things did happen with a delightful synchronicity.

She made her way through the residence wing, where the staff's sleeping quarters were, and into the shared space of the courtyard. It was a gathering place that allowed the residents, who spent the excavation season here, to unwind after a hard, dusty day of work out in the field. Pre-dinner-drinks time was a much-anticipated, long-standing evening tradition for the staff at Chicago House. Alex had no qualms about crashing their party.

The early evening light cast dramatic shadows in the courtyard. Alex wove through the small clusters of chatting residents, looking for a safe harbor away from the others. What she didn't need right now was to feel socially obliged to engage in happy conversation. At the moment there was one thing she needed, and it was at the bar. Alex rarely drank, but her nerves needed calming.

Buxton and Niles stood in a far corner having an animated conversation. Buxton was red-faced and Niles looked . . . well, the only word for it was *angry*. Alex wanted nothing to do with their drama or either of them. She redoubled her nothing-to-look-at-here psychic camouflage and walked past them to the self-serve bar.

As a child, she'd read in a tabloid that celebrities would dial back their star power, allowing them to go unnoticed into the regular world. Alex spent hours perfecting this approach to a point where she at times felt like she was a ghost moving around the living. It came in handy, especially in moments like this when she wanted to blend in with the wallpaper or, in this case stuccoed walls.

She grabbed a bottle of bourbon and poured two fingers in a glass. She splashed in a hint of ginger ale. The mix was strong, but in this case she was looking forward to the burn.

She cut through the courtyard to a secluded table in the corner, away from the chattering masses, but where she could still keep an eye on Niles and Buxton. Niles was doing much of the talking, and from the look of it, it wasn't good news. Maybe that personal errand Niles went on didn't go so well?

Alex held her glass up, enjoying the bourbon's rich

amber color. She sniffed at it tentatively; the fumy liquid smelled of gasoline. She tipped it back and drank deeply. The bourbon burned as it traveled down her throat. Its ready heat spread quickly through her chest. Almost instantly she could feel it rise to her head.

Alex leaned into her chair and closed her eyes. She breathed in a deep breath, filling her lungs to capacity, then slowly let it out. A small layer of tension slipped away with each breath. She opened her eyes and gulped down more gasoline. A warm numbness wrapped itself around her like comforting arms.

She gazed across the room, taking a voyeuristic pleasure in watching Bird Boy unawares. Her eyes roamed slowly over the length of his body, taking in his tall, lean, powerful form. His dark almond-brown skin was luminous in contrast to his crisp white cotton shirt that lent an air of careless elegance to his rumpled jeans and wind-tousled hair. Alex shivered against the sultry Egyptian air. It was too bad he was such a jerk.

Alex lifted her glass. It was now empty except for the quickly melting ice. Time for another. She pushed back on the wrought iron chair. Its raw scraping noise filled the courtyard.

Conversation halted and all eyes turned to Alex. She wobbled a little as she stood and flushed at the attention. She tipped her glass toward them and smiled as if to say cheers, then made a beeline to the bar. Maybe another drink wasn't such a good idea, but at least it would guarantee her a dreamless sleep.

Alex, drink in hand, returned to her table. Buxton and Niles were no longer in their corner. *Oh shit.* They were heading straight toward her, dour expressions and all.

"May we?" Buxton asked as he swept his hand over the table.

"That depends," Alex said, feeling a little devil-may-care.

"On what?" added Mr. Sexy.

Her impulse was to toss out some clever verbal banter, but she could only stare blankly. The bourbon had already doused her intellect. "Whether it's good news or bad news. I don't know if I can handle either one."

"So I take it you reached your mother?" asked Buxton.

Alex nodded and tipped her glass at him. An uncomfortable silence hovered over them.

Buxton cleared his throat. "I am sorry about our exchange in the courtyard. I only—"

Alex cut him off. "Yeah, I know, you were worried about me. It may not have been the smartest thing for me to go out on my own. But I needed time to myself."

"Well, I am glad you made it back to us. I know I'm not the only one who wouldn't be able to forgive himself if something happened to you." Buxton glanced at Niles and flashed a fleeting smile. "I've got business I need to take care of before dinner. I'll leave you to it; I am sure you have a lot to say to each other." Buxton seemed to stifle his smile as he walked briskly away, as if he were trying to flee to a safe distance from a just-released grenade.

Niles looked after him a moment. "Don't be hard on the old man. He acted the way he did because he cares."

"You're one to talk." Alex smiled at Niles. He shifted in his seat.

Alex enjoyed seeing him squirm at the discomfort of trying to decide which of the sentiments she thought applied to him. "Old, that is."

Niles chuckled. His shoulders slumped, presumably at ease now that the conversation moved toward a safe, emotion-free direction.

She tipped her glass on the table and rolled it along its edges. The ice cubes clinked as the silence grew between them. Was this another round of whoever was first to speak loses? She was growing weary of navigating the layers of suspicion around her. She wanted a moment to talk with Niles unguarded. There were so many things that needed to be talked about. Ugly and uncomfortable things like the strange creatures that live in the deepest parts of the sea. *Did you kill my dad? Are you working against KHNM? Why do you make me act like a schoolgirl?*

Niles laid his hand on hers, silencing the clattering ice. Her hand twitched at the unexpected contact. His hand found hers again, resting heavily atop hers, almost daring her to move it. His warm pulse gently throbbed against her skin. She cocked her head and searched his eyes for a navigation point. She longed to trust him, to immerse herself in his universe.

Whenever he touched her it was as if their skin melted away and knitted an entirely new fabric of *them*. Could these feelings be one sided? Was she mistaking the God-human connection for something more personal?

Niles broke the silence. "I couldn't believe it when Buxton told me you went out on your own. Out there. Raymond could have gotten you. And that would have been it. For a number of things." He broke eye contact with Alex. "A lot is resting on us being able to stop Raymond. Or more to the point, you stopping Raymond. I can see how you might feel like you are being dragged along by KHNM on this wild ride."

"Correction, hell ride," Alex interjected.

"Glad to see you still have a sense of humor. I haven't seen much of it since Chicago. And here you are again, lushing it up."

"From the heights of champagne down to the mean streets of bourbon. You could say that KHNM is doing wonders for me."

Niles leaned in toward Alex. His eyes shone with amusement. "I will never forget, and for me that is a terribly long time, the look on your face when I insisted you bought that drink for me back in Chicago." He leaned back and smiled a toothy grin. "It was priceless."

"Glad this lowly human was able to give you some entertainment."

His smile disappeared. "Once I'd heard about Marceline I knew I had to connect with you. I promised your dad a long time ago that I would look out for you. I've had you in my sights for quite some time. I wanted to be sure if things went sideways, I would be a known quantity to you. It was a spur-of-the-moment decision on my part. I wanted to interact with you before you got swallowed up with KHNM. Now it looks like we are both entwined with the agency. Ask me whatever is plaguing you."

"So you are the living embodiment of the KHNM FAQ page?" Alex laughed a punchy sort of laugh. She needed a moment or two to process what he'd said. Had Niles been watching over her all her life? She reached for her glass and gulped some liquid strength. *Let's start with simple and move on to complex.* "Do you know where Salima is?"

Niles's expression clouded over. "No, I don't know. Buxton seemed to think she will be gone for quite some time."

What was the wounded warrior look supposed to mean? Was he heart-torn at Salima's absence? Was he worried about her? Alex looked away from Niles toward the glass-paned courtyard doors bookended with potted palms. One of the resident house cats was stalking a small songbird resting in the green foliage. Alex turned her attention to Niles. "What's with the cinnamon?"

"Cinnamon?" asked Niles, his eyebrows pinched together in confusion.

"Salima." A thump sounded in the distance. The cat misjudged its attack. The small bird took flight. The cat stalked away as if the outcome was intentional.

"Oh, that. It's a representation of her three forms. Kind of an indicator light. When she is angry, cinnamon . . . amorous, clove . . . The third is quite a mystery. Honestly, I don't think anyone has ever smelled the scent of Salima's contentment."

Alex chuckled. "I know I sure haven't. So, where were you today?" Much to her chagrin, her voice came out sounding like a suspicious lover. "Buxton said you were on a personal errand, but judging by the way you two were debriefing over there, I would be willing to guess it was agency business."

"Everything with this mission could be considered personal. He's already killed three of my family members. I had to find a safe house for my last two living family members on Raymond's kill list. Isis and Osiris—their Immortal names are Isadore and Oscar. I agree with Buxton that for Raymond to become the Aten he needs to kill the five major Gods—Isis, Osiris, Set, Nephthys, and Horus. Hathor, Bes, and I are relatively minor characters compared to them. Who knows, maybe he wants us dead too. But I think his must-haves are those five."

"So all he needs is a few more pieces to the puzzle. Do we have a chance?"

"Missions can go two ways. Success and failure. The outcome is unknown now. All we can do is soldier on the best we can."

Suddenly Alex realized they were alone. Everyone else had headed to dinner. Now that they had the courtyard to themselves it was time to bring out the big guns. "So how many missions have you been on? I heard you have been flying under the radar for quite some time."

"I lost my taste for active duty a while ago. I figured I would serve the agency best if I did not serve at all."

"What made you lose your appetite? Was it a specific mission?"

"I'm sure your mom said a thing or two about it."

"She certainly did. As a matter of fact, she said more than a couple of things."

"Enlighten me."

"She said to tell that son of a bitch that she's never forgiven you, and that you ruined her life and mine. When I asked her what you did, she said I would have to ask you."

"So, she still blames me." He said it softly, as if talking to himself. He gazed into the distance, seeming to be miles away in thought.

"It's the one thing that has plagued me my entire life; the fact that my father was taken away from me when I was so young. My mother always told me his death was an accident. Now I find out he was killed. For some strange reason, I don't think you killed him. But I know you know something about it, and I need you to tell me what you know." Overcome with emotion, her instincts told her to flee. She grabbed her glass and stood. "I'm getting a refresher, and by the time I come back I expect an explanation."

Her short walk to the small bar gave her the time to gather her thoughts. She poured herself a double, and one for Niles. *Hell, if he doesn't want it, the way tonight is going I might just drink it myself.* She set both drinks on the table.

He grabbed one of the glasses and set it on the table in front of him. "Alex, I know your mother blames me. I have inflicted mountains of blame on myself over the years. The hard truth is, and Alex, I need you to hear this, the decisions that led to your father's death were both of ours. There is not a day that goes by when I don't rehash what happened. But no matter how many different scenarios and how many alternative endings I try to come up with, it changes nothing because he is still dead. I know it was the blackest day of your mother's life. She loved your father so intensely that when he died it was as if someone had severed half of her soul. She was never the same again. I know she blames me, and I know that she blames Buxton. But I would have you know that if there was anything I could do to bring him back for you, I would do it. That day I lost one of my dearest friends, my partner. His death left a hole in me so large that I felt I would no longer be of any use to the agency."

He took a sip of his drink. "Whoaawee." He coughed as he lifted his glass up to Alex. "Damn, Alex, now that is a drink." Once he recovered, his expression returned to serious. "Your dad was a great man. I have lived for eons, and men like him come once, maybe twice, a millennium. He sacrificed himself so I might live."

Alex couldn't believe what she was hearing. "Sacrificed?" Her response came out a little slurred. The bourbon was hitting her hard.

Niles leaned forward, his eyes soft with emotion. "Alex, please listen. Don't jump the gun and say something you can't take back. Hear me out. He sacrificed himself so I may continue to guard the secrets we unearthed together. He knew when he made that decision all those years ago he would never again see your smile, or hear your giggle as you dug in the backyard looking for dinosaur bones. But he also knew it was the only chance for saving your future. He loved you so much. Before he died he made me promise to watch over you. To make sure you come to no harm." Niles gently brushed her cheek with his hand. "You were his world."

Alex gazed at the now-dark sky, trying to take in what she'd heard. The palm trees overhead rustled gently. Tears welled up in her eyes and spilled over, uncontrolled. Niles squatted by her chair and put his arms around her, pulling her toward him. She leaned her head into his neck and breathed in his scent of desert and bourbon, enveloped in his strong arms. Her tears ran like hot, wet caresses down her neck.

"I will do anything to protect you, Alex. Anything," he whispered into her ear.

CHAPTER TWENTY-FOUR

The worst thing wasn't the god-awful hangover; it was the blur of last night. What little she did remember had a good news–bad news quality to it. The good news was Niles didn't kill her father. The bad news was she drunk-cried on his shoulder until the cotton fabric of his shirt was nearly transparent. Alex cringed as she recalled the awkward expression on Niles's face as she extracted herself from his embrace.

Her stomach churned with a thick volcanic heat, threatening to make what remained within a sick souvenir from last night's overindulgence. She staggered to the kitchen in hopes of scrounging up an offering that would appease the angry fire in her bourbon-abused belly.

At first glance, all the kitchen had to offer were remnants from last night's missed dinner of lasagna. Alex shoved the metal tray back into the refrigerator. She would have to miss it even longer. She played it safe; her repast would consist of mint tea and a stack of saltines. She loaded them onto a tray and carried her bland bounty to the empty courtyard. At this time of day everyone would have left to work out in the field. Fresh air and solitude sounded like a good start to slowing her spinning head. Why did she get that second drink? Or the third for that matter.

"Good morning, sunshine." Niles's voice came from out of nowhere.

Alex nearly dropped the tray as Niles stepped from the shadows. His handsome face twitched in an odd way, as if he was struggling to suppress a smirk.

Her heart sank. *Could today get any worse?* The last thing she wanted was to face him.

Not only was she embarrassed as hell over her loss of control, but the situation was compounded exponentially as she knew she certainly had to look like death warmed over.

She pulled her watch up close to her eyes. "Morning? I am sure it is somewhere." Alex shambled to one of the tables in the courtyard. They sat across from one another in silence as Alex sipped her tea.

"Headache?"

"Just a little."

"Not surprised."

"Whatever, Mr. Holier than Thou."

"On the dot."

"So is that how you end all your conversations? 'Uh, don't even try because I'm a God.'"

"Wouldn't you?"

Alex laughed, which made her head throb even more. She closed her eyes and cradled her head in her hands.

"Man, you've got it bad. Didn't know you were such a lightweight."

"Three doubles? A lightweight?" Alex tilted her head and squinted at him in disbelief. Niles got up and walked to the bar. "I've got the thing for you."

"Please, no hair of the dog. It's a wives' tale, you know. Studies show it does nothing for a hangover. And quite frankly, the way I feel, I don't think it would stay down."

"You underestimate my powers. I have been alive since the beginning of time. Don't you think I may have picked up a few helpful hints here and there?"

"Are you going to conjure up an ancient hangover spell for me? I think there was a remedy referenced on one of the papyri at work that listed ground sycamore bark and scorpion venom as a cure. Have you got any of that?" she asked, trying to sound playful.

"Normally, if I were at home, I would concoct a cure that is an oldie but a goodie. It's a headache paste consisting of coriander, poppy seed, juniper, and honey. You grind it into a paste and then smear it all over the patient's head. I could also crush a hog's tooth, if it weren't so hard to come by, and bake it in a sugar cake for your indigestion." He bent over and reached into the bar cabinet. "But since I'm not and I don't, this will have to do." He placed a box on the bar top and smiled his best life-coach smile.

"Alka-Seltzer?"

"It'll fix you right up."

He set a glass of water and the blue box in front of her. "Drink up, princess."

Alex gave him a sour look as she plopped the tablets into the water. But their effervescent sound had a Pavlovian effect on her; the crisp, reassuring fizz strengthened her constitution. She grabbed the glass and chugged it. The saltiness made her gag a little. "Ahhhh."

"Now comes part two of this ancient hangover secret. Close your eyes." Niles rounded the table toward Alex.

Uncertainty filled her. She wasn't in a game-playing mood. Was he going to play a silly prank on her?

"Really, Alex. Close your eyes. It's the only way it will work. Trust me. I'm a God, you know."

"Immortal."

"Suit yourself. This Immortal tells you to close your eyes."

Alex complied. He was standing so close she could feel the pleasant heat of his body as he leaned against her. There was a small tug behind her ears as he lifted her glasses off her face. They made a small tap as he placed them on the tabletop. Her eyes twitched, threatening to open out of curiosity, wondering what was to come next.

"Keep 'em closed, princess."

His fingertips gently rubbed her scalp, making soft and warm circles, swirling her hair into a divine chaos. A shiver ran through her as his hands traveled down her neck, gently pushing into her flesh. Tension fluttered away with each stroke. He worked her shoulders, solidly thumbing away their tightness. Her whole body and mind softly melted like ice cream abandoned on the kitchen counter. She became lost in his magic soothing touch.

Niles whispered in her ear, "I've found this to be the best remedy yet." His breath tickled against her neck, making her wonder if he could feel the goose bumps his touch was causing as his hands swept up her neck to the crown of her head, where his gentle caresses evaporated.

Alex slowly opened her eyes as Niles sat across from her.

"The coriander paste is a lot more fun," Niles said in a matter-of-fact voice.

"Why is that?" The words came out a little slurred. Alex wiped at her chin to make sure she hadn't drooled on herself.

"I don't know if it does much for the headache, but it sure makes the wearer look hilarious." Alex chuckled.

"Better?"

"Worlds." Alex replaced her glasses. Maybe today wasn't all gloom and doom. It didn't feel like a massage one would give a little sister. Unless he was a pharaoh, of course. Alex smiled at her little joke. The word *pharaoh* rang around in her mind like an alarm bell. Wasn't there something she was supposed to ask Niles about? Something her mother told her? About a woman her father knew? That was it.

"Last night my mother mentioned to me that I should try and find a woman my dad used to know in Luxor. She seemed to think this person might be able to help us. Maybe she can give us intel on where Raymond might be."

"Did your mother say anything specifically about this person? Was it someone from KHNM or one of the locals?"

"She mentioned this woman's name sounded like a sneeze. But I am sure that makes it about as clear as mud. She'd also said this woman believes she is—"

"Akh-Hehet? Wow, I haven't thought of that old bird for ages. Your father and I once saved her from a particularly sticky situation. Your father felt bad for her, considering her unstable mind, and, well, he kind of took her under his wing. She was like an adopted auntie for him. It's possible he told her something that might help us. But it is strange he didn't mention it to me." Disappointment salted his words as if he thought there was nothing her father hadn't told him. "If you want, we can go to her. If she is still alive, I know exactly where she is."

"We?" asked Alex.

"Do you think I'm about to let you out there alone again? Buxton would have my ass on a platter."

Alex rolled her eyes.

"Something to keep in mind when we are visiting her, a visit to Akh-Hehet can be a journey into the fantastical. She is purely mortal, but she absolutely believes herself to be a seer of the yet unknown. She believes the ability comes from her exposure to the Netherworld from her continued visits in this realm by her long-dead lover. Apparently, the afterlife has a conjugal-visit plan. In the Immortal community she is, well, tolerated. Keep in mind while we are there we are strictly on a fact-finding mission."

"I think I can manage that." Alex pushed her chair back and stood.

In a flash Niles stood very near; his deep sea-blue eyes held a decidedly stormy look. "And another thing. Don't stray from the path. I want you near me at all times. You are not to ever get out of my sight line."

Be still my little heart. She wished with every ounce of her that he really did mean "ever."

Alex followed Niles through the crush of humanity into the Egyptian souk, becoming lost in its current. The vibrant colors, sounds, and smells of the mazelike alleyways assaulted her every sense. Glinting gold, bronze, and silver drew her gaze simultaneously like anxious hosts, each begging her for her visual attentions. It felt as overwhelming as trying to absorb a chaotic spattered Pollock painting in a glance.

The bazaar pulsed with life—men wearing long robe-like galabeyas in the traditional grey and blue, women with bright and sometimes bejeweled head scarves carrying shopping bags that hung over their forearms, tourists in shorts, overheated and ruddy with sunburn, Egyptian shopkeepers wearing jeans and polo shirts smoking with gold-ringed fingers as they hawked their wares. Alex breathed in the unusual cologne of cooked meats, sweat, and cigarette smoke. The color, the sounds, and the push of it made Alex think everything she experienced in her life up to that time was lived in black and white.

Tapestries and scarves of every color imaginable floated overhead from unseen lines as if suspended by magic. Row upon row of satin slippers sporting upturned toes lined the walkway. Across the way was a spice shop, its open front erupting with huge bins containing perfect peaks of exotic spices—rich browns, golds, and oranges. She stopped and marveled at the gorgeous pixie-sized mountain range.

"Come on, Alex. We are almost there." Niles tugged at her, pulling her back into the crowd.

Alex wished she had time to play tourist. The warm glow of faux gold and dark-blue lapis lazuli in the prolific trinket stores enchanted her. If only she had time to window-shop all the cheesy tourist remakes of tomb goods and God fetishes.

As they walked deeper into the souk, the crowd thinned substantially. Niles turned down a dark alley. At its end was an almost blinding glow. Niles's pace quickened. He stopped in front of the store. "Here we are."

"A chandelier store?" The shop was filled with brilliant light and contained thousands of refracted rainbows from the hundreds of cut crystal chandeliers within. She couldn't think of a single person who had one and didn't imagine the average Egyptian had much use for them either.

"British," Niles said succinctly, as if the one word explained it.

"What do you mean?"

"She's British."

"Oh," Alex replied, understanding, but at the same time, not.

Niles leaned in close. "And if that weren't enough, she's also batshit crazy." He swept his hand through the threshold, directing Alex to step in. "Entrez-vous. Be careful. If I remember correctly there is an odd step down."

It was a good thing Niles mentioned the stairs. Alex was blinded as she stepped in from the dark alleyway. When her vision cleared, an extraordinary and elderly woman stood a mere three feet away from her. What made her unique wasn't the turquoise Egyptian-style robe she wore, her hennaed hands, or the ornate jewelry and heavy makeup à la eighteenth dynasty Egypt. It was that her head was completely bereft of hair. It was as smooth as an alabaster bust and shone brightly in the light from the sparkling cloud of chandeliers surrounding her.

"Dears, welcome. Just in time for a spot of tea." The old woman paused and turned toward Niles, patting him on the arm. "You are a naughty one. Staying away from Auntie Hehet for too long. Oh, have I been longing for a nice visit. Perfect day for it. Although I wasn't expecting company." She touched her head. "Best I could do quickly. Couldn't find my special-occasion wig. The one with the beads and such. You know you always want to treat your guests with—"

"Akh-Hehet, seer of the unknown. I would like to introduce you to Miss Alex Philothea."

Akh-Hehet's eyes went wide. "My, aren't we in a rush? Whatever happened to a little cordiality? Philothea? Hmmm . . . I did wonder when this day would come. Join me for some tea. It's about to boil."

Niles rolled his eyes as Akh-Hehet turned to navigate them through the dense jungle of chandeliers. They were hung at varying heights, giving an illusion of a connected, illuminated forest canopy linked together here and there by a dangling crystal ball or metal arm reaching out to its neighbors. Everywhere Alex glanced she caught the flash and sparkle of prismed light.

Alex stopped for a moment to take it all in. Akh-Hehet stood next to her. The old woman's face was illuminated with the joy of sharing her treasure. "Isn't it delicious? It's been a long time since I have had such an appreciative visitor."

"That it is." Alex smiled at the old woman's creation. Even if this foray proved fruitless, Alex knew this was a moment she would never forget.

Akh-Hehet reached up to the chandelier nearest them and unhooked a large dangling crystal from its center and handed it to Alex. The old woman looked like she was going to say something but then seemed lost at the high-pitched scream of a tea kettle. "Oh dear, tea's on." She pushed on toward a black curtain ahead. It flashed closed behind her.

"Batty? She seems perfectly sweet to me," Alex whispered in Niles ear as she dropped her new treasure in her scribe's bag.

He opened his mouth to say something, but before he could reply Akh-Hehet emerged from behind the curtain. "I thought you said you were in a hurry, Niles dear." Her face held a look of consternation. "Don't dillydally—chop-chop, time's a-wasting." She motioned with her hands for them to hurry along.

The back room was more like a small apartment than an office. In the furthest corner, there was an alcove with a bed and accompanying privacy curtain half pulled across. Next to the alcove was a door. It most likely led to a bathroom.

Alex and Niles stood as Akh-Hehet gathered the tea things in her makeshift kitchen. "Don't be shy. Have a seat, you two." She placed the tea set on the table.

Alex was no china expert, but the tea set looked like the real deal. Judging by the gold edges, the beautiful rendering of blue roses, and wafer-thin appearance, it must have cost her a mint. It was odd the woman would have a Spartan living space and such a luxurious tea set. Alex lifted the delicate cup to her nose and inhaled the malty aroma of the black tea. The strong yet delicate flavor of the tea was refreshing. Alex hadn't realized she was chilled until its pleasant warmth soothed her.

"So, to what do I owe the pleasure of this visit?" Akh-Hehet asked.

"Not much of a seer, are you?" Niles winked and gently tapped her hand.

"Oh, Niles. You have always been a cheeky one. You know better than anyone how this goes. Of course, I know why you are here, but you know I need to hear why you are here."

Alex shook her head. "What?"

"Akh-Hehet can see things in the past and numerous possible futures."

Alex smiled, realizing that Niles must be playing along with the old woman's delusions.

"She can see many different possibilities of what will be or what can be. But what she can't do is see what you want. It is the questions you ask that will blaze a path to what she can see."

"Well put, young man." Akh-Hehet smiled in a wistful way. "I so miss having a flesh-and-blood man around. But alas, all I have is my dear Horemheb's Ba-soul visitations."

Niles coughed into his hand and turned away. Hopefully, Akh-Hehet did not notice his shoulders were shaking. When he swiveled back to face them, Niles's perma-smile was securely plastered on his face.

Alex cut to the chase. "I spoke to my mother, Roxanne, last night."

"How is she?" Akh-Hehet's flat tone revealed she was merely asking out of courtesy.

"She is as well as she can be, but we aren't here to talk about my mother. At least not directly." Was it relief Alex saw on the old woman's face? "She mentioned that my father told her years ago that you might have something for me or be able to help me someday. That is why we are here."

Akh-Hehet's face radiated with delight as she leaned

across the table and grabbed Alex's hands. "I must do a reading for you."

"A reading?" Alex looked to Niles for direction. Was this a road they wanted to travel?

His expression was completely blank.

"So, I see," Akh-Hehet said in an offended tone. "Niles didn't tell you my story. Is it because he doesn't find it worth telling? Is it because of what they say about me?" Akh-Hehet's voice shook with emotion. "I know everybody does. Talk about me, that is. Like I am some sort of freak show. Look at you." She pointed her finger at Niles; her expression now held a threat of unstable aggression. "You are one to talk. Caught between two worlds and no way back. I can see you are like the rest. Use me as you will. You all want to brush my story under the carpet. Her father was the only one to treat me with dignity."

Niles stood and walked to the trembling old woman and placed his hands gently on her shoulders. He spoke low and soft, "Akh-Hehet, dear Auntie, you do me a great disservice. Please calm down before you cause yourself to meet your beloved Horemheb in the Netherworld before your time. The reason I didn't tell your story to Alex is because I saved it for you to tell. Nobody is better."

Akh-Hehet smiled broadly, as if his words were the needed balm to quell her rising tide of emotion. Behind the old woman, Niles shrugged his shoulders, as if to say, sit tight—we are in it for the long haul now.

As Auntie told her story with great dramatic aplomb, it occurred to Alex that maybe Niles's assessment of Akh-

Hehet was spot-on. But then again, who was she to judge stability? How sane was it to be falling for Niles . . . an Immortal?

Akh-Hehet's story meandered from her earliest years as a priestess in Horemheb's court during the eighteenth dynasty in Egypt, to her rebirth in the present time as Emily Loren. How she emerged from a public-school childhood in Great Britain to a chandelier shop in Luxor. After sitting through the long and detailed telling, Alex felt she had a newfound empathy for the doldrums of being immortal.

Once Akh-Hehet's storytelling desires were sated, she led Alex and Niles back into the crystal maze. This time she took them deeper into the heart of the crystal cloud, till they stood in its center in a small triangular-shaped clearing. Overhead, capping the space, was an extremely large inverted crystal pyramid suspended above them. The floor below was covered with a large oriental rug with an ornate floral pattern.

Akh-Hehet sat with her legs folded on the rug with a surprising amount of flexibility for a woman of her advanced years. She rubbed her hand over the carpet and closed her eyes. "This carpet was woven with magic threads. Each thread tells a story of what could be and what will not be. This is the carpet we must sit on." She motioned to Niles and Alex. "Come. Sit."

They formed a triangle that mirrored the one that hung above them.

"The crystals above and around are a tuning mechanism

for me to hone my sight. Each chandelier strengthens my signals exponentially into the unseen world from which we seek answers. Now, let's connect our spirits by holding hands."

Akh-Hehet's hand was like ice. Niles's thrummed with warmth.

"Okay. I'm ready," Akh-Hehet said. "I will need you two to be utterly silent as I attempt connection. It may take a while. The older I get the harder it becomes and the more crystals I need. When I was young . . ." She sighed. "Oh what does it matter? Remember, complete silence."

A breeze whispered by Alex's face as the crystals above her gently tapped against each other creating a sweet tinkling. The soft wind continued to pick up speed until the prisms sounded like a thousand determined wind chimes playing a capricious melody. Akh-Hehet's voice rose above the beautiful yet raucous noise. "Oh mighty Hehet, Great Goddess of the Immeasurable, please hear the voices of those who come to ask."

Alex opened her eyes. Akh-Hehet appeared to be deep in trance.

Akh-Hehet spoke in a breathless, wavering voice. "Alex Philothea, ask what you came to ask."

Alex glanced in Niles's direction for some sort of cue, but his eyes were slammed shut. It struck her as odd that someone who had such dubious feelings about the seer's ability was playing along so dutifully.

"Oh Great One." Alex didn't know where to start but figured you couldn't go wrong inserting a little formality, especially when addressing a Goddess. It would have been nice if Akh-Hehet would have gone over some ground rules first. Was this a one-shot deal? Did she only have one question to ask? It made sense to start big. They wanted to find Raymond. So why not start there? "Please guide us to where Re dwells."

A great wind rushed in, and the chandeliers swung back and forth in a chaotic dance. Alex's pulse raced at the thought of the chandeliers crashing down on top of them. Then, as if ordered to halt by an unheard voice, the room became deathly still.

"You must descend into the primordial soup, beyond the stones of eternity. There you will find your answer." Akh-Hehet clapped her hands and fell backward.

"What the hell?" Alex rushed to the old lady's side.

"I guess her trance is over." Niles scooted over and lifted her head onto his lap. He reached into his pocket and retrieved a small white packet.

Alex shot him a questioning glance.

"Smelling salts. Old-fashioned, but then again so am I." He winked at Alex and leaned over Akh-Hehet. He held the packet under her nose and then broke it open.

The old woman coughed and sputtered back to life. Her eyes fluttered open to the handsome down-turned face and deep blue eyes of Niles. She smiled wide. "I had no idea the afterlife would be this good-looking."

"You're anything but dead," said Niles.

Akh-Hehet rose and staggered back. Alex caught hold of her before she could fall. "Niles, could you do an old woman a favor? Go into my kitchen and grab me a glass of water. These trances always tend to make me dizzy these days."

Niles turned to make his way back to her apartment.

As soon as he was out of sight, Akh-Hehet spun around and grabbed Alex by the shoulders, her eyes blazing with an unexpected clarity. "I don't have much time. Don't say a thing. Just let me talk. Your dad used to come to ask about visions of the future. I saw many things, many possible outcomes. I had one vision in particular that made his heart go cold. He made me promise to help. I told him I would do what I could." Akh-Hehet let go of Alex's shoulders and stepped back to look her over. "Not much here to work with."

"Thanks," said Alex.

"Remember, me talking, you listening," Akh-Hehet asserted.

As the old woman's eyes roved along Alex's neckline, a spark lit in the old lady's eyes. "Perfect." Akh-Hehet grabbed the coffin pendant that Alex bought on the promenade yesterday. She held it in her hand. The old woman's flesh glowed red as if she were covering the end of a flashlight with her palm. Akh-Hehet jerked her hand away as if shocked with an electrical pulse. The seer brushed her hands on her thighs.

The pendant was warm as it fell against Alex's collarbone.

Akh-Hehet grabbed Alex's forearm, her touch still

warm from the magic. "Please, always remember, in your darkest hour, there are helpers awaiting the call."

"Darkest hour? What do you mean?"

The old woman's eyes grew wide and pleaded for silence.

Niles returned with the water and handed it to Akh-Hehet. "What have you two been up to?"

Akh-Hehet instantly slipped back into her previous persona of batty old seer. "Oh, just a little girl talk." She took a sip of her water and tipped it toward Niles. "You two best be on your way. I sense you have a lot on your to-do list."

Why was Auntie keeping secrets from darling Niles?

CHAPTER TWENTY-FIVE

Alex and Niles exited the mazelike souk onto a narrow shop-lined street as they made their way back to Chicago House. An occasional taxi or tourist carriage passed them by, but mainly pedestrians populated the dust-filled roads. The quiet atmosphere was more residential than tourist. In the distance lay the broad and bustling Corniche, and beyond it the mighty Nile.

It was disappointing that Akh-Hehet's visions regarding the location of Raymond's lair were obscure hints at best. Alex was hoping for something a little less cryptic. What exactly did the old seer mean by primordial soup and stones of eternity? It was almost as bad as a fortune cookie. Maybe Niles was right. The old woman was simply an expat with vivid delusions.

As they approached the main thoroughfare, Alex stopped dead in her tracks. Luxor Temple lay directly in front of them. Her eyes lingered on the site. She knew deep within lay a monument built by her ancestor Alexander the Great. An odd tingling sensation filled her chest at the thought of it.

The temple's beauty stood out against the pink-orange sunset painting the western sky. Alex reached into her bag and grabbed her phone. Its basic digital camera wouldn't come close to capturing the majesty of it, but at least she would have something to remember the moment by.

Niles turned around. His face pinched with annoyance that softened as he noticed what caught her attention. "She's a beauty, isn't she?"

Alex took a quick picture. "I have always dreamed of being here, of exploring all there is, and now I am here and all I have seen of Egypt is the inside of Chicago House and a batty old woman's chandelier shop."

"What's wrong with now?"

"Shouldn't we be bringing Akh-Hehet's information back to Chicago House?"

Niles hooked his arm in hers. "Yes, but Buxton left early this morning working on a lead and won't be back until after dinner tonight. I don't think there is much we can do in the interim. And, life is too short."

"And how would you know?"

"I stand corrected, improper cliché use by an Immortal. How about, your life is too short."

"You really think you're funny, don't you?"

"Sometimes. You know what they say, all work and no play. . ."

"Ensures the work gets done?"

"It's been a while since I've visited Luxor Temple. The last time I was here I recall some intriguing texts on the chapel Alexander the Great built. Maybe there is a clue buried within the hieroglyphs." He leaned in close to Alex, awakening within her a small flock of fluttering butterflies. "Looks like there is going to be a full moon. It's hard to get any better than that. There was a time when I embodied the power of the moon." His tone had become wistful.

Niles was right. A full moon had already risen in the pale dusky-blue sky.

As they approached the entrance to the temple grounds, it was surrounded entirely by temporary barricades, beyond which a private party was in full swing.

Alex sighed in disappointment. "Just my luck."

"Quitter," Niles said as he nudged her with his shoulder.

"It's a private party."

"There are few things I enjoy more than going to parties. Especially those I wasn't invited to."

Alex put her hands on her hips and narrowed her eyes at Niles. "For some reason that doesn't surprise me. Obviously, it's a private affair. They've got gatekeepers and supersized security guards. They're not going to welcome crashers."

"I've got an idea." Niles led her to the short line at the entrance. He whispered in her ear, "Speaking of affairs . . . act natural. Act like you're into me."

His breath tickled her neck and sent chills down her

spine. *Act, really?* Niles had a natural tendency to hit the nail on the head and simultaneously miss the mark altogether. Was he being egotistical, humorous, or heartbreakingly oblivious? Did the Immortals have their own spectrum of cluelessness that he happened to fall within? The warmth of his flesh radiated through his cotton shirt to her bare arm. All she knew in that moment was she never wanted to let go.

As the couple in front of them wandered through the gate, the security guard asked Niles for a ticket. He pushed up on his toes and lifted his hand to shade his eyes. He turned in the direction of the couple who had just crossed over as if visually tracking them. "Oh damn, there they are." Completely ignoring the guard's request, he waved his hand high in the air and shouted, "Michael." The couple turned around. With an authoritative air Niles strode through to the other side, pulling Alex along with him.

Alex yearned to look back to see the expression on the guard's face, but sensed this moment called for the nonchalant aura of belonging and entitlement. She marched on, ignoring the impulse and following Niles's lead.

When they caught up with the pair, Niles held out his hand to Michael. Niles's face contorted into a look of befuddled confusion that softened into a mild embarrassment. "Sorry, my mistake. I thought you were somebody else completely."

The man shook his head and wandered toward the enchantments of the fantasia beyond.

"So, do all of you have that power?" asked Alex.

"Power?"

"I thought only Isis was the sole knower of all names. Do all the Immortals share in that ability?"

Niles turned and faced Alex, his face a mask of absolute seriousness. He tapped on his chest. "Name tag."

Alex laughed in spite of herself.

Niles once again slipped his arm through hers as they strolled through the open courtyard. The pale moon hung low in the now darkening sky, its silver-hued light creating an illusion that the temple's limestone walls were lit from within. The massive twin seated statues of Ramses the Great that fronted the temple's entrance humbled Alex. They held court over all who dared approach the sacred threshold. Alex wondered at the stories they might tell if she had a magic adze like the ones used in the funerary rites of the pharaohs to bring the breath of speech to their silent mouths.

On her left lay rows of recently excavated sphinxes lining the boulevard that once linked Karnak and Luxor Temples. In ancient times, during the annual Festival of Opet the golden statues of the Gods would travel from Karnak Temple along this sphinx-lined road to Luxor Temple. She'd read how the Gods' images would be carried in sacred ritual boats, great curtains hung to keep their holy statues from the brazen eyes of commoners. Apparently, it was a joyous state celebration where citizens, priests, and nobles alike took part in dancing, music, banquets, and beer.

Alex peered down the avenue of sphinxes. A line of young men dressed as pharaohs spilled into the courtyard. They were accompanied by hypnotic Middle Eastern music, the rhythmic thump of drums combined with high-pitched pipes. Each performer held a blazing torch as they formed a circle.

The music gained in tempo and the young kings started to dance. The speed became frenetic as the young men tossed their fire-tipped sticks to each other in a complex juggling exercise. Suddenly the music stopped. The performers broke into smaller groups and walked amongst the crowd of onlookers.

The musicians fell back as they played a charming melody. Two of the young men made their way to Alex and Niles. The smell of burning woodsmoke accompanied the brilliant flash of fire as the young men deftly tossed their flaming torches to one another.

The music and the moment were simply enchanting. A lightness of heart filled Alex.

Niles noticed her smile and chuckled. "Isn't it funny how they always manage to dress the servants like kings? I wonder how the old man would have taken it." He nodded toward the silent statues of Ramses the Great.

"You would know." She playfully whacked him on the chest. "One of these days when all this is over, I'd like to pick your brain for about a decade or two."

"Oh, I see how it is. That's all I am to you." Niles continued in mock high drama. "A living encyclopedia of human history."

Until that moment, it hadn't hit her how old he was. He actually had known the Great Pharaoh. The thought of his true age completely and momentarily immobilized her ability to come back with a witty reply. She stood, silently, trying to absorb how different they were from each other. Her short-lived moment of joy was doused. What was she thinking? What a foolish lovesick puppy she was. *He is an Immortal.*

"What's up?" Niles asked.

"Just thinking."

"Oh, that's never a good thing to do." He pulled her away from the flame jugglers and whisked her toward the heart of the party. "Especially when we were just starting to have some fun."

The main party area was less like a stage and more what Alex imagined the inside of a genie bottle would look like. On the ground, hundreds of carpets were strewn, creating an inviting mosaic of color and pattern. Overhead, pastel paper lanterns swayed in the evening breeze. Small round tables surrounded the dance floor where many partygoers surrendered their inhibitions and were whirling around as if overtaken by a wild desert spirit. At the center of each table lay a small, thin-lipped oil-filled bowl with a tiny wick at its center smelling of oranges and coriander.

"Red or white?" asked Niles.

"Do you think they have champagne?"

He smiled briefly, then charged away like a man on a mission. She watched him as he carved his way through the crowd.

Small blue ceramic favors made to look like ancient faience artifacts were scattered on the table. Each was a rendering of Hathor, the cow-eared Goddess of love and beauty. Salima. Alex couldn't understand how someone so cold and calculating could be the Goddess of something so beautiful and intangible. It seemed so out of range for her personality. But then again, love isn't always what fairy tales make it out to be.

Alex sighed as she snagged a Hathor head and dropped it in her bag. It was pathetic amongst all the romantic moments and relationships that could be sparked tonight that the tiny head of Salima would probably be her only takeaway.

Niles returned in a flash with two flutes of champagne. He handed one to Alex and held his up. "So what will we toast to?"

To you? Alex smiled to herself. "How about . . . tonight, the fantasia, the moonlight, the music, and—"

"And the temple."

"Took the words right out of my mouth." *Well, not exactly.* Alex lifted her glass. Their eyes met with the soft clinking sound. For a brief, unguarded moment his eyes burned with an intensity that left her breathless. Alex knew exactly what her wish was as she took a sip of the crisp, tart champagne.

Niles's mellow expression turned to a scowl as he tipped his glass back to drink. He peered away as if looking into a faraway universe. "Speaking of the temple. It is a beautiful sight by full moon. Let's go check your great granddaddy's chapel. What do you say?" His tone spun from engaged to glib in a heartbeat.

What was with him? Each time they connected on any personal level, he distanced himself from her. One second it was there, and then it was gone, like a plug jerked out of an outlet. "Nothing I would enjoy more," Alex said flatly.

They walked silently in an unhurried pace toward the grand temple, champagne in hand. Alex was shocked to see how few partygoers took the opportunity to explore the site. It was as if she and Niles had it to themselves.

As they passed through the temple grounds, Alex was drawn to the statues of Tutankhamen and his wife/half-sister Ankhesenamun. Niles wandered off to the other side of the courtyard. Since they left the party the air between them became thick with complications. She struggled to focus on the statues and ignore the insistent interruptions of her mind calling forth the pleasant burn as Niles gazed hungrily into her eyes.

Alex pushed up on her toes as she tried to clear her mind of Niles. She concentrated on trying to find any tell-tale lines of Ankhesenamun's recent facial restoration.

"Precision nose job."

Alex jumped, startled by Niles's voice suddenly near. "Damn you're quiet," she said.

"Famous last words." He grabbed her hand. "Before we make our way to the chapel, I've got something I want to show you." Niles led her to a wall at the far end of a smallish alcove.

Alex scanned the wall decorated with a bevy of naked

ladies dancing in a row. "Oh . . . I can see why this is your favorite."

Niles rolled his eyes. "No, not there. Come over here to this corner." He pointed to some bulls carved in relief. "You see them?" He motioned at the horns. "What do you think those are?"

"It can't be."

"Just tell me what you see."

It was a relief that depicted bulls leaping and jumping in a presumed arena. Their horns were adorned with what looked like poorly made hand puppets of human figures. "Horn puppets?"

"Exactly."

"What was the point?"

"Fun, I guess." He rubbed the wall. "I think that is why this is my favorite part of the temple. Forget the hall of eternity. Forget the great rulers and all their trappings. This right here is what matters. Grabbing a moment of happiness within an eternity." Niles brushed his fingers against her face and cupped her chin with his hand, tilting her head upward, his eyes searching hers. "This." His voice cracked. "This is what matters to me. All your life I have looked out for you and have always held a certain sort of love for you. One of protection and duty. But the moment I saw you in that ridiculous champagne bar, that changed. My love for you became something different. I've tried so hard to ignore what I've felt. In part because I know how it would grieve your father. To involve you with something so impossible."

"Oh, Niles—" Her words were halted by his lips as they gently brushed against hers. She closed her eyes as his fingers softly whispered down her neck. He pulled away.

Alex blinked open her eyes. "What's wrong?"

"This can't be right," he said, his voice rough.

Alex leaned into him, feeling the welcoming warm throb of him. She tilted her head as she pushed up on the balls of her feet and whispered in his ear. "Then all I want is to be wrong, Niles."

He laughed. "So, everything eventually ends up being a country-western song?" Amusement lit his eyes as he leaned into Alex, pressing her against the ancient wall and its fanciful dancing bulls. Alex was lost in his embrace. The music faded and the world disappeared as they melted into one another, slipping into their own singularity as they explored this newly created universe of them.

When they parted Alex was not sure if minutes or a lifetime had passed. She gazed at Niles in wonderment, as if seeing him for the first time. She was filled with a warm glow of contentment and a sense of home in this strange land with this strange man.

Niles cleared his throat. "As much as I would enjoy staying here until the cow-headed Goddess comes home, we should probably make our way back to the house. Buxton is probably beside himself." He ran his hands through Alex's hair. "You got a little rumpled."

"I'll say." Alex looked at him and grinned.

Niles grabbed her hand, and they walked through to the main temple complex.

As Alex stepped into the courtyard, a flash of movement registered in the corner of her eye and everything went black.

CHAPTER TWENTY-SIX

A dull throb came to life in Alex's skull as she tried to maneuver in the dark, tight space. Her reward was abraded elbows from the rough, unfinished wood that surrounded her. The strong scent of the pine box cut through the mental fog that coated Alex's mind like marshmallow cream. Where was she? The last thing she remembered was walking hand in hand with Niles. She gasped for breath when she realized she was in a small coffin.

Breathe. Breathe steady. Clear your mind. Breathe. She was struggling to overcome the fears that were hijacking her mind. *This is out of your control. Breathe in . . . Breathe out, slowly . . . calmly. A calm mind is the only way out. Calm.* With every breath her anxiety level dropped just a little. Her father had coached her in this technique when she became locked in an old steamer trunk while playing hide-and-seek as a child. The key to it had been lost for ages. He calmed her by repeating those words over and over, while he struggled to pick the lock. She was thankful to have this skill and smiled at the thought that this was one gift he'd given her that she would never lose.

With a calmer mind, her attention shifted to the external sounds around her. The grunts and groans made her realize humans were carrying her. Or minions.

"Don't drop her, you fools," yelled a familiar female voice.

Salima? Alex's stomach lurched as the box was hefted quickly upward. She attempted to kick at the box lid. Her heart thumped hard, as if trying to escape through her rib cage. The sound of her own pulse pounding in her ears renewed a sense of panic from within. *Calm . . . breathe . . . calm.*

"She must not be harmed. We cannot offer bruised fruit to the Gods," said an unfamiliar male voice.

"Careful, you imbeciles. One more stumble like that and she'll have some company on her trip to the Netherworld." The malice in Salima's voice made it clear this was no empty threat.

The box once again shifted and landed with a bone-jarring crash. The lid momentarily cracked opened, and blessed fresh air rushed in like cold water, punching Alex back into a keen focus. The lid to her coffin was slammed shut once again.

"Down on your knees, you useless sons of Set," said the male voice. "It is time for you to meet Ammut, the devourer of souls." There was an unmistakable whisper of a blade sliding out of its sheath. The blade swished through the air, and a meaty *chthunk* sounded. "Their carcasses will remain to sustain the scavengers of the desert."

Over time the wooden container had gathered heat and became stiflingly hot. Where was she? Where was she being taken? Her parched, cotton-dry mouth signaled she was on a long desert trek. Apparently, they didn't have any qualms about giving dehydrated fruit to the Gods. She chuckled at the thought. She must be losing it if she thought that was funny.

The temperature around her dropped substantially. Was she going into shock?

"Set her down over here." Salima's voice echoed, revealing they were no longer in the open air. Had she been working as a double agent all this time? Or, was Salima here in hopes of helping Alex escape? And who was the stranger who had apparently beheaded the two sons of Set with one stroke? Was it Raymond? Was Niles in a similar box? Or worse?

Alex slid down as the box was propped up against something. When it came to rest she was in a half-standing, half-leaning position.

"Pry it open," commanded Salima.

The wood creaked and groaned as the lid was removed. Alex's heart sank. They were in a burial tomb. Salima stood directly in front of her with a self-satisfied look. Next to Salima was a well-built man with boyish good looks. His golden-blond hair and his placid smile were made all the more terrifying as in his hand he held what looked like a smiting rod.

What were they going to do to her? She struggled to break free, but her movement was completely restricted. She had to stay calm and come up with a plan if she wanted to survive this.

Salima slinked toward Alex.

Alex struggled to get free, but only managed to whack her head on the wooden container that now served as her support. Salima's expression was completely unreadable.

"What have you done with Niles?" Alex yelled.

"Done? Why would you think anything would need to be done with Niles? You are precious. Didn't you find it even the smallest bit odd that his feelings for you had suddenly become transparent?"

"Niles is—?"

"Niles is my blood, which is always thicker than water, darling. Don't look so sad. You had to know you'd eventually lose. Who are you to fight against a God? Especially one as strong and brilliant as the noonday sun," said Salima.

The man with the golden hair approached Salima. Alex struggled against her bindings. "Raymond?"

He placed his hand on Salima's shoulder and laughed. "I guess you could call me that, at least for a little while longer. Thank you, my daughter, for bringing me this prized mouse. Did she have the artifact?"

Salima snorted a laugh and pulled out Alex's scribe's bag. "So how do you feel now, Alex? Do girl Gods really rock?" Salima laughed as she upended it. All of Alex's possessions tumbled to the floor. Horus's eye rolled into a far corner. Alex wondered if Salima took note of it. She didn't seem to take a second glance at it as it passed by.

"It looks to me to be only random bits of crap . . ." She reached in and picked up the faience Hathor head. "Aww, isn't that sweet, a little Mini-Me."

Raymond came so close to Alex, she could smell his myrrh-scented breath. "What a shame. It could run in our favor, though; maybe the prophecy is wrong."

Alex jutted her chin out. "Why am I here?"

"Well, first things first." Salima poked her finger at Alex's chest. "You . . . are going to die."

"Die?" The word came out of her mouth with a dry croak.

"'Die' as in *dead*, as in not breathing, as in going West." Salima smiled.

Alex struggled to find a physical advantage as she moved. All she could manage was to ineffectively move her head from side to side.

Raymond sneered at Alex's feeble attempt at escape. "You should relax. You can't go anywhere. Why spend your last minutes in torment?" His words dripped with a sense of personal enjoyment. "You won't be able to move your body.

It has been magically bound. There is no escape for you."
His face had an open expression of enthusiasm, as if he was
relishing a particularly good memory. He rubbed his chin
with his fingers. "This reminds me of a time long ago, when
I had the life of your father, Phillip, in my hands. I think the
terror in his eyes before I killed him was very similar to what
I see in yours. The apple does not fall far from the tree."

"You killed my father?" A shock of anger pulsed
through her at the revelation. Why hadn't Buxton just
come out and told her? A fury raged within her as she
spoke through gritted teeth. "I will raise heaven and hell to
make you pay."

Raymond laughed and softly brushed his hand across
Alex's cheek. "Oh, I doubt that very much. You are a bound
captive. And you are in a long-abandoned tomb far away
from anything and everything. No, Alex, this is where you
will die. It was fated before you were born."

Alex burned with anger. "Go to hell!" she said, and spit
on Raymond's face.

He retrieved a handkerchief and wiped it away. "I may
do that. After I attain the Aten, I can move through any
realm that pleases me. And after I subdue humankind, I
will create order in their realm." His eyes blazed with the
hot light of a true believer.

"How could you, Salima? You are a KHNM agent, set
with the task of protecting humanity."

"How could I not? My efforts against the mortals are
going toward a very good cause. Me. My father has
promised I will be brought to my third state, Sekhmet, the

destructive eye of Re. I've been pacing the cage of life waiting for this moment. I have hungered for two thousand years to feel the bones of your kind splinter beneath my rage." Salima's fiery voice directly conflicted with the dull, listless look in her eyes. Was she putting on a show for Raymond?

"You don't have to do this, Salima. I know deep down in your heart you care about humans. If not me, what about Buxton? All the KHNM agents you have worked with? Captain Medjay?"

Salima's cheeks flashed red as if she'd been slapped. "You think you are so clever, don't you? Philothea . . . lover of Gods . . . how quaint." A weird smile pulled across Salima's face. "I bet in your tiny human mind you made up a soppy reality where I was in love with Captain Medjay? Do you think mortals matter to us? Captain Medjay could never be anything more than a plaything to a creature like me." Salima locked eyes with Alex. "Take that lover boy of yours. Where do you think he is right now? Do you think he fought valiantly when we took you? Do you think he is bound and ready to die, as you are now? Or was he having a little fun with a mortal? Like a hawk enjoying a game of chase with its prey."

Alex tried to struggle against the magical binding that held her. There had to be a way to escape.

Salima's smile broadened. "How do you think we knew where to find you?" Salima turned from Alex and walked to a large granite block in the middle of the tomb. She picked up something that glinted sharply in the dull light. It was a small obsidian ceremonial knife with a crescent-shaped blade. "I am actually doing you a favor. This way you will die knowing the truth. You were nothing to him."

Alex closed her eyes. Her heart was racing. She wouldn't give Salima the satisfaction of thinking she'd retreated into fear in her final minutes. Alex forced her eyes open. If she must die in this moment, it would be with dignity. She would honor the life she lived in the last few moments she had in this world.

Salima chanted in a low, husky voice. Her eyes closed as her body swayed back and forth, lost in the rhythm of the spell.

A hot gash cut across Alex's left palm. Blood oozed and trickled down her fingers. She tried to look at her wounds, but her neck couldn't crane that far forward.

Two minions hefted Alex out of her box. Her body remained as stiff as a board as they carried her horizontally and placed her on the altar.

Salima leaned over Alex's body. The strong scent of cinnamon enveloped Alex. "It is unfortunate for you that death will not come quickly."

Raymond took Salima's arm and they headed to the entrance of the tomb. Salima dropped her grasp on her father's arm and returned to the altar, her expression completely unreadable. Salima drew closer, and Alex caught a flicker of . . . sadness? Regret? Was she trying to communicate something to Alex? Salima's eyes turned cruel and dark once more.

"Come, daughter, leave that wretch to die," Raymond shouted.

Salima loomed above Alex with cold, hard eyes. "I didn't want to leave without savoring the moment a little." She turned her head and smiled at her father. "I wanted to leave Miss Alex with a thought or two." Salima made a sweeping motion with her hands, indicating the broader room. "These torches are not magicked in any way. They will burn out shortly, then you will be in pitch black until your end. Enjoy the light while you can; your darkest hour is yet to come." Salima turned and walked away.

A heavy grinding noise sounded. *They must be sealing the tomb.* Alex struggled against her magical bindings, but all she could do was to gaze up passively at the painted night sky that arched above her with its gilded stars in their midnight-blue background.

As time slipped away, both the lighting and her consciousness became faint. She was light-headed. It probably had something to do with the cold stone vault and her loss of blood. She fell in and out of consciousness in a strange, dreamy waking state. A carousel of memories and fantasies trailed through her head. Was this what it meant when people said their lives flashed in front of them?

Something Salima said before she left kept trying to emerge from the fog that encircled Alex's mind. It appeared and disappeared like a skittish feral cat uncertain if it wanted to be captured or flee.

Maybe centuries from now her remains would be found here on this altar for some hapless archaeologist, breaking the seal and wondering at the mystery of why a twenty-first-century woman was laid to rest in this ancient tomb.

As time passed Alex was overwhelmed by darkness. The torches must have died. A dull bell of memory softly chimed. Refractions of rainbows and showers of glowing crystals by the thousands filled her mind. Was this heaven? Was she in the afterlife or waiting in line to have her heart weighed in the hall of truth? Was she standing there in front of the scales, waiting to be judged, with her ancestors looking down on her? She had failed them. Most likely she would be devoured by Ammut, not because of an untruth told, but because she ruined the world for all of humanity.

"I am sorry, Dad." Tears streamed down her face. "I have let down my ancestors. Oh beautiful Meyret, I am not worthy of your trust. And the great Alexander, as you look down from the heavens on my helpless and bound form, I am sure you have a wish in your heart you'd found a better vessel for the prophecy."

Alex relaxed into a dull haze. She turned her head and stared into the darkness. As if in a dream, she thought she saw an ethereal form of the Goddess Maat step down from the tomb wall and walk toward her as her consciousness faded.

CHAPTER TWENTY-SEVEN

After leaving Alex for dead in the desert tomb, Raymond and the others made their way back to his boat. As his grand vessel came into view, he smirked at the memory of the architect's unease when Raymond made it clear he'd meant to gut the entire square box of a vessel. A sleek, modern giant yacht would stick out like a sore thumb as it traveled up and down the Nile against the hundreds of cruise ships and feluccas. This way he could hide in plain sight.

Raymond walked hand in hand with Salima, followed by a cadre of minions, deep into the center of the ship, where he'd built his throne room. As they passed its threshold, the splendor of the space managed to please him as always. It stretched ahead of them in a long oval shape intentionally mimicking a cartouche. In place of the usual stylized rope around the cartouche's perimeter there stood the remnants of the forty-seven stone representations of Sekhmet he'd deftly procured from the recently excavated site near the Colossi of Memnon. You could get practically anything in Egypt, if the price was right. The statues were excavated from the forgotten temple of Amenhotep III. It was a fitting retribution for Raymond to raid the sacred space of Akhenaten's father.

He'd learned his lesson from that aborted attempt to become the Aten, the One True God, when that weakling of a king failed him. This time Raymond wasn't going to rely on a human to further his plans. He had his daughter. He glanced at Salima, his chest filled with pride. This time it would work, and this time he would have someone to share it with.

They climbed the black granite steps of the dais. It was crowned with a throne constructed of midnight-black obsidian trimmed with rich red-orange carnelian. The black stone was carved into an intricate and organic pattern depicting the wind as it cascaded over the desert sands in swirling lines. The material could be mistaken for an ornate wrought iron work if it weren't for its shiny-sharp appearance. The seat and backrest were covered in a mosaic of carnelian tiles in varying tones of yellows, oranges, and reds.

Raymond let go of his daughter's hand and lowered himself into his throne. Salima seemed a little pensive since leaving Alex underneath the ancient temple. A temple that had been dedicated to Salima in her Hathor form, in ancient times. She stood next to him and placed her hand on his forearm. Raymond laid his other hand over hers. "Are you anxious to embody your third self, my daughter?"

Her gaze was fixed on something in the distance. Silence grew between them. What thoughts held her captive? Was she thinking of the failure of the last time, eons ago, when she attained Sekhmet? "This time will be different, dear."

"When you last called me forth to rage upon humanity, I did what you asked, nothing more. I harvested the crop you wished of me. I killed the humans." Her tone sounded weary.

He tried to comfort her, but he only seemed to have angered her. He squeezed her hand. "Patience, my love."

Sounds of pushing and shoving came from the doorway. The minions brought Niles from his holding cell as Raymond had ordered. Niles's arms were tied behind his back. The creatures dragged his struggling form to the dais. *Let the show begin.*

Niles stilled and looked at Raymond. His eyes blazed with hatred. "What makes you think you can get away with this? You failed at this before. This whole One True God thing. It will never work."

Excitement sparked in Raymond at seeing Thoth held against his will. He'd had it coming for some time now. "It's pointless to struggle. Where would you go, anyway? If you leave the sanctuary of my boat you are dead. Run if you want." Raymond flicked his hand dismissively toward the door. "All it will accomplish is to ensure I won't have to put up with you any longer. You step one foot off this boat or tamper with the implant that I gave you, it will explode, releasing the venom. And you will be gone forever."

Salima leaned toward Raymond's ear. "Let the idiot go."

"Unhand him, minions," Raymond commanded.

Niles rubbed his arms where the minions had held him.

Raymond was surprised at how much he enjoyed antagonizing Niles. It might be entertaining to reconsider his end. Maybe when Sekhmet arrived it would be fun to watch a little cat and canary. A charge of excitement shot through him, and he thought he caught a glimmer in his daughter's eyes. Maybe she was thinking the same thing.

"Why am I here? Why haven't you killed me like the Others?" asked Niles.

"You are not important enough," said Salima. "The calling spell requires only the Great Five. Not you. After my father becomes the Aten, the Others will fall under his thumb."

"Including you?" asked Niles.

As Salima leaned in, the scent of clove enveloped Raymond. "After my rampage to subdue the humans is over, I will take my rightful side next to my father for the eternal reign of the Aten."

Salima's voice was oddly flat. Maybe he'd been asking too much of her. They would have to take a nice long break after all of this.

"Early on, my daughter and I deemed it would be helpful to keep you around. Your additional powers could make my transition smoother. You are the scribe to the Gods and Lord of the Sacred Word. Come travel with me once more on my sacred journey, stand beside me once again as my protector. I have rewarded you greatly in the past for your services. If you deal with us fairly, we'll be a happy family of three for eternity. But, know this: your life hangs in the balance. And now we no longer need you for leverage. It appears that you are becoming less and less useful."

"Leverage?"

Raymond smirked. "Your little human friend, the one of the false prophecy, the one you were getting so close to at Luxor Temple. Miss Philothea, God lover. So quaint."

Salima laughed. "I don't think they'd made it that far, Father. Had you?"

Niles ran toward the dais. A defensive line of minions blocked him from the throne. "What have you done with Alex?"

The tortured look on Niles's face struck Raymond as comical. "We left her to die in the very same tomb her father died in all those years ago."

Niles fell to his knees. "I will kill you, old man."

Raymond's hackles rose as Salima gazed down at Niles with a strange intensity. Then it occurred to him, she must be contemplating all the fun ways she could kill Niles.

Salima's eyes glinted with a sharp excitement as she spoke. "By now, Alex is dead or extremely close to it. She will never see the light of day again. Her blood will slowly seep into the thirsty limestone and meld with the dried blood of her father. That family vine will wither in that tomb."

"We made certain she would have time enough to think about the beautiful symmetry of it all," said Raymond.

"You bastard!" Niles yelled.

"Take him away from my sight. I have no more use for this one. Let him go, so he can sulk for his lady love in private." The minions dragged Niles to the throne room's entrance and unceremoniously tossed him out.

"Father, should I head back to KHNM headquarters to see if they have figured out where your sacred space is?"

"How would they figure it out with their tiny little brains? No, I don't care what they think anymore. We have Oscar and Isadore. All is at the ready. You won't need to return to Chicago House."

Salima turned away from him. "So we are heading to your sacred place?"

There was something in her voice that made him pause. He stood and held his hand out for her to take. She tentatively grasped it. He would have to keep an eye on her. Something was not quite right with his daughter.

They walked into the main corridor. It was an exact but downsized version of the Hall of Mirrors from Versailles. Every time he walked through he couldn't help but look at his reflection in each mirror. One day soon he was going to rule everything and everyone. His chest expanded with a deep breath.

A flash of movement caught his eye. In a distant reflection, he could see Niles reach down to pull Jorge up from the floor.

CHAPTER TWENTY-EIGHT

Alex focused on the stars above as her consciousness drifted toward them like a downy feather caught in a lazy breeze. A golden star-point shimmered ahead. A sensation of warmth and peace flowed through her as fear and desperation melted away. In the distance, Alex could make out a figure that held a bright light in one hand. She wore a pleated linen dress. Her familiar face hung like a friendly moon, then disappeared.

"Meyret?" Alex's dry vocal cords croaked at their sudden use. She blinked to clear her vision. The stars and sky that surrounded her ancestor's head were merely painted. She was still in the tomb. Her heart sank at realizing it was a mirage. But it was no longer dark.

"I'm glad to see you are awake, dear one."

Meyret's soft and comforting voice was a balm to Alex's

soul. Alex pulled herself up and leaned on her elbows to look around the room. Could it be her ancestor was conversing through her mind as she did when they first met? A hand gently rested on Alex's. She winced at the slight touch and looked up to see Meyret looking down at her.

Meyret pulled her hand away. "Sorry, I bound them the best I could. They must still pain you. It's a lucky thing. The cuts Salima made were not too deep."

"How is it you are here? They sealed the tomb."

"You called me."

"And you were able to appear?" Alex sat up a little too quickly, making her head spin. She stretched her arms, feeling the burn as she pulled her tensed muscles back to life.

Concern softened Meyret's face. "It's fortunate Akh-Hehet was able to apply the calling spell to your coffin pendant. The ushabti inside worked as a touchstone for me to reach you, even in this half state."

Alex brought her hands close to her face and examined them. Her hands were well- tended. Alex noted the binding material consisted of strips ripped from her torn shirt.

"I've ruined your shirt. I needed to stop the bleeding quickly. It was all I had. The wounds were not deep, but you must have been down here for some time. Your body was cold as the stone they'd laid you on. For a moment I thought I was too late." Meyret's face slackened into an expression of deep sorrow. "You must understand I could only come when I did. Magic has strict rules. The spell

Akh-Hehet used would only work if you called to me at your darkest hour."

"I'm glad you are here, Meyret. Thank you for bringing me back and binding my wounds." She shrugged as she lifted her hands toward her ancestor. "I truly appreciate all you have done. Now that you have come, can you magic us out of here?"

"If only I could. I am limited in what I can do in this form. There is no word in the human experience to name what I am right now. In this state I have limited abilities which do not include transporting solid forms buried deep within the earth."

"So you brought me from the edge of death, and lovingly bound my wounds, just to keep me company until I die?" Alex laughed at the thought of it. Meyret's sorrow-filled expression cut her laughter short. "Sorry. Gallows humor has always been a fallback for me." The last thing Alex wanted to do was to hurt Meyret. She truly appreciated the fact that she'd come, even if she had no idea how they would escape the tomb.

Meyret smiled and put her hand on Alex's shoulder. "It was many years ago the seer Akh-Hehet revealed a vision of this possible future for you. Your father searched me out, desperate for an answer. This is our imperfect solution. The hope was that, when the time came, we could figure out a way forward."

"Can you make the granite slab move?"

Meyret shook her head.

Alex sighed. She visually scanned the room looking for

any sort of implements or tools that might have been left by Raymond and Salima or their minions. She slipped off the altar to investigate the room more closely. Her legs buckled as her feet made contact with the ground. She straightened herself up and shook her tingling legs to encourage circulation. "So, Akh-Hehet really has visions?"

"What made you think she couldn't?"

"Niles."

"Niles is a different story altogether. You can't take much of what he says too seriously." Meyret shot Alex a knowing look.

Alex's heart tightened as she turned away from Meyret's pitying expression. Maybe Salima was right after all.

"I guess I should see if I have anything useful." Alex wandered around the tomb and collected her scattered belongings. "Salima dumped everything out. They both seemed to think I had some sort of artifact. And they were ecstatic when they realized I didn't."

Alex returned to the altar and emptied the contents of her bag. The pile included a ticket to Luxor Temple, her passport, a pack of gum, lip balm, Niles's pen, the crystal from Akh-Hehet, the blue bead from the Met, the Nile river rock, the faience Hathor head, and, of course, the large glass marble that was Horatio's eye. She shuffled the items around on the granite altar. "A sad inventory." She picked up the lip balm, popped open the cap and spread it across her parched and dry lips. "At least I can go to the Nether-world with a supple pucker."

"More gallows humor?"

"Sorry." She chuckled as she looked down at the paltry items from her bag that now lay in an ordered line on the altar. She had, without thinking, lined the objects from her bag from largest to smallest, starting with the passport and ending with the blue bead. Apparently her inner researcher needed to make order of the pile.

Niles's pen stood out to her. Niles was Thoth. She had Thoth's pen. Maybe it possessed magical properties. She picked it up and studied it. "To your knowledge, does Niles, I mean Thoth, have any magical items?"

"There was a time when he had a pen filled with magicked—" Meyret's words halted as her eyes reached the pen. "You have Thoth's pen? If that is it, it holds strong magic."

"So you are saying it is possible I might write myself out of this tomb?"

"In a matter of speaking." Meyret chuckled.

Alex could feel the mood lighten as she screwed the pen apart. The ink cartridge glowed softly as if it were filled with a luminescent gold ink. "I think we have a hit here. But, what do we do with it?" Alex scrutinized the minuscule volume of liquid the tube contained. They'd only have one go at whatever it was they were going to try. "Would this magic ink be able to eat through a granite slab?"

Meyret wandered to the tomb entrance. "No, I fear it is too thick. I think we need to be thinking less about the physical world and more about the world of spells."

"What do you mean, exactly?"

"With magic the approach is more indirect. Instead of the liquid melting granite, the spell used in conjunction with the ink can bring to life or enhance an already magical item."

Alex was more confused than before. What did Meyret mean? Thoth was the God of writing. Could it be this pen would have the ability to bring the written word to life? Alex crossed to the side of the tomb that was covered with hieroglyphs and ran her hands over them. She wished her ability to read them was stronger. If there was a spell in the text, she could find it along with their way out.

She looked over her shoulder at Meyret, and an idea sparked. How could she have not seen it before? Meyret was standing next to a false door. The ceremonial exit that would allow the tomb's resident Ba-soul to venture into that of the living. Could this be the magical object that would allow them to escape?

Alex joined Meyret and pointed at the false door. "Do you think a spell on the false door in conjunction with the pen fluids could create a physical portal to the outside of this tomb?"

Meyret's eyes lit up. "It's possible."

"Do you know any spells that might work for the false door?"

"I can read the spell around it. With the magicked ink it might do the trick."

"Let's get rolling." Excitement welled up in Alex— maybe this was going to work.

"I must caution you. Although this is a great plan, it

depends entirely on whether or not the magic within Thoth's essence has been corrupted."

They squatted in front of the false door that was hewn from the native rock of the tomb. Its sharp, clean lines made it look as if it were carved yesterday. For the first time in her years of study, Alex noticed a resemblance of the ancient false door to a craftsman-style door. It was made from very different materials and was much smaller, but the stone pattern of nested squares held a strong resemblance. Around the door's lintel were lines of delicately rendered hieroglyphs that wished safe passage to the deceased's Ba.

Meyret rubbed her hand over the rock and closed her eyes. "Let's give this a try. I will need you to stay completely silent while I spin the spell. I will need to focus all my magic toward this end."

"Understood."

"Have you got your passport?"

"Are you the tomb's customs officer? Will you not let me pass without one?"

Meyret laughed. "I need a palette for the ink. I think out of all the items in your bag, it would work the best, as the surface won't absorb the liquid."

Alex returned to the altar and grabbed her passport. She quickly shoved the other items in her scribe's bag. If all went well, she wouldn't be in the tomb much longer. When she returned, Meyret had snapped the ibis head clip from the pen's cap. *I guess I won't be returning Niles's pen anytime soon.* Alex handed her the passport.

Meyret deftly snapped the pen tube in half. A cracking sound filled the tomb as it broke apart. A golden, glowing liquid pooled onto the flat surface of Alex's passport. "Remember, silence," Meyret said.

Meyret placed the ink-laden passport in front of her and the silver ibis-headed figure next to it. She cupped her hands as if in prayer, then closed her eyes and rocked back and forth. A sweet meditative hum emanated from her as she swayed. The chant ceased as she sat stock-still. Her eyes flashed open as she picked up the ibis head and gently swirled it in the glowing substance, then lifted it to the hieroglyphs. Meyret spoke in a low mumble as she wrote. The symbols illuminated with a queer blue glow. The text expanded and melted into its neighbor. The blue light spread over the false door like a crazed virus until it overtook the space and turned it into a glowing mass of blue.

Meyret leaned forward and pressed her hands onto its surface. The once-solid stone wiggled as if it were filled with gelatin. Her chanting built to a frenetic crescendo. Meyret leaned forward and pushed her torso into the void. The surface gave way and the top of Meyret disappeared. She pulled herself back into the tomb. Her smile was radiant as she handed Alex her passport. "You've cleared customs, dear one. Leave now— I can only hold it so long."

"But what about you?"

"The touchstone around your neck leaves when you leave, then so will I. Go, before the spell breaks."

Alex crawled into the blue void, holding her breath, uncertain if this unknown space contained any air. The substance she pushed through had the consistency of chilled pudding. Her lungs fought against the lack of air. As she struggled to keep her mouth clamped shut, she sensed a thin barrier that gave way against her hands. She leaned forward with all her might, her head breaking through the surface, and she gasped for air. Alex thrust her arms out and then pushed down with all her strength. Her body was suddenly flung outward, ejected like an assembly-line reject. She lay on her back, breathing in the night air, finding herself on the desert floor looking at masses of brilliant stars. The ground was cool below her.

She'd made it. "Meyret?" Alex said in a hopeful whisper. Her heart sank with the realization that she was alone. Alone in a vast open expanse of desert. As if on cue, a jackal howled somewhere in the distance. At least she hoped it was in the distance.

Alex stood and scanned the landscape that spread out before her, wondering how she could make her way back to Chicago House without a map or any navigation tools. Yes, she'd escaped, but the clock was ticking. Anxiety flooded her as she realized it might already be too late. Raymond could have already seen his plan through, and the world as she knew it would be altered forever. But regardless, she knew she couldn't give up. She needed to get to Luxor, one way or the other. She gazed out to the horizon. The sun would be rising soon. At least when it did, she would know which direction was east.

She brushed the desert sand from her pants and peered toward the first light of dawn illuminating the early sky.

Was she seeing things? A large dust cloud traveled toward her, and it was making great time. Could it be a sandstorm? Knowing their dangers, she needed to search out shelter.

She climbed a small mound behind her in hopes of finding a safe nook in which to crawl. As she crested the hill, in the distance she saw a tiny Stonehenge-like structure in the shape of a circle. The stones stood about three feet high in varied sizes. Their tops were jagged and pointy, forming a triangle shape in the center of the stone circle.

Raymond and Salima had taken her to the Nabta Playa, a site far away from anything resembling civilization. Now it was certain she was hundreds of miles away from Luxor. Rocks skittered down the small hill in her wake. Some scholars believe it was an early worship site for the Goddess Hathor. There was no way she could walk to Chicago House. If she recalled correctly, the site was closer to Aswan than Luxor. Even that shorter distance was deadly.

She planted herself in the center of the stones and surveyed the area. No shelter to be seen for miles, and the dust storm was quickly closing in. Alex knelt with hands raised in the air and yelled, "Ancestor Meyret, Priestess of Maat, I call to you again in this dark hour."

Nothing. No miracles. It would be nice to know the rules around calling forth your magical ancestor. In hindsight, it would have been a good thing to have nailed down with Meyret when she'd had the chance.

She sat against one of the larger upright stones and pulled herself into a tight ball, hoping she could protect most of herself from the oncoming abrasive wind. The sound of the storm came to a stop. Then she heard . . . a door slam? Alex stood. A man was approaching her from atop the berm.

"What on earth?" the man asked as he stumbled down the sand hill toward her. "He was right. She is here."

Relief flooded over her until she noticed who it was. Jorge. How on earth did he manage to end up here? She knew his memory had been wiped, but had it come back? Would he remember who she was?

He half fell, half walked down the sand dune to Alex. Jorge's face didn't register any recognition of her. When he got close, he prostrated himself, pushing his face into the sand. "Oh great incarnation of the Golden One, Hathor, Great Wild Cow, Lady of the Sycamore, I bow to you as your humble servant."

The brown tentacles of gel-encased hair quivered as he addressed her. He thought she was Hathor? Right now, all she cared about was getting back to Luxor. If that meant acting like Salima, so be it. She channeled her deeply buried inner bitch. "You insignificant toad. How dare you interrupt my daily meditations? You dare address she who keeps the desert safe at night, when the new day has yet to begin? If you do not please me, danger will stalk you and your entourage through to the afterlife, you lowly fly."

He raised then lowered his torso with his hands outstretched in supplication. His eyes were shut tight. "Oh Great One of love, music, and dance, please forgive this unthinking fly."

This was too good to be true. Was this another spell concocted years ago by her father and Akh-Hehet? "Lift your gaze to rest it on my glory, fly."

He flipped his body up as he continued to kneel in the desert sand. His eyes flickered at her. Then he turned away in deference, as if avoiding looking directly into the eyes of a holy one. He must truly believe.

"Yes, Mistress. Whatever you command."

Beyond Jorge, the dawning light was starting to warm the morning sky with its washed-out glow. Atop the hill stood four other men who watched the scene below. The sand dune was low enough that Alex could pick out the adoration that washed over the faces of all but one. He stood there, arms folded and body pitched to one side, as if waiting for the show to be over.

She puffed her chest out and said in the deepest and loudest voice she could muster, "Who have you brought to the Lady of the Western Mountain? Are these robust souls here for my pleasure?" The inference of what she'd said quickly sunk in. A sudden unease overtook her at the thought of how Jorge and his companions might interpret those words. For all she knew they thought this was a fun little role-playing game. There were five of them and one of her. It was hard to believe, no matter how dense Jorge might be, that he would attempt to . . . presume to . . .

"They are weary travelers like me, who search for wisdom," said Jorge as the bored-looking man with crossed arms coughed. "And Mohammed, our guide."

Alex breathed a sigh of relief. "And how did you locate me, my disciple fly?"

"I had chanced upon a wise man on a boat." He dramatically cast his hands in big rolling circles as if offering holy adulations to her with his words. "He entrusted me with a map to your sanctuary. Saying I might find you here, taking on your human form during the darkest hours of the night, just before morning dawns, at your most ancient site of worship."

"And why did this wise man send you?"

"He said you must be taken to Luxor. A convening of the Gods is coming, and you must be there."

"And he sent a mere fly to fetch me?" Alex shot him what she hoped was an expression of unbridled disgust.

"Your sand chariot awaits. We have a great land ship to whisk you away to Luxor. Like in the sacred barques of old, within you will find a private chamber, away from our admiring eyes, Goddess."

"You may rise. Lead me to your ship." As she crested the dune many questions swirled around her tired head. The most prominent one was *Where on earth did Jorge get ahold of a military-grade hovercraft?*

CHAPTER TWENTY-NINE

The look on Buxton's face had been priceless when Alex disembarked from the sand chariot. Jorge and his followers had fallen to their knees, eyes averted as she walked by, creating a path of humanoid sphinxes on either side of her.

The memory of that moment made her smile as she stood in the shower and let the hot water run over her body. It streamed down her like a warm river that stung the fresh wounds on her palms. Although Buxton had carefully tended the cuts, the water made them burn.

While Buxton had worked on her injuries, Alex recounted the basic facts of her capture and escape and of Akh-Hehet's cryptic vision. She added that Salima was working for Raymond. When she'd shared that last bit of information, Buxton's expression went flat. Had he already suspected? Or was he supremely disappointed? In retrospect, it embarrassed Alex that she didn't touch on her other suspicions. That it was feasible that Niles was in league with Raymond as well.

All the way to Chicago House, Alex had hoped Niles would be there and prove Salima wrong. But he had been nowhere to be seen. Could he have joined with Raymond? Was everything he claimed to believe a lie? Was that kiss a lie? How could she have allowed herself to have fallen for him? Throughout her life she believed she was good at reading others, but maybe it only worked with mortals.

Alex leaned into the shower's stream, allowing her tears to get lost in the brackish cocktail of blood, dirt, and sorrow cascading toward the drain. She rested her head on the shower wall and turned the dial as far as the red arrow could go. The scorching water was painful and somehow soothing at the same time. *Snap out of it—everyone is waiting for you downstairs.*

She turned off the water, threw on some clothes, and headed to the inquisition, or welcoming crew.

In the courtyard, Alex caught the eye of Buxton, sitting at a corner table in the distance. She waved and gave him a grim smile, knowing they would need to have a long chat in private. What she had to say to him was not for mass consumption. Would he be shocked to think Niles working for Raymond?

It surprised her to see Gormund standing behind the bar, apparently boosted to average height by standing on a chair. His expression was aglow with mischief, or scotch, or possibly both. "So what will our returning Goddess of Love have to wet her whistle?" Gormund snickered. "Your throat must be mightily parched after cruising around the Red Lands with Mr. Alien Adventurer and his mighty dust chariot."

Alex grimaced. "Bourbon with a splash of ginger ale, please. If you are here, I would have to guess Meyret is around."

Gormund poured her drink and handed it to her. "Oh, don't worry, she's resting securely. Buxton put out an all hands on deck. Even Luke is here." Gormund pointed to the far corner. "He is chafing at the fact that Buxton never seems to give him any real challenges. He's an archivist, what does he expect? To suddenly be Indiana Jones or something? Saving damsels in distress? Anyway, it seems as if we've lost some powerhouses. Everyone is needed just in case."

So it must be true. Niles is working for the other side. Alex knocked her drink back. "Another, please. Did Luke bring Jeeves?" She was surprised at how the thought of seeing the grumpy little schnauzer lightened her mood.

"I think you would definitely know if Jeeves was in the house." He poured her another. "The One of Prophecy is thirsty."

"If you want to call it that, I can go with thirsty. Hey, have you seen Niles around lately?" Alex tried to make it sound like it didn't matter one way or the other.

"Not since you disappeared. Speaking of disappearing, has Buxton told you about Big Oscar and his lady?"

"Osiris and Isis?"

"They were removed from their safe house the same night you were snagged."

The evidence against Niles was growing. Raymond was able to quickly locate Alex as well as Isis and Osiris. KHNM must have sealed their fate by trusting in the three Immortals who supposedly swore to protect humanity. Where did Gormund stand in the mix? Could he be trusted? "So Raymond has them all?"

"He's checked off his shopping list."

As Gormund rubbed her forearm, Alex must have looked dejected. "It does seem pretty desperate. I am sure Buxton has a plan hatched." He nodded in the direction of where the old man was sitting. "He's probably waiting for you to come over so he can lay it out for you." He smiled a wide smile. Alex was certain it was meant to be encouraging, but his sharply pointed teeth made that all but impossible.

She crossed the courtyard to Buxton. The Egyptian sun had sunk below the western horizon. A cool breeze made the palm fronds and the fiery pink bougainvillea petals rustle. In an alternate reality, she would find the experience idyllic. In this imagined world she might have sat in this courtyard and joked with her colleagues about Re finishing with his work for the day and now starting his journey through the Netherworld. However in this reality, she knew, one way or another, everything was about to change.

She sat across from Buxton. Shadows weighed under his eyes.

"Gormund told me the bad news," she said.

"We're running out of time. We must move out against Raymond tonight."

"Who is we?"

"You, me, and Gormund. We need to find Raymond's lair and stop him."

"What about Niles?"

"He can't help us now. We need to recognize that reality. It will be far better for all of us." Buxton shot Alex a knowing look.

He said it so bluntly it shocked Alex. "Raymond and Salima were looking for an artifact. Apparently they thought I would have it. Do you know what it is?"

"You don't have the artifact? Didn't Niles ever give it to you?" A dark shadow passed over Buxton's face.

"All he ever gave me was his pen, but it is ruined."

"Ruined. What do you mean?"

"I used it to escape from the tomb. It no longer exists."

"Damn it." Buxton hit the table with his fist. "This changes everything."

"What?" His unexpected show of anger was jarring.

"I am willing to bet that if Niles gave it to you, it is the artifact. We have nothing to battle Raymond with." Buxton slumped into his chair, his frown and dull expression filled with resignation.

Alex couldn't believe he was about to give up. After all they'd been through. "You and Gormund can stay here and wait for Raymond's reign. I don't care if I have to kill him with my bare hands. I am going to raise heaven and hell to stop him from becoming the Aten. I will avenge my father or die trying."

"If I didn't know better, I would say you have amazing powers of foresight. At least about the hell part."

"What do you mean by that?"

"It took a while, but I think I understand Akh-Hehet's vision. Raymond has set up shop in the Duat."

"The Netherworld?" Alex was staggered by the thought. How could they travel into another realm?

"Of course Gormund and I will go with you. We'd already determined this could be a suicide mission. I am glad to hear you are game, Alex. Your dad would be proud."

Alex smiled at Buxton. He sat up straight and had a newly lit fire in his eyes. Suddenly, it struck her as funny. This kind old man was literally sending her straight to hell.

CHAPTER THIRTY

The reconstructed concrete ramp to the Seti I mortuary temple at Abydos lay ahead. Its slight slope beckoned Alex forward and up. The site was eerily absent of tourists. Buxton must have a contact high in the Egyptian chain of command for the tourist police to have cleared out the area so quickly. A steady stream of air-conditioned coaches whizzed by them as they made their way to the temple site. Alex imagined them full of red-faced angry tourists, the tour guides sweating against the air conditioning as they tried to unruffle the feathers of their cargo.

Alex and her unusual battle team, an ancient professor and smart-ass dwarf God, stood before the temple entrance. What could go wrong?

She'd only seen this grand monument to Seti I in pictures, but it always managed to capture her imagination.

It set itself apart from other temples in its squareness. As she approached the main entrance, it resembled a monumental limestone harmonica. Instead of great round pillars, this temple was fronted with large square ones.

"It casts a captivating spell, doesn't it?" Buxton asked. "Abydos has always been a place of wonderment for me. Excepting the circumstance, I am so glad to be here with you, Alex." He had an odd smile on his face. "Your father was fond of it too."

They walked through a vast open courtyard toward the blocklike pillars of the temple's portico. On close inspection Alex could see they were adorned with hieroglyphs. She knew the texts welcomed the Theban triad of Gods— Isis, Osiris, and their son, Horus. She also knew the entire family was somewhere within this complex. Horus was dead, but what about his parents? Had Raymond killed them yet or were they still alive?

As they entered the massive structure, Alex was surprised at the openness of the initial chamber. Moonlight poured in through open shafts in the ceiling, illuminating the space before them. At first glance it appeared to be as large as a football field. This was where priests would cleanse themselves at ablution wells before continuing into the holy sanctuaries beyond. Alex wondered how the great temple's builder, Pharaoh Seti I, would feel if he knew that modern travelers who were unwashed, cranky from the heat, and probably hungover wandered aimlessly within its sacred walls.

Alex exited the large chamber and found herself

standing in an impressive forest of pillars—not a wild grove teeming with life, but a rootless landscape that created a contemplative stillness in its regularity. Alex knew hypostyle halls were an attempt to architecturally mimic the clutches of reeds that once banked the Nile's shores. Although the pillars failed miserably to create the effect, standing among them was astonishing. The hypostyle hall simultaneously impressed upon Alex the genius as well as the insignificance of humanity.

A dove cooed, breaking the haunting spell that had been cast on Alex. The sound of its wings flapping made her glance up. A small white feather danced down through a shaft of light from above. It landed softly on the ground. She bent over, picked it up, and dropped it in her scribe's bag.

"Alex, we must move on." Gormund took ahold of her hand.

Buxton leaned in and touched Alex's shoulder. "I promise. If we survive this, we will have a celebration, a fantasia like no one has seen at this very spot." His face lit with a smile. "And you, my dear, will have the time to scour as you will."

They continued on, blithely passing by the chapels that were built for the Gods. Alex had to stifle her urges to break away from the group and wander with abandon. Temptation called her around every corner.

They ducked into a hallway inscribed with deeply carved reliefs. The close walls amplified Buxton's voice. "I think Raymond has located a portal to the underworld within the

Osireion. It is my best guess." Buxton stopped for a moment and turned to gaze at the wall to his right. "When we have our celebration, you will want to come to this wall. I know you will find it quite fascinating."

Alex brushed by cartouche after cartouche carved into the temple wall. It had to be the Abydos King List. "Damn," was all she could say as she trailed behind her companions, who led her away from the list and through a narrow, unadorned hallway. In comparison to the rest of the temple complex, its lack of decoration made it seem like an ancient servants' entrance. When the corridor abruptly ended, Alex found herself standing at the crest of a hill in the cool night air.

The moon was low and large. Its light was like a spotlight focused on a megalithic structure in the pit below. Huge blocks of granite were stacked on one another in a manner atypical for an ancient Egyptian site. At its base was a dark pool of water. Around the centermost standing stones were what appeared to be doorways to chapels or niches. Arched corridors in the distance led away from the submerged structure. Could this be the primordial soup and stones of eternity that Akh-Hehet foretold?

Alex was familiar with images of this temple and recognized they were standing above the Osireion. She knew if it were daylight, the water would look like murky pea soup. In the moonlight, the groundwater was as dark as India ink. The massive vertical granite blocks appeared to rise out of the muck with enough space between them to imply that they were intended as giant columns. Twin horizontal slabs crowned the columns, connecting one to the other.

Some believed this site was the burial place of the God Osiris and somewhere nearby was his symbolic tomb. As they shuffled down the dirt hill, Alex noticed a wooden structure leading into the pit where the massive blocks rested. "What is that?"

"It allows tourists to hover over the murky water and enjoy the ambiance of this strange site. But it is of no use to us," said Buxton, his voice wavering.

"How so?"

"We are going to wade into it," said Buxton.

"Eww," added Gormund. "It is a lucky thing it's night-time. I think my imagination would run rampant in daylight, wondering what unseen thingies lived in the depths of that murky mess."

"Thank you once again, Gormund, for adding some creepy zest to the moment before we plunge forward," said Alex. "I am just glad that . . . unlike for you, Gormund, that murky mess will only be mid-thigh on us. You, on the other hand, might have to swim to keep your head above water. Or one of us could give you a piggyback ride."

Gormund's face clouded and he defiantly waded in.

"Be sure to make smooth strokes. That will probably help minimize muck movement." Alex enjoyed giving Gormund a little of his own medicine.

They made their way through the dark liquid, pushing through its stagnant brew. With every ripple, no matter how small, a vile and pungent stink of rotting debris assaulted her nose. She wanted to retch. The contents of her stomach threatened to return to the outside world. Alex swallowed hard, not wanting to add to the already rancid brew, then pinched her nose. Both Buxton and Gormund wore expressions of great discomfort, especially Gormund, whose nose skimmed the surface as he attempted a sad, slow dog paddle.

"Is there something in particular we are looking for?" asked Alex as she followed Buxton toward the underground corridor.

"I think we will find what we are looking for in there." Buxton pointed to the massive square lintel ahead of them.

They arrived at the dark passageway. Buxton stepped up into it and pulled Gormund with him. "The water will be shallower in the mouth of this man-made cave."

"Thank God I can stand now," Gormund breathed out in relief. "I was starting to lose steam. However, the idea of drowning in that glop was a great motivator."

"I think it is time to don the headlamps." Buxton pulled his out and strapped it around his head. "Switch it on and let's get going."

Eventually, the corridor came to an abrupt end.

"Oh dear," said Buxton. "It looks like I was mistaken."

"Mistaken? You mean I swam across that crap for nothing?"

"This looks like a blank wall. I can't see a hint of a door or even a latent magic spell."

"Or a gigantic arrow pointing down with the words *Underworld This Way* in glowing neon?" Gormund's voice dripped with sarcasm. "I can't believe I let you talk me into this wild-goose chase. If I weren't so tired from swimming through that primordial soup I would—"

"Hey, wait a minute," Alex said. A little speck of light at the end of the wall caught her eye. "Come check this out." Alex ran her finger over a hole so smooth and perfect it had to be intentionally created. It had a definite shape and size, like a dollhouse-sized keyhole. Around it were tiny hiero-glyphs. Alex rubbed them with her fingers.

"Can you read it, Buxton?"

"It says something about the strength and power of Osiris will lead you safely through the Duat."

No, it couldn't be that simple. However, Alex hoped with all her might that it could be.

CHAPTER THIRTY-ONE

Alex slid the djed pillar pendant off its gold chain and wondered if she was grasping at straws. It had worked as a key of sorts in the portal at the Met to the God machine. Could it possibly allow her access to the Netherworld too? She re-clasped the chain and let the coffin pendant fall against her chest under its own weight.

She studied the small gold charm closely. The ridges of the pillar, depicting the spine of Osiris, did have a certain resemblance to the teeth of a key.

"Here goes nothing."

"You think your pendant is a key?" Gormund's tone implied that he certainly didn't.

"Have you got any better ideas?" She held the broad, flat end between her thumb and forefinger and slipped it into the small hole. Alex turned it slightly to the right and thought she heard an ever-so-slight chinking sound. A small glimmer of hope rose in her. She turned to her companions. "Did you hear that?" Her fingers burned with a sharp intensity. She quickly let go of the pendant and blew on her newly singed fingers. Smoke fumed out of the hole, accompanied by the hard-edged smell of molten metal.

"Damn it." Her heart sank as she watched one more rare remembrance she had from her father fizzle away into nothing. "There goes that idea. Any other ideas on how to break into the Duat?" Alex poked at the spot where her djed pillar disappeared into the limestone wall with a lame hope that maybe she could retrieve it. Her hand jerked back as a shock charged through her index finger as it made contact with the rock face. She leaned in close to look at the area. A white speck of light caught her eye. It was growing larger and larger. She stepped back from it. "What the hell?"

The opening continued to expand. A warm breath of air billowed out, gently puffing at her hair. There were no sparks or flames, only an expanding burn. She leaned in close and peered through the hole.

"What do you see?" asked Gormund.

"Wondrous things," Alex replied, dumbfounded at the world she'd caught a glimpse of.

Buxton moved closer to Alex. The hole expanded enough for them to both see while standing side by side. "We've found our portal. We must cross over before it closes."

"Maybe if we wait, the hole will keep getting larger and larger." Alex wasn't sure if it was big enough for them to pass through. The light had a sparking-bright electrical quality to it. If they nicked an edge, would they get jolted with deadly currents?

"We can't take that chance. We must go through," said Buxton. Gormund chuckled. "Like Nike says, just DuAT."

Alex couldn't help but chuckle at the pun as she moved through the portal, ducking under the surprisingly cool white embers that continued to enlarge the hole. The acrid scent of the magical fire burned her nose with an unpleasant smell somewhere between burnt plastic and singed hair. Her hand instinctively reached up and patted her head. Nope, it wasn't her.

Once she landed on the other side, she switched off her headlamp, which was no longer necessary. The odd smell hadn't gone away. She wrinkled her nose and hoped she would get used to it.

The landscape was different from anything she'd ever witnessed before. It was as if she had stepped inside a Dalí painting colored in a collection of reds, oranges, and yellows. She stood on a plateau that over looked a hill-laden valley with a river snaking through it. In the far distance there was a range of mountains. Everything was visually distorted as if she were trying to view it through a curtain of cascading heat waves—though the temperature of this world was neither hot nor cold. All that lay before her was so peculiar it felt like an illusion.

Buxton jumped next to Alex. Gormund rolled into them

like a bowling ball, knocking them to the edge of the plateau. "Sorry," he said as they stood and brushed themselves off. "The portal was starting to close, and I didn't want to be left behind."

Alex turned to see the circle of flames shrinking inward, closing the portal.

"So where to next, Buxton?" asked Alex.

Buxton turned back and peered at the strange vista ahead. "From here on out, your guess is as good as mine. Let's head there to the river."

They carefully picked their way off the plateau and down the rocky slope into the valley.

Gravel the color of a vibrant sunset was continually cascading down from above them as they walked. Could it be possible someone was following them? Alex fell back and stopped for a moment to look behind them. There was nothing but large boulders that jutted from the side of the plateau, aside from the few small rocks that skittered by. Their progress must be causing some sort of delayed reaction with the rockfall. Was she getting paranoid in thinking someone was constantly following her?

As they made their way to the riverbank, Alex kept her eyes trained on a golden glimmer that flashed like a beacon. As they got closer, she realized it was a large golden boat that rested on its side on a small beach of bright-red agates. A feeling of dread rolled through Alex when she touched it. "This seems a little too convenient. Do you think it's a trap?"

Buxton sighed heavily, then crossed his arms. "The Boat

of Re. This will more than likely take us right to him. But, of course with everything given, there will be a cost."

"What sort of cost?" asked Alex.

"All that is known is that it can't be known. It could be Re abandoned it here to use later, or he could have called it here for us. Either way the cost will be great." Buxton rubbed his hand against the solid-gold hull.

"We have two choices. Alex, the choosing must be up to you. This boat could be either our salvation or our undoing. We can blaze our own trail through the Duat, which is filled with countless deadly traps and tortures beyond imagining. Getting lost in the underworld does not take much. If we choose the wrong path, we could wander this void for eternity, never finding Re or even a way home. Or we can take this boat, which may or may not have been sent by him. It will bring us to him if we survive the trip. Either choice is harrowing and deadly. No matter which you choose, we could end in success or failure. Which do you choose, Alex?"

Both were equally dangerous, but at least the boat could carry the promise of finding their target if they were able to survive the journey. She knew, no matter the cost, it was the only choice. "The boat."

Gormund kicked a bright-orange river rock. "Damn, I knew she was going to pick that." "You can always stay behind, but I wouldn't advise it," said Buxton as he climbed into the golden boat. "Countless unexpected and peculiar things lurk under every rock and behind every hill."

Gormund tilted his head as if contemplating the choice, then quickly climbed in behind the old man.

Alex followed them in and sat down. She rested her back against the boat's curved hull as it shifted, righting itself. Her stomach flipped as the boat unexpectedly moved on its own, making a soundless and smooth transition over the rocks and toward the water.

"Whatever you might expect down here, expect something different and you'll still be dumbfounded. This is after all the Netherworld," said Buxton.

Gormund cringed as he surveyed the area. "Hell. That's what I like to call it."

Alex peeked over the edge of the boat at the river below. Its water was a dark inky black. She switched on her headlamp. When the beam of light touched the surface, Alex gasped as she planted herself on the floor of the boat.

"Blood," said Buxton, his voice flat.

"Blood?" Alex was queasy, and it wasn't from the boat's motion.

Gormund's stocky little body twitched with an agitated repugnance. "The . . . river . . . is . . . blood. God how I hate this place. It gives me the willies."

"Whose blood?"

"Does it matter?" Gormund's words snapped out at Alex. He seemed to be getting punchy. "Blood of the dead, blood of the eternal, Blood of Nut. Why does it matter? It's blood, okay?"

"Calm down, Gormund, you can't fault Alex for wondering." Buxton patted Alex's knee. "You will see many things down here. The ancient and the immortal surround us. We are traveling in a time that has never existed but has always been. This is a land of consistent inconsistencies and infinite conundrums."

Alex took in the alien landscape around them. Red-hued mountains sprang up at sheer angles from the thin strip of the river's shoreline like a predator's sharp teeth after a kill. She glanced downriver and saw the churning red-black liquid ahead. "Oh shit. Rapids?" The boat's pace quickened and rocked from side to side as it picked up speed.

Gormund pulled his knees up close and wrapped his arms around them, forming a compact man-shaped ball. He rocked back and forth. "Oh man, this is the worst. I've heard about this part."

"They're only rapids. Right?"

"Nothing, my dear, is only anything in the Duat," Gormund said in a matter-of-fact tone. "Look for yourself."

Alex peered over the side of the golden craft, grasping tight onto the boat's edge, not wanting to get bucked out. She screamed and flung herself back in. With each thump against the boat's hull Alex couldn't help but have the image of the floating severed heads flash through her mind.

"Made you look." Gormund's weary tone was still more matter-of-fact than playful.

Alex slapped her hand over her mouth, hoping her body would understand. The thought of peering over and seeing that horror again frightened the molten contents of her stomach back down.

"Need you be so cruel, Gormund?" Buxton asked.

Gormund glared at Buxton, then tilted his head in Alex's direction. "She needs to stop acting like Alice lost in some wonderland."

Gormund was right. She needed to bring her A game to the situation at hand. There were so many questions. It would be nice if she had someone who could give her some sage advice like Meyret. Alex recalled how the priestess had spoken through her mind. She closed her eyes and relaxed, trying to call Meyret forth. She focused intently on the mental image, concentrating hard, trying to connect with her ancestor through the void of space between them. Nothing.

Her eyelids popped open as there was a loud thunking sound. The boat jostled violently, as if it were being lifted from underneath. "What the hell? More heads?"

"This is the worst possible scenario," Buxton said gravely.

Gormund's face blanched into an odd grey-white. "Sobek?"

"Worse. Hippo dirges," said Buxton.

"Shit." Gormund turned a despondent gaze to the bottom of the boat.

"What's going on?" asked Alex.

"They are powered by fear." Buxton's voice wavered. "They are hunters for Amduat. They will turn over our boat and pull us to a deep death. Then we will be wound, like mummies, in river grass and kept as food stock for the great devourer."

The boat continued to rock from side to side. Buxton

was yelling now. "If we calm ourselves, it will come slow. If we let the fright run wild, it will be a quick death."

Alex was torn as she tried to calm her thumping heart. Her anxiety was ratcheting up. The more she acknowledged it, the more it seemed to build on itself, turning to a panic.

A hazy pink fog rolled in toward them from both sides of the river. It smelt of cloves and roses. It overpowered the continuous burning-plastic smell. Maybe they had entered into a softer, nicer area of hell. Alex found herself giggling at the thought. Buxton and Gormund were moving toward her in slow motion. Her body went slack and her eyelids were overtaken with a sudden and overpowering drowsiness. She could barely hold them open. Maybe she should rest. Just for a moment.

CHAPTER THIRTY-TWO

Alex jolted awake as the golden boat landed on a bright-orange beach. Both Buxton and Gormund lay at the bottom of the boat in an apparent deep sleep. As they slumbered, their expression lacked any concern, like the faces of babies napping.

She rubbed her eyes, trying to wipe away the residual drowsiness from whatever it was that had knocked them out. She gently nudged her companions with her feet. "Rise and shine." The memory of the pink wispy fog crept into her mind. What was that? How did they manage to survive what was almost certain death? Could it be that Meyret had somehow intervened?

Buxton stretched as he sat up. "It looks like we will live to see another day."

"Yay," said Gormund half-heartedly as he stretched.

"Somebody must have intervened. I have never heard of anyone surviving the Hunters of Duat."

Maybe Meyret was their guardian angel, or maybe Raymond wanted live captives.

Alex scanned the long strip of land that lay before them. It was covered with a dense low-growing ivy. She squinted, trying to get a clearer view. *Oh shit. It's not ivy.*

Alex raised her arm and pointed toward a swirling mass of snakes that completely covered the land ahead. They twisted and writhed like a living carpet of black, green, beige, and red. In the far distance, beyond the reptilian rug, was a vast, yawning cave.

"Hey, guys. We've got a bit of an issue here," said Alex.

Gormund was the first to speak. "Gross." His tone was flat.

Alex rolled her eyes. "Is that all you've got? Gross? How do you expect us to get through them?"

"We'll just walk through," Gormund said blithely.

"I know you think you are funny, but . . . I don't think snake venom is a good way to start the day."

Gormund sat up and puffed out his chest. "But you forget who you are traveling with—Bes, protector of the home and hearth. Snakes will not come near me."

"That's great . . . for you. But it only gets one of us over there," said Alex.

"Ye of little faith. I may be short, but I am strong. I can carry each of you over, one at a time."

"Delightful," Alex said flatly. She wasn't sure what bothered her more about the proposition: having

Gormund's small hands god knows where on her body as he transported her, or the fact that he could at any minute decide to dump her ass in the snake-scape around them.

"Don't try and sound so excited, Alex." Gormund rubbed his hands together. "It will be a good way for us to get to know each other."

Alex stood at the mouth of the cave, waiting for Gormund to bring Buxton over. Although Buxton exceeded her body weight by at least thirty pounds, it seemed as if Gormund was making the trip twice as fast. She closed her eyes. That crossing was something she wouldn't soon forget. She didn't like having her life so literally in someone else's hands.

Alex turned away from her companion's progress and decided to explore the cave. It was massive, like the great sea caves on the Pacific coast, but there was no ocean in sight. The sparkling sand below her feet was so sugary soft. She had to fight the urge to take her shoes off and wiggle her toes in it. Where did this cave and sand come from? What sort of geological event could have created them?

Gormund's words came back to her. It is the Nether-world; it just is.

In the far distance, midcave, stood two rows of massive silver statues depicting some of the Egyptian Gods. By their dress, Alex inferred there were seven males and seven females segregated by sex— men on the right, ladies on the left. At the end of this great causeway was a large temple crowned with an enormous silver disk.

Gormund gently set Buxton in the sand, then wiped his brow. "I need to rest a little. It might be a good idea to cut something out of your diet. I nearly dropped you a couple of times toward the end."

They sat on the small rock outcropping at the mouth of the cave, their backs to the sea of snakes below.

"I had a chance to look around after Gormund left to bring you over. As soon as you are rested, we should move on. I sense our time is drawing short. I've noticed this cave has many similarities with the mythic cave of Sokar, in which the snake Apophis, adversary of Re, lives. If that assumption is right, it would stand to follow that the temple ahead is the shrine of Osiris. In the temple should be a passageway commonly known in Amduat studies as the Hidden Place of Osiris."

"I bet that could lead us to Raymond's lair," said Buxton.

"That's what I was thinking," said Alex.

"The temple is known to hold sixteen hawk-headed mummies at rest. Their sole purpose is to kill the enemies of Re. Once we find the hidden passageway, all bets are off," Buxton added.

"So, in other words, we have our work cut out for us," said Gormund.

"Do we ever," said Alex.

Buxton was starting to look haggard. Alex wondered what sort of toll this adventure was taking on his old bones. He was keeping up all right, but it must be taking everything he had to do so.

"While we are exploring the cave, we need to communicate with one another silently through hand gestures. We don't want to wake the defenders of Re." Buxton stood, signaling it was time to move on.

Alex marveled at the gigantic silver statues as she passed them by. She eyed them for the slightest movement. Growing up she'd loved to watch the vintage stop-motion fantasy movies from the sixties and seventies like *The Seventh Voyage of Sinbad* and *Jason and the Argonauts,* where the statues come to life and decimate the unwitting adventurers.

At the temple entrance Alex's senses were on high alert. As they crossed the threshold, Alex noticed its unusual layout for an Egyptian temple. Instead of being constructed in a linear form, it was circular. All along the interior were sixteen rectangular chambers, each containing an upright mummiform creature with a hawk's head. It seemed her deductions were spot-on. She wasn't sure if that made her happy. Following her companions' lead, she gave the stationary defenders of Osiris a wide berth.

In front of the temple was a statue of a rearing snake she'd guessed was Apophis. Next to it was what appeared to be a large, flat offering table.

Buxton raised his finger and swirled it in a circle,

signaling it was time to round up and swap notes. They quietly wandered out of the temple and stood in the open space between it and the massive silver God statues.

Alex kept her voice low. "I think the path is pretty clear. I fear my deductions were right. Out of the three snakes of the Netherworld, it only makes sense that this is Apophis."

"You are certain it isn't Mehen, the protector of Re, or Pestu, the devourer of stars?" asked Buxton.

"Mehen makes more sense to me. Why would the defeater of Re be guarding the entrance to Re's lair?" asked Gormund.

"That I can't answer. In the myth of the sixth hour of the Amduat, it speaks of the mummies that protect Re from his enemy as well as the cave in which Apophis dwells. It seems to describe the temple before us perfectly. In a way, it makes sense that the mummies would stand at the ready and surround the greatest threat to Re, Apophis. I believe that statue is Apophis and could be the key to locating Raymond," said Alex.

"So you are saying we should avoid the mummies and explore the snake?" asked Gormund.

"Exactly," she said.

Buxton leaned in close. "We must move with stealth to Apophis. Once we arrive at the statue, you two will search for a lever or mechanism on the snake. Your eyes are keener and will be much more efficient in this task. As you investigate, I will search the other parts of the temple. If we do locate a device, the finder will silently let the others know. Once it is activated, we will have to act on instinct. If we wake those mummies, it will be sixteen against three."

Gormund face turned smug. "Uh, two and one Immortal."

"Whatever, Gor." Alex rolled her eyes.

Buxton pointedly ignored their theatrics. "So, as I was saying, we will need to be ready to spring into action immediately. We will have to move and think as one mind. Whatever presents itself to us, our first priority, no matter what, is to make sure Alex is able to progress further into the Netherworld. Got that? Nothing else matters at this stage in the game other than getting Alex to Re so she can finish this business once and for all, as the prophecy says." Buxton's face held an intense and determined look as he gazed toward Gormund. "No matter what. Get my meaning?"

Gormund kicked at the orange sand. "Of course I do. I wouldn't be here if I didn't understand the importance of it all."

"You and I know that this is when things get hairy. I need to know you will do what needs to be done, Gormund." Buxton locked eyes with Alex. Concern sharpened his warm gaze. "Alex, promise me on the memory of your father that no matter what you see and no matter what happens, you will find a way forward, whether it comes down to fighting Re's mummies, running down a passageway, or jumping through a portal . . . whatever it may be, I need to know you will go through with it. Whatever comes, you must embrace it with everything you have."

Alex turned away from his hard stare. She didn't know why, but she could feel a burning threat of tears. Why did this moment feel so final?

Buxton moved toward her and tilted his head to catch her gaze. "Promise. You must."

Alex wished she could wipe away the concern in his eyes. She knew she had to give it her all, to make things right for her father's memory, her mother's future, and the imperfectly beautiful world. "I promise."

Alex slid her hand over the cool, smooth stone surface of the snake statue as she searched. They didn't know what they were looking for. She hoped it would be evident when she ran across it. It was frustrating that they were still fumbling around trying to get to Raymond, and for all she knew it might already be too late. As was her way with anything that seemed insurmountable, Alex endeavored to push negative thoughts out of her mind and focus on the task at hand. The pyramids would never have been built if those who desired them were not patient and had not persevered, block by block. She kept this in mind as her hunt for the unknown continued.

Eventually, Alex found herself near Gormund as they worked their way around the large statue. She was drawn to an intricate pattern of diamonds that was carved into the entire top length of the snake's body. Her hand moved softly over the grooved area, applying gentle pressure as she explored, tense in anticipation. Disappointed, Alex returned to the front of the statue and reached up to rub the underside of its chin. She felt a slight movement of a grooved cog spinning at the touch of her finger. She motioned to Gormund as a clockwork sound came from within the snake.

Alex jumped back at the sound and knocked into Gormund. The unexpected momentum tumbled them into the offering table, toppling it over. A loud crash reverberated through the room. Suddenly, the ground started to shake violently. A crack fractured the temple floor and out of it a stairway appeared. It was unfolding upward, building each new level upon the last; each step flipped up, reaching toward the temple ceiling.

"Run to it, Alex," yelled Gormund. "Buxton and I will follow."

Alex peeled away to the staircase as it rose toward the temple ceiling. A nugget of concern for her friends' safety burned through her as she ran, but she dared not look back. The guardians ahead charged out of their niches straight at her. She imagined the ones behind her were doing the same.

Alex clambered onto the first stair and glanced over her shoulder to see where Buxton and Gormund were. Gormund was nearly to the staircase, his short legs pumping hard. Buxton wasn't far behind, but the hawk-headed mummies were closing the gap quickly.

"Don't stop, Alex. Run!" Buxton yelled through his gasps for air as they sped toward the staircase.

Alex charged up the stairs two at a time. As she jogged, her elbows were pointed outward to keep her balance. She tilted her head upward to see what lay up ahead. She was shocked to see it looked like she was running straight toward the night sky.

When she reached the top her upper body met no barrier. Her head pushed through to a vast open space with the heavens stretched above. Alex scanned what lay before her and picked out an almost imperceptible line above her waist. She reached up and pushed down to lift her body up. She hefted herself onto this ledge and shimmied forward. Whatever her body rested on was strong enough to support her weight.

The surface she lay on was transparent. Her stomach flipped at the disconcerting illusion of floating and yet at the same time being solidly planted as if she was hovering above the action below. Gormund and Buxton were charging forward. As Gormund approached the top step, Alex dropped her arms down. "Lift up your hands, Gor."

Alex grabbed Gormund's outstretched hands. His unexpected weight tugged at her arms, making them strain. Alex wondered if she would be able to lift him up and over. She pulled with all her might as she deadlifted his small but hefty body.

Gormund unexpectedly shot toward Alex. Buxton was pushing him from below.

"It's now or never," shouted Buxton.

Alex heaved with all her strength, and with the help of Buxton was able to swing Gormund over the edge.

Gormund scrambled beside Alex. They peered over the opening. A hawk-headed mummy was closing in on Buxton.

She reached down, arms at the ready to grab him. Buxton reached up. Her fingers brushed against his.

As Buxton pushed up on his toes the clockwork noise loudly resounded. The staircase collapsed upon itself. Alex reached down and grasped at the air as Buxton swayed to steady himself.

Step by step, Buxton was being delivered to the waiting crowd of hawk-headed defenders of Re. Her heart broke with every tick of the clockwork sound as he was pulled further away.

Buxton looked up at Alex. His eyes held a mix of love and pride in them. But unlike the time of their first meeting at the Met, this time Alex did not find it odd. As he descended, his steady gaze never wavered from hers.

"No!" Alex screamed.

The surface under her turned from clear to opaque grey. The portal she and Gormund climbed through closed completely, sealing them off from Buxton. He was gone. If only she could wind back time and save him. If only she had been able to grab onto him. She shuddered to think what his last moments would be at the hands of those . . . things.

CHAPTER THIRTY-THREE

Alex dropped to her knees. She could only imagine the horrors that played out below them for Buxton. She beat at the opaque surface with her hands.

"I'm sorry," said Gormund. "He was a good man."

"Why?" Alex asked the unanswerable.

"I know this is hard to take right now. But no matter how hard it is to deal with, Buxton is gone. You and I cannot afford the time to think about what happened."

"What happened?" A surge of anger-tinged grief rolled through her. If only she would have reached down sooner. "What happened? How can you say it like that? Like a vase just got broken or a car was smashed up. Buxton is down there." She pointed emphatically with her finger. "Having god knows what done to him by those creatures, and that is all you have to give?"

"That's not fair." His broad face flushed red. "Don't turn on me. I am only facing the stark reality." He touched Alex's forearm. "You and I have made it. We need to move on. It's not what I want to do. But it is what we must do. It is what Buxton would want us to do. And not to make too fine a point, but it is what we both promised."

She uncurled her body and stood. "Sorry, Gor. I know this isn't easy for you either." The surface now glowed in the moonlight like a blue-hued Australian opal, the night sky arching over them like a vast dome. "Where are we? Could we really be standing in the night sky?"

Gormund shifted his weight from side to side. "Must be a cloud platform. I have heard about these before, but I have never run across one."

"How far do you think it spans? Do you think it goes all around the world? If we walk, could we go on forever, or would we just fall off somewhere?"

"There's only one way to find out." He grabbed her hand and walked forward. "We can only hope there are no abrupt endings."

Alex gazed at the astounding night sky that spread above them. "Do you think the celestial arc above us is real, or an illusion?"

"It's hard to say. We could still be in the Duat, or we could have been transported by a magicked staircase to the night sky, or both. Or we could be in an exceedingly large room with an IMAX 3-D projector."

"You're no help."

"I can't tell you what I don't know. Would you rather I continue to make things up?"

Something struck Alex as odd about the star formation around Orion's belt. "Wait a minute." She pointed in the direction of the constellation. "Do you see that?"

"Just a bunch of twinkling— Hey . . . his dangling sword seems to be absent."

"Let's head that way. It looks like there is something in the way of the sword. Like something is blocking it."

It could have been a few minutes or hours that they walked under the canopy of stars. Or what appeared to be stars. It was just as likely that someone would hang millions of LEDs in a supercomplex and literal cosmic joke. As they walked, Alex kept her sights on Orion. Her mind wandered as her feet plodded forward one step at a time in a seeming infinity. The space around them was so vast it was difficult to tell if they were making any progress. The distance between objects never appeared to compress or minimize in any way. It was as if they were in a void that lacked time and distance. Were they walking through an invisible eternal labyrinth? Had they stumbled upon the Catholic limbo in the Netherworld? Or had they merely ceased to exist, but their consciousnesses hadn't yet been notified?

As Alex turned to say something to Gormund, her body thwacked against something solid. The momentum threw her backward like a bird hitting a picture window. She lay on the ground, glasses askew. "What the hell?"

"Unbelievable—you humans are so clumsy. How can you possibly trip in a room full of nothing?"

"That certainly wasn't nothing." Alex straightened her glasses and pointed. "Look, there is some sort of rectangular seam."

Gormund walked in front of Alex's prone body. He swung his arms forward and struck something solid. "I think we found a stellar wall."

Alex stood and placed her hand on her lower back as a small spasm twitched through her muscles. "You wouldn't happen to have a stellar key, would you?"

Gormund shook his head and chuckled. "No, I didn't think I would need it, so I left it at home." His expression turned impish.

Alex leaned against the wall. "Maybe this is a holding cell for new constellations. Sort of a green room before hanging out in the night sky for eternity."

"I would seriously doubt that."

"I was kidding, you know."

"I wasn't. I mean I can see how there might be an interest in creating a constellation of me . . . I am Bes, one of the best-loved Egyptian Gods . . . and what are you?"

"Thanks, Gor." She patted him on the shoulder. "You know, you really know how to make a person feel special."

"Anytime." He pushed his hands against the wall, grunting as he strained to topple it.

"Well, now that we've found this, we could look on it as

an anchor. So long as we are near the wall, we at least know one thing." Alex ran her hands over the cold, smooth surface.

"What?"

"That we aren't in the void. I say we stay close together. You take the low part, and I will take the high. We will run our hands down this wall until we find a crack or tear or—"

"Or plummet through the heavens and splat onto the surface of the earth like a big fat bug!"

After what seemed like ages searching the wall, Alex plopped down on the floor. This wasn't getting them anywhere. Maybe there was a better approach. She reached into her bag to grab a ginger chew. The crystal Akh-Hehet gave her caught her eye. She popped the chew in her mouth, then flipped the crystal into the air. The steady rhythm of throwing it up and catching it soothed her.

She held the crystal close to her eye and peered through it. Once, when she was a child, she looked through an antique crystal ocular with her father. It was beautiful and fascinating. Her father took great pains to explain to her how it all worked.

As Alex looked through the crystal it multiplied the infinities of stars through its prism. A green flash caught her eye where Orion's sword would be. She pulled the crystal away and it was gone. Alex looked through it once again, and there it was, glowing like a traffic signal.

Alex walked toward it. "I think I found something." Gormund followed behind her. "What is it?" he asked.

"I'm not sure, but it looks like an elevator button." She handed the crystal to Gormund. "I'll be dammed if it isn't." He pushed his index finger at the stellar wall. A bell sounded, followed by a swishing sound. Two sections of the wall pulled apart like mirrored elevator doors, revealing a small square interior all done up in red damask silk. He handed the crystal back to Alex and rolled his hand dramatically toward the elevator. "Entrez-vous, mademoiselle, your carriage awaits."

Alex stepped into the blood-red lift with Gormund following close at her heels.

Her stomach fell as the elevator rose. The sensation made her realize how fast it must be. There were no buttons to push; this elevator either read minds or it had only one destination. The thought pleased and disturbed her at the same time.

She and Gormund stood in silence as they were being pulled into the unknown. Alex was jolted sideways, falling to the floor as the elevator shifted its direction horizontally.

Alex laughed as she stood back up. "What's so funny?" asked Gormund.

"Oh, the fact that this elevator goes upwards, downwards, sideways, and crosswise makes me think of Willy Wonka's glass elevator. And well—"

"Ha. Ha." Gormund's laugh was full of sarcasm. "Another Oompa-Loompa reference. How original. You need to freshen up your repertoire. Anyway, his had many buttons. This one has none."

"I will concede that point—this elevator is more limited in choices. There is another possible difference to ponder."

"The decor?" he asked.

"No, not that." She smiled at the little beast who somehow managed to become her friend. Alex and Gormund had no idea what they were walking into, what the situation might be, or who they would be up against. With as much mischief and teasing as she could muster, she said, "No, I doubt Willy Wonka ever actually allowed the Oompa-Loompas in it."

"Nice," said Gormund.

The elevator doors parted and they stepped into the unknown.

CHAPTER THIRTY-FOUR

The dim, flickering torchlight made it hard to decipher how large the chamber was. Alex and Gormund stood on one of seven small islands that encircled a large mound. A silvery-black liquid lapped up against the mounds. Long spoke-like piers led to the center mass.

As her vision sharpened, she could tell the islands were boatlike in appearance, each shaped like a cupped hand. A walkway stretched before them to the center mound, where Raymond and three Others stood behind a large altar. Beyond them were three massive thrones. In the shadows, Alex thought there might be six or so minions standing at attention. Ten against two. The deck was decidedly stacked against them.

The middle and largest of the three thrones appeared to have a depiction of Isis atop its high stone back. Alex couldn't identify the iconography of the smaller ones. Their unusual order was confusing. If they were depicting the Theban triad, the mythological first family of Thebes, Osiris would have stood dead center, with Isis and Horus flanking him. It didn't make sense, but then again it was the Netherworld.

A strange mix of dread and elation filled Alex. This was the moment. The moment Buxton had been sacrificed for. The moment of truth. Would Alex be able to fulfill the prophecy? *May you banish the God's abomination and ensure man's salvation.* The abomination of Raymond's murderous power grab, which had shifted the celestial weight to one side and displaced Maat, upsetting the balance of the world. She had to do whatever she could to stop him.

In the far distance it appeared that two of Raymond's crew were struggling against each other. Was there a division between them? Alex's heart skipped a beat with hope. Could it be Niles? Was he fighting against Raymond? As the tempo of the struggle increased, masses of long dark hair flung about like twin agitated horsetails. One pinned the other against the altar. The victor's head snapped up, their eyes blazing at Alex, boring into her. It was Salima.

The woman Salima had pressed against the altar resembled Meyret. Could it be her? Alex struggled against the instinct to hurtle herself toward the mound. With no artifact, all she and Gormund had to fight with were their bare hands and their intellect. She couldn't go off half- cocked.

When Alex identified the fourth form, the reality hit her hard. The shadowed figure was Niles. A surge of anger mixed with disappointment coursed through her. He had joined Raymond. Both of her betrayers stood before her as plain as day, and Gormund, the unexpected friend, true of heart, stood with her now.

"Hey, can you tell if Salima is still Salima?" asked Alex. "Is this a Grant's Tomb–type riddle?"

"Ha ha, very funny. Has she transitioned into Sekhmet?"

"If she were in the form of Sekhmet, there would be no questions . . . just dead bodies."

"Good to know. I guess." Alex wasn't sure how much Gormund's input boosted her confidence. "Let's get a move on. I'm guessing they must be getting tired of looking menacing over there."

Gormund jumped and landed in an aggressive squat— knees bent and arms flung out to the side. "Right beside you."

Alex surveyed the area as they traveled down the wooden pier. The mummified bodies of Nephthys, Set, Horus, and Osiris occupied four of the seven islands surrounding the mound.

Their bound remains stood upright, feet together and arms crossed against their chests. Directly behind each mummy stood a large black diorite Ka statue that would allow their Ba-soul to find its way home.

Three of the islands stood empty. If Niles and Salima were with Raymond, who were the expected occupants of the remainders? Gormund and who else? Was Raymond planning to double-cross them both? Or could those islands remain forever vacant?

Her gaze drifted toward Niles. He wore a hood low over his face, but there was no mistaking that it was him. She didn't want to look at him and at the same time couldn't help but rubberneck at her own heartbreak. His head cocked to the side, and the hood fell back. His eyelids drooped, heavily, as if he'd been awakened from a drug-induced sleep. His posture was unnaturally stiff, and his arms disappeared behind his back. Niles was tied to a post. Alex gasped. He was a captive.

A flood of conflicting emotions overtook her; she was relieved he was still alive, yet alarmed he was Raymond's prisoner. His head bobbed up and down, as if he were battling against sleep. She must find a way to free him. Her mind spun with the possibility as she and Gormund moved toward the Others. If she could free him, maybe he could help in the battle.

His head slumped forward once more. Her hope plummeted. He could barely hold his head up. What good would he be in a fight?

"It's about time," said Salima as Alex and Gormund approached the mound. Salima finished binding her captive and pulled the woman's head up by the hair. Alex knew at once the gagged woman was not Meyret.

"Isis!" yelled Gormund as he charged the mound. Alex's arm shot out, stopping his progress. His shoulders slumped in compliance. She was relieved he had held back. They needed to wait for their moment, and Alex was certain this wasn't it. She didn't know how long she could try to orchestrate control over his reactions. Any emotional hold she might have on him was tenuous at best. They were his family, not hers.

Salima smirked. "Oh come, come little one. What made you think Isis, out of all of us, would live?"

Gormund's lips pulled back, revealing an angry snarl.

"That is no way to make friends, daughter," said Raymond in an odd, syrupy voice. Was he trying to sound like Mister Rogers, or was that his talking-down-to-humans-because-I'm-a-God voice? "This doesn't have to be an us-against-you thing, Alex. We can all come out of this winners. It takes a little quid pro quo. You know, I scratch your back and—"

"You kindly take over humanity?" asked Alex.

Isis's head tilted toward Alex. The captured Immortal's eyes pleaded as Salima secured her to the altar with large leather strips.

Alex steeled herself against an upwelling of emotions caused by the memory of Horatio, Isis's only son, dying in her arms back in Central Park. When his Ba-soul departed, Alex was struck with a deafening sadness. A hopelessness tied to losing something that was integral to life, without ever knowing it existed until it no longer did. It was as if a large branch from the tree of life had suddenly snapped off, weakening the connection between humanity and the unknown alchemy of their realm. This feeling revisited her as she witnessed Isis, the powerful Goddess- mother of Horus, trussed up like common livestock, awaiting the slaughter. Alex needed to focus, to find a way to save her, save them all. But for now, all she could do was stall them, keep them talking until she could formulate a plan.

"You could be a part of a ruling team. You, me, Salima . . . even Niles. If I could get you on board, I am certain I could talk some sense into Bird Boy." Raymond tipped the golden mace he was holding toward Niles.

As Raymond spoke, Alex surveyed the platform and beyond for options. Her heart sank—there were no other exit points and no handy weapons that happened to be lying around. Just her luck. Would this all come down to lopsided hand-to-hand combat? Her gaze rested on Niles as his head rolled sideways. His face drooped drowsily.

"You know it could all stop now. You could untie Isis," yelled Alex.

"She has to die." Raymond's expression morphed from conviction to a look of sad desperation as he toyed with a loose end of the rope that bound Isis.

"No!" Gormund yelled at the top of his lungs. "You can't do this, Raymond. This isn't right. And you know it."

Alex realized Gormund's control must be costing him dearly. She placed her hand on his shoulder. His head turned to Alex. His sorrow-filled eyes pleaded for action.

Alex gently tightened her grip on Gormund, hoping he would hold on.

Salima rubbed Raymond's back and whispered something into his ear. For a moment, it was as if Salima and Raymond had forgotten Alex and Gormund stood there.

"Of course, dear," Raymond responded to Salima as he set down his mace.

Alex saw a glimmer of hope where before she had none. *If only I could somehow retrieve that weapon.*

His previous dark demeanor was replaced with the sharp illumination of a true believer. "You couldn't be more right, daughter; what is past is past. Now we must move on to the inconveniences that stand here before us. It's a good thing you arrived when you did, Alex. You are just in time to enjoy the show." His hand flashed upward and came to a stop. He held a jewel-encrusted dagger.

Alex's breath caught in her throat. Was he actually going to kill Isis in front of them?

"Come on," Gormund said between his clenched teeth.

"Please," Alex whispered.

"Raymond, drop the knife," said Niles, his voice was weak. He leaned his head against the post he was tied to as he attempted to stay upright. His face was a patchwork of bruises and cuts.

Salima and Raymond smirked at each other. "Oh, I feel so scared right now. What are you going to do about it?" Raymond ran the knife a hairsbreadth away from Isis's trembling chest. He slowly played it down her torso. "We could rule, the four of us—think about it. We could bring order to chaos."

"Chaos?" asked Alex.

"You see what is going on in the world. It was a careless thing to allow humans to think they could manage themselves. They are slowly strangling the perfect utopia, the

Eden we call earth. They can't comprehend the treasure they have been gifted. All the wonder and magic of nature is not enough for their consumption. They need more things until there is nothing to give. Their bellies are swollen with their constant rape of the abundance."

Alex knew Raymond had to be lying about them all ruling together. Her appearance must have made him rethink the prophecy. Now that they were face to face he would try to use whatever emotional trickery he could to bring her in and defeat her. She figured if she played along, she could buy some time. "So, what would you do for me if I decided to throw humanity to the wind and join Raymond's army?" asked Alex.

Niles jerked to attention, his haggard eyes sparked. "Don't . . . Alex." Niles struggled against the ropes.

Salima strolled over and slapped Niles in the face. She leaned in and sniffed his neck. "Smells like chicken to me." She laughed aloud and turned to Raymond. "Do you think he would run around the roost if I cut off his head?"

"Settle down, Daughter. You know we have other plans for him."

"Spoilsport." Salima reached into her pocket and pulled out a heavy-duty syringe and plunged its needle into Niles's chest. His head fell forward. "A little negotiating currency." Salima grabbed a handful of Niles's hair, lifting his head up like a prize. His eyes were barely open, and the small spark of life he'd struggled to gain was now dimmed. "Sorry." Salima's mouth turned up in a wide grin. "You can't jam it in like that without a little of the poison escaping. So we are crystal clear. Your boyfriend's life is in your hands."

The flash of Raymond's knife pulled Alex's attention from Niles to Isis. "You can't kill her like that," Alex yelled.

"You know, I believe you are right." Raymond tilted his head.

"You do?" Alex was confused. She knew he couldn't be convinced that easily.

"Of course, this is not a killing knife. Nor was it ever meant to be. This is a ceremonial knife." He slipped it across Isis's shoulder; a dark red line spread across her flesh. Raymond leaned over with a vial and collected some of the blood. It turned golden as he handed it to Salima. "This is what will make my daughter strong, enabling her to become her most powerful self. She will drink the blood of Isis and become my destructive eye, destroyer of humans, her third self, Sekhmet."

As Raymond talked, Alex watched Salima out of the corner of her eye. Salima turned away from Raymond and toward Niles. Alex caught an odd flicker of emotion on Salima's face. It came and left in a millisecond. Was it disillusionment? Sorrow? Or was Alex's imagination playing tricks on her?

Alex returned her focus to Raymond as he continued. "If you don't agree to join us, I get a second try at killing my second Philothea in so many generations."

A hot wave of rage rolled through Alex at the reminder that she stood facing her father's killer. She found strength in it. Come hell or high water, she was going to do her best to take a piece out of this asshole. She had to be sure to keep an eye on the mace and pounce on it if an opportunity opened up. It looked like a powerful weapon. If Alex was in luck, it might also be magical. Maybe it was the artifact after all.

"Join us now, and you and Niles can live together forever. As soon as I have killed the last of the Theban Royals and cast a calling spell on all their powers, I will become the Aten. No secret of this universe will be inaccessible to me. I will move and bend time as I choose. I will have the ultimate power over life and death. I could make it so you could live forever. Killing Niles and my daughter would add a modicum of power to my Godhead, but it would be negligible."

"What about Gormund?" asked Alex, still trying to buy some time.

Gormund looked at her; his brows pulled together, then softened. He must have understood what she was trying to do. "Yeah, what about me, Raymond?"

"Are negotiations open?" asked Salima.

"Think of it, Alex—you'd have an eternity," said Raymond.

"But I don't get it. Why would you want me around?" asked Alex.

"There is one thing I have learned over my long life. Eternity is a long time. The five of us could be a family of sorts, be the pillar of home and hearth for the other. Not everyone is lovable, and I have found that it can also be oddly satisfying to have those who despise you around. It keeps things lively." He smiled what he probably thought was a warm and tender smile, but it had all the warmth of a shark's open mouth. "But I don't expect a mortal to understand." Raymond signaled and the minions filed out from behind the thrones.

"Don't be a fool, Alex. He is afraid of the prophecy." Niles's weakened voice managed to cut through the air.

His neck muscles appeared to be straining mightily to keep his head up. Alex guessed it must have cost him a great deal to fight through the poison that coursed through his body to try and warn her. It tore at her heart to think he'd used what little strength he had to talk her out of something she never really considered.

Raymond punched Niles hard in the stomach. He coughed and made an odd wheezing sound. There was a fierce look in Raymond's eyes. "I am afraid of nothing, Niles. You should know better than that. So, Alex, where is the artifact?"

"I don't have it. I don't know if I ever did." This couldn't go on much longer. The time to act had to be near. "I don't even know what it is."

"I expected you to say nothing less than that. But you must have it. You must have shielded it from our eyes in Nabta Playa. I can't imagine you would have come to battle without it. Give it to me. We can destroy it and move on to happier days."

"I told you I don't have it."

"Salima, why don't you share a little more of the poison

with Niles. Maybe we can see if we can get our little bird to sing a song we like the sound of."

"I'm telling you the truth. Niles gave me his pen when I first met him. I used the fluid within it to escape from Nabta Playa. If it was the artifact, it no longer exists."

"I don't believe you," said Raymond.

Six minions caged in Alex and Gormund. They formed an impassible wall around them. Two broke ranks and tore away her scribe's bag and dumped the contents in a pathetic pile near her.

"It looks like the same pile of crap," said Salima.

Raymond's voice chimed with victory. "So she wasn't lying after all. Good news all around. This has been so much easier than I expected."

"What about killing your entire family?" Gormund yelled. He pushed forward toward the mound, eluding Alex as she tried to ensnare him once more. A minion snapped him up. It held him overhead as his small legs pumped, trying to run through the air.

Raymond walked over to Salima and held the vile of Isis's blood to her mouth. "Time to drink, my dear. Open wide."

For an instant a look of disgust passed over Salima's face at the illuminated liquid.

How odd. If she were a willing participant, why did he not let her willingly drink it herself? Did Salima not want to drink the blood of Isis? Why did she hesitate? Did she not want to become Sekhmet, or was Raymond's control over her distasteful?

Alex glanced at Niles. His eyes had a dull glimmer in them as if he'd somehow gained a modicum of awareness. His expression was cut through with grief.

Raymond grabbed Salima's chin and tilted her head back. As her mouth opened, he poured Isis's blood in. Salima's throat contracted, making her cough as she swallowed the Goddess's blood. Raymond stepped away. "Drop the little one."

Gormund tumbled to the floor.

Salima covered her face with her hands as she rocked back and forth. Her movement became frenetic as her form became a blur, unrecognizable as herself. A hot red light burned in the center of the mass and spread like a rapid flame to the very edges of the space Salima occupied.

The surface of Alex's skin prickled with heat as the core of the mass turned to white. The strange fire collapsed on itself like a supernova, there was a flash of light, and Salima was gone. In her place stood a fierce lion-headed creature with glowing yellow eyes.

"Daughter, you may kill my enemies. You are set free to destroy my undoers as I command."

"I must call my brother to battle. Mehen, Protector of Re. Come kill with me." Sekhmet jabbed the syringe into Isis's neck. "Oh Brother of Death, I sacrifice this one for you."

Alex screamed as Sekhmet plunged the poison into Isis. The Goddess's body convulsed as she gasped for air.

"Oh brother, heed my worthy sacrifice and join me," yelled Salima, now Sekhmet.

The floor of the chamber shook. Large waves of the oily black liquid violently rocked back and forth. Salima roared as the magic waters erupted with the head of a massive snake. Its gigantic head thunked down onto the chamber floor, and it slithered out of the depths, curling itself around Raymond's feet. The snake's long silver fangs glinted in the soft torchlight.

Alex peered up to the mound. The throne she thought was a likeness of Isis was actually the Goddess Maat. She hadn't noticed earlier, because the Goddess was missing her trademark Feather of Justice. Alex looked at the small white dove feather lying among her pathetic pile of treasures. The feather, was it the artifact? Could it be?

She grabbed the feather and retrieved the Eye of Horus from the small compartment at the base of her scribe's bag. Horatio mentioned it held the power of the moon. She hoped he hadn't been throwing around hyperbole and that it held a powerful force within. She knew what she had to do. Armed with a marble and a tiny feather, she had to get past Raymond and Salima to the throne of Maat.

"Mehen, I command thee to kill the little one," yelled the lion-headed beast. "I'll take care of the girl."

Confusion muddled Gormund's face. "A snake?"

With that one word, Alex knew they were on borrowed time. It seemed unlikely, but had Salima as Sekhmet forgotten and sent a snake to defeat Bes? Had the protective will of Isis carried over in her essence within the fluid that transformed Salima into Sekhmet? Could that essence be, even in a small way, working against the destructive will of Sekhmet?

As Sekhmet and Mehen charged toward them. Alex yelled at Gormund, "I need to get over to the throne. Free Niles, if you can."

Gormund's eyes were bright as he turned away and ran.

Alex charged forward toward Sekhmet. A desperate hope propelled her forward. She threw the marble toward Sekhmet. It hit the ground with a pathetic knock. Alex's hopes plummeted as the lion-headed beast continued to speed toward her. Her face was alight with a predatory grin, golden eyes aglow. Sekhmet stopped in her tracks. She spun to face the small glass ball as if being pulled by a magnetic force. A loud concussive clap sounded, and waves of a silvery energy radiated outward, punching both Sekhmet and Raymond backward.

Alex shot past them, hoping the blast bought her enough time to make it to the throne before them. She glanced behind her. They were in hot pursuit, and gaining. Her legs burned as she scrambled up the throne. She placed the feather into the top of the Goddess's head. The tiny feather looked utterly ridiculous atop the head of Maat. Nothing happened.

They charged toward her, even Gormund and the snake. Soon they would converge on her.

"Nooooo!" Raymond's eyes were wide and his arms flailed about frantically.

Raymond's outrage confused her. Wasn't he about to get everything he'd wanted? Alex let go of the feather as it burned into her flesh. A small red flame hung in the air, consuming the small white form that disappeared altogether in a delicate wisp of smoke, along with any hope she'd had. She'd chosen wrong, the feather was just pigeon molt, not the artifact. Alex's mind spun at the idea of Raymond as a cruel master to all humans. What a cruel master he would be.

A small light glowed weakly from the crest of the statue's head. Alex looked more closely. It wasn't a glowing light, it was gold. It was as if an unseen hand was pouring molten gold in a transparent mold above the Goddess's head, stacking layer upon layer of thick metallic honey. The form was instantly recognizable . . . The Goddess Maat's Feather of Truth.

Alex turned around to see everyone stopped in their tracks, but the chemistry was inverted. Everyone lost interest in Alex and was now focused on Mehen. Bes stood in front of the huge snake and warded off Raymond and Sekhmet. Why would Gormund be trying to protect the creature who was trying to kill him mere moments ago?

Alex jumped off the throne and quickly unbound Niles. She yanked the syringe from his neck. His body slumped to the ground. She wasn't sure if he was alive or dead. If he was alive, and came around, at least he could escape. She turned around in time to see Sekhmet unsheathe a large sword and slowly approach Gormund.

"Out of my way, little man," yelled Sekhmet.

"Get back, She-Beast, this is out of your hands now. Alex found the artifact, and you are no longer in control."

Alex ran toward Gormund. Mehen was transforming. His fangs were retracting, and his scales were slowly turning from gold to black. Did the artifact of Maat change Mehen into Apophis, defeater of Re?

"You stupid . . . little . . . man." The words spat from Raymond like sparks from a hot fire. "If you don't let your sister take care of this beast before it changes to Apophis, none of us will survive. Let her pass."

Gormund stood his ground. "This ends here."

Alex tried to catch her breath as she stood by Gormund. "Apophis? The Destroyer of Re?"

Gormund's face broke into a wide smile. "The one and only."

Sekhmet swiped her sword through the air, as if testing the heft of the blade as she neared Gormund.

"Kill him. What are you waiting for?" Raymond pulled his dagger and charged forward toward Gormund.

"No, Father, don't," yelled Sekhmet. Raymond rushed toward Alex and Gormund.

The snake grew to an immense size. Alex stood her ground as Raymond bore down on them, but a shove knocked her to the ground. She tried to break her fall by flinging her hands behind her but ended up landing painfully on her elbows. She glanced up to see Gormund curl up like a moving cannon ball toward Raymond's knees, knocking him to the ground. His dagger skittered across the floor.

Sekhmet rushed forward with her sword held high and arrived a few clicks too late. The snake Apophis, Defeater of Re, grabbed Raymond by the midsection and lifted him high into the air. Apophis began thumping Re's body like a wrecking ball against the boats holding the God's mummies.

"Look what you've done!" Sekhmet ran to Apophis and jumped on its back. She planted her sword deep into his flesh. The snake was unfazed and continued its destruction. She pulled her sword out and scaled up its swaying body.

Gormund yelled over the din around them. "Sekhmet must be stopped. Apophis once awoken has an insatiable bloodlust. He will most certainly kill us, but at least humanity will have a chance. He is our one chance to make this right. He can kill us today, but he can never leave this realm."

Alex ran to Raymond's dagger and turned to Gormund. "I will be the one to stop her. If I have to die today, at least I will die fighting."

"Give me the knife, Alex. You don't have to do this."

"No. This fight is mine. It'll be easier for me to climb that beast than you, with those short little legs of yours." Alex touched Gormund's shoulder and winked at him. She ran, dagger in hand, in pursuit of Sekhmet.

The scales of Apophis were smooth and sharp. She had to push her fingers between them to pull herself up. It was like sliding her hands into a box of razors, causing hundreds of tiny cuts all over her hands. The sight of her own blood solidified her determination as the snake's body swished and jerked back and forth. She hung on with all her might as she climbed higher.

Alex heaved herself up and over the serpent's flat head. It was about the size of an old station wagon. She pulled herself up and crawled on all fours as she grappled to stay upright. At the far end, above Apophis's eyes, Sekhmet stood steady with an effortless grace, her huge sword submerged in the creature's head. She pulled the bloody blade out and immediately plunged it into another spot close by. Her lion face was contorted with confusion. "The stupid bastard won't die."

Alex crawled toward Sekhmet.

"You know, Alex," Sekhmet leaned on the hilt of her sword, pushing it in farther, "I don't see any point in us fighting. There is no way you can win against me. As a matter of fact, at this point you should be fighting along-side me. As you can see, Raymond is beyond help. Apophis has bashed him to a bloody pulp. Killing this beast is the only way you, me, and Gormund can get out of here alive. Even Niles, if he's still with us. We shouldn't be fighting against each other. Let's let bygones be bygones and live to see another day."

"Like how Isis will see another day?" Alex made slow but steady progress toward Sekhmet.

"You know what you can do when you are dead? Nothing. What's the point in dying now? How would that help anything? Certainly didn't help your dad. For all I care, you could spend the rest of your life coming after me. Don't be so shortsighted."

Alex stood and carefully walked toward Sekhmet. The swaying snake's head made her progress slow. But she had to be extra careful. She'd tucked the dagger in the back of her pants; falling was not an option. "You know, you are right. Why die today if you can live to fight another day?" She neared Sekhmet as the lioness retrieved her sword from the snake's head. Alex grabbed Raymond's dagger and plunged it into Sekhmet's neck.

Sekhmet pulled the dagger from her neck with her free hand and tossed it aside. She reached up and touched the gold and glowing blood that streamed down her chest. Her expression was one of startled amusement as she held her bloodstained palm out to Alex. "Thank you, Philothea. I always knew you had it in you." Sekhmet fell backward off the snake, still clutching her sword, laughing all the way down.

The snake's head jerked as if being called to attention.

Alex grabbed onto the sharp black scales to steady herself, wincing in pain as she peered over the edge. Apophis had dropped Raymond's battered body to the ground. It swiveled quickly, lowering its head toward the fresh meat of Sekhmet that just landed in front of it.

Alex held on with all her might as the snake's head dove toward Sekhmet's prone body below. As it neared the lion-headed Goddess, a flash of steel glinted then sliced clean through the snake's flesh, decapitating it. The separated head dropped into the dark, mercury-like liquid below.

Before Alex could react, she fell like a stone into the bone-cold metallic sea. Her skin burned in the frigid liquid as she plummeted downward. She turned herself, her lungs straining for air as she swam-pushed her way up through the viscous liquid. As her head broke through the surface, she gasped. Her legs pumped to keep herself afloat as she made her way to the nearest wooden pier. She pulled herself onto the timbered planks.

Gormund was running toward her. The chamber filled with a glowing golden light. As Alex stood, she saw the light was coming from an orb that emerged from Apophis's lifeless body. The air hummed with electricity. The light flashed and collapsed on itself and formed into an illuminated curl of glimmering mist that slowly wound its way upward, reaching to the ceiling like a rising trail of gilded smoke.

"The snake Pestu?" gasped Gormund.

Could it be Pestu? Swallower of the stars who ends the night?

A bright flare emanated from Raymond's crumpled body and rose toward the shimmering swirl. As it got close to the snakelike curls of light, the flare expanded and shaped itself into a resemblance of Re's ram-headed God form. As Re's specter rose into the air, it picked up speed and intertwined with Pestu's glimmering light.

All around the chamber, similar points of light, like stars, rose from each of the mummified Gods and then morphed into silhouettes of their God images before combining with the celestial swirl. Salima's took the form of the cow-eared Goddess Hathor.

Alex's gaze turned to the central mound. The star-lights drifted upward from both Niles and Isis. Niles was gone.

Her heart broke into a million pieces as she watched his ibis-headed form twirl up and join the Others. It never could have been. The sheer beauty of the moment made her realize her shattered heart had expanded into a universe unto itself. She was filled with unexpected joy. Maybe wherever he was going, Niles or Thoth or whoever he was would be able to find peace at last. Maybe they'd all found peace.

As Niles's and Isis's glowing forms joined the Others, a sudden blinding white light made Alex look away. With an electric jolt, she fell back hard onto the wooden deck.

Alex opened her eyes to the breaking dawn, surrounded by desert sands.

EPILOGUE

Alex stepped through the threshold of the ancient hypostyle hall in the temple of Seti I in Abydos. A small light in the distance dimly illuminated a depiction of the Goddess Maat on the temple wall. This was the site Buxton promised her she could luxuriate in once they'd finished their quest. By special arrangement, she and the KHNM agents had the place to themselves. Although she relished being there surrounded by the magical ambiance of the inscriptions and artworks, the experience fell short of her expectations in the shadow of her losses. Losses that were so deep she feared nothing ever would fill them.

This fantasia was a celebration, but to her it became mostly a memorial.

Since her return, everyone at the agency tried to bring her out of mourning. But they were set with an impossible task. How do you console the inconsolable? She tried to put up a strong front from the time she formally accepted Buxton's old position.

Alex taking on the reins of power was a hard thing for her mother to take. Alex not only had fallen into the KHNM fold but was leading it. The world had no idea how close they came to being enslaved by a narcissistic and crazed God, her mother included. Alex had made some progress recently with Roxanne. She credited it in part to Roxanne's new recovery process. The approach included joint counseling sessions. Together, Alex was certain they would find a way through the past, the future, and the now.

The small burst of light and the snap-crack sound made her realize they must have started the fireworks. Yet another thing Buxton promised but others had to fulfill. Soon she would have to join them all in the festivities and plaster on her business-as-usual attempt at a happy face.

Leaders had to be strong and resilient. A lesson she learned quickly. With the Gods back in their realm, the agency's role was in question. All of their futures were up in the air.

Upturned floodlights illuminated the ancient reliefs in stark white light, making the hieroglyphs jump off the wall. The memory flashed through her mind of her rushing through this very site with Buxton and Gormund. At the time all she could think of was losing herself in the texts, but now that the temple was all hers to explore, the experience felt shallow because of the absence of those she'd lost —Buxton, Niles, and even Salima.

Alex was haunted by the loss of them all. When she pondered how events played out, she still didn't have a firm grasp of which side of the fight Salima was truly on. Did she sign on with Raymond to rule by his side, or was she a mole to bring him down? No matter how many times she replayed the events in her head, Alex could never come out with a solid answer for those two questions. In the tomb at Nabta Playa, why did Salima make Alex's wounds shallow? Had she really wanted to make Alex's death long and agonizing? Or was she trying to buy her some time? Did she kill Apophis knowing that Pestu would appear? Or did she only want to escape the Netherworld with her hide intact? Alex was certain of one thing—she would probably never know the truth.

The click-clack of high heels pulled her out of her musings. Her body stiffened with recognition. Dr. Thorne was coming to retrieve her. *Great.* Once Alex took the agency over Thorne's attitude immediately changed. Good old Thorne had become quite a brownnoser, but every once in a while Alex noted the familiar flicker of hatred spark behind those steely eyes.

A slight breeze passed by as the temperature seemed to plummet. A garish shadow of Thorne's thin and pencil-like form lengthened across the room, a portent of the misery to come.

Thorne lifted a pashmina scarf up to Alex as if making an offering to a god. The harsh floodlights carved Dr. Thorne's features into high relief, making her smile look sharp and inauthentic. "I thought you might need this." Thorne handed the brightly hued scarf to Alex.

"Everyone is hoping you can come out and join the festivities," she said, her smile still refusing to warm up those cold eyes. "The fireworks have started."

Alex took the scarf and wrapped it around her neck. "I'll be out in two shakes. Has Gor arrived?"

Thorne gave her a pinched look. "He arrived with the fireworks. Of course." Her voice reeked of disapproval. Alex wasn't sure what Thorne was trying to imply about Gormund with that statement. But Alex stopped trying to figure out the twisted nooks and crannies of Thorne's mind. Since she and Gormund were retrieved from the desert, all of Thorne's blatant disapproval, previously directed at Alex, was now transferred onto Gormund. "He was very agitated." Thorne paused dramatically. "I mean, more than usual, about seeing you."

Thorne stared at Alex expectantly. She must have been tasked with bringing Alex back into the fold.

"I guess there is no time like the present."

Alex and her minder turned to join the party outside. They walked in silence, surrounded by the ruckus of celebration in the main courtyard.

"He mentioned something about finding information on the books of magic you have been searching for."

For the first time since returning from the Netherworld, a small hope blossomed in Alex's chest. Leave no man behind.

ACKNOWLEDGMENTS

The story of Alex Philothea and KHNM could not have been told without the help, love, and guidance of so many people.

To my amazing husband, thank you for introducing me to this obsession called fiction writing. I wouldn't have taken the first step towards writing this novel without your support, understanding, and gentle nudges. Thank you for being the first reader of countless drafts, and all the while being a loving and supportive sounding board.

I want to thank all the friends and family who have (hopefully) missed me while I have been plugging away at this novel. I appreciate your continued understanding and support over the past few years.

Thank you to Michael Gooding, Heidi Hostetter, Bridget Norquist, Ann Reckner, Emma Rockenbeck, Laurie Rockenbeck, Heather Stewart-McCurdy, and Elizabeth Visser; my wonderful and talented writer's group who have helped me in countless ways. I am supremely thankful to have each one of you in my life. A special thank you to Heidi and Laurie for blazing the way forward.

Thank you to my alpha readers Shelitha Blankenship, John and Linda Creed, Melanie Henry, and Irene Wojciechowski for helping me make this book the best it can be.

A special shout out to my peeps in the Seattle Office of Arts & Culture. Thank you for being gracious listeners as I've been continually bending your ears regarding the joys and pitfalls of writing.

I want to thank Pam Binder and the Pacific Northwest Writer's Association for their support. Pam, you have been an amazing inspiration for my writing practice and an invaluable instructor. I wouldn't have gotten this far without your encouragement and mentoring.

Bob Brier and Pat Remler, thank you for sharing your vast knowledge about ancient Egyptian history, myth, and culture with me. I have learned so much from you both. Pat's book *Egyptian Mythology from A-Z* was a constant companion as I wrote this novel. You've both played a major part in spurring me on to engage in my interest of ancient Egypt.

Thank you to Kristin Carlsen for your brilliant copy editing skills and to Mariah Sinclair for your spectacular cover design.

In this novel, I endeavored to represent the ancient Egyptian pantheon of gods and their myths as accurately as I could. Any missteps were completely my own.

ABOUT THE AUTHOR

 Sandy Esene is a self-professed ancient cultures geek. Traveling to ancient ruin sites around the world is one of her great passions. Over the years, she has traveled to over twenty countries including Greece, Malta, Jordan, Turkey, Belize, Peru, Thailand, Japan, and of course Egypt.

When not traveling or writing, Sandy enjoys making jewelry, going to museums, and taking long walks in Seattle parks with her husband and their miniature schnauzer Sneferu.

In addition to her creative pursuits, Sandy is the registrar for a civic art collection.

CPSIA information can be obtained
at www.ICGtesting.com
Printed in the USA
LVHW092028261118
598272LV00004B/224/P

9 781732 810518